JADE

Books By Sally Watson
by year of original publication

Highland Rebel 1954
Mistress Malapert 1955
To Build a Land 1957
Poor Felicity 1961
Witch of the Glens 1962
Lark 1962
Other Sandals 1966
The Hornet's Nest 1968
The Mukhtar's Children 1968
Jade 1969
Magic at Wychwood 1970
Linnet 1971

JADE

by Sally Watson

Image Cascade Publishing
www.ImageCascade.com

MANUFACTURED IN THE UNITED STATES
OF AMERICA

A hardcover edition of this book was originally published by New York: Holt, Rinehart and Winston, Inc. It is here reprinted by arrangement with Ms. Sally Watson.

First *Image Cascade Publishing* edition published 2002.

Library of Congress Cataloging in Publication Data
Watson, Sally, 1924-
Jade.

(Juvenile Girls)
Reprint. Originally published: New York: Holt, Rinehart and Winston, Inc., 1969.

ISBN 978-1-930009-67-7

for my cherished niece Karin Glinden,
who is not altogether unlike Jade.

Author's Comments:

I'm particularly glad to have *Jade* republished! For one thing, it's the heroine most people like best; me, too–I think–for another, my niece, Karin (to whom I dedicated it) now teaches school and has been reading it aloud to classes, and demanding that I get it republished so that her pupils can read it for themselves.

Well, it wasn't that I didn't *want* to! Karin isn't the only one. Everyone asked for *Jade!* Gratifying but frustrating. How wonderful it will be not to have to answer letters from lovely people earnestly wanting copies, to say, disappointingly, "Sorry, but I *can't* sell you a copy, I have only a single battered one left myself."

(By the way, every male who reviewed *Jade* back in the '60's simply *hated* it. Females were not *supposed* to behave like that; much less with the tacit approval of the author, who was clearly no better than she should be, and in danger of Corrupting the Young. What was more, two of them, despite the careful historical notes, simply refused to believe that Anne Bonney and Mary Read really existed– so there!)

Acknowledgments

For my long-time fan-friends: Carla Kozak, Darice McMurrey, Donna Trifilo, Joy Canfield, and Michele Blake, who all conspired beautifully to make this reprint possible; and Caryn Cameron, who put me on a website, among other supportive things.

Contents

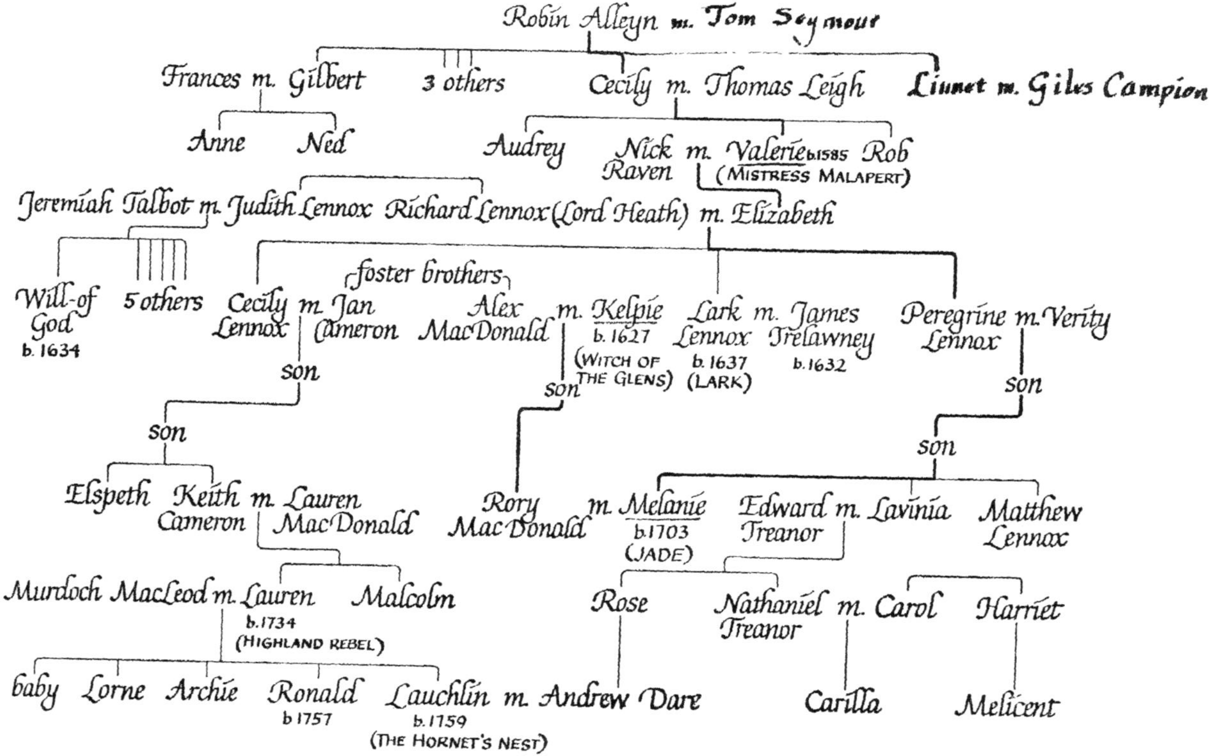

Robin Alleyn m. Tom Seymour
Frances m. Gilbert
3 others
Cecily m. Thomas Leigh
Linnet m. Giles Campion
Anne
Ned
Audrey
Nick Raven m. Valerie b.1585 (MISTRESS MALAPERT)
Rob
Jeremiah Talbot m. Judith Lennox
Richard Lennox (Lord Heath) m. Elizabeth
Will-of God b. 1634
5 others
foster brothers
Cecily Lennox m. Jan Cameron
Alex MacDonald m. Kelpie b. 1627 (WITCH OF THE GLENS)
Lark Lennox b. 1637 (LARK) m. James Trelawney b. 1632
Peregrine Lennox m. Verity
son
son
son
son
son
Elspeth
Keith Cameron m. Lauren MacDonald
Rory MacDonald m. Melanie b.1703 (JADE)
Edward Treanor m. Lavinia
Matthew Lennox
Murdoch MacLeod m. Lauren b.1734 (HIGHLAND REBEL)
Malcolm
Rose
Nathaniel Treanor m. Carol
Harriet
baby
Lorne
Archie
Ronald b 1757
Lauchlin b.1759 (THE HORNET'S NEST) m. Andrew Dare
Carilla
Melicent

JADE

CHAPTER ONE

The Lopsided Smile

"Of course I did it!" said Jade at once. "You *know* I did it! Who else could have done it?" And her green eyes glittered defiance at her parents.

Her name wasn't Jade at all, of course: it was Melanie. She had been christened Melanie Lennox right there at Bruton Parish Church, her parents called her Melanie, the town of Williamsburg called her Melanie (when they weren't calling her that shocking Lennox minx), her governess called her Miss Melanie, her brother and sister called her Lanie, and the slaves called her—lovingly—Missy Lanie. No one had *ever* called her Jade except her grandparents (who had been dead these five years) and old Monsieur Maupin. But these were the three people she loved the most, and so, with perfectly characteristic obstinacy, she went on thinking of herself as Jade. Her family would have been astounded had they known.

Mistress Lennox sat down with a rustle of lilac silk panniers and agitated lace, and regarded her oldest daughter with the expression of a perfectly respectable duck who has unaccountably hatched out a sea gull. "Oh dear!" she sighed, fanning herself. "I *don't* know why you're so wicked, Melanie! You don't get it from *my* side of the family, I'm sure." And she looked with faint reproof at her husband, whose parents had always been eccentric to say the least of it, and whose worst tendencies seemed to have been inherited by Melanie.

Mr. Lennox ignored the implied reproach. He was regarding his daughter with strained calm. "You simply walked into the Howes' back gardens and turned young William's fox loose?" he demanded. "But why? You must have had a reason. What has William ever done to you?"

Jade's head tilted and she smiled a little on one side of her mouth. William, as a matter of fact, had done many things to her, mostly of a sneaky nature calculated very successfully to get her into even more trouble than she managed for herself. But she was not a tell-tale, and anyway, past was past, and irrelevant.

"William's a bad taste on my tongue," she said reflectively. "And a thief, besides. He stole that fox's freedom. I just gave it back." And at an impatient exclamation from her father, she puffed suddenly into anger. "No one has any *right* to take away someone else's freedom, whether it's animals in cages or human slaves!" she spat, glaring at her parents. "It's wicked!"

They looked at her with tightened lips and despairing eyes. Was she wrong in the head? She had been conducting this argument for years now, refusing to listen to any reason whatever. Nevertheless, her mother tried once more, though without much hope.

"It *isn't* wicked; it's a perfectly natural and ordinary fact of life, as right and natural as keeping dogs and horses. Why do you keep *on* this way, Melanie? We treat them all kindly and fairly, don't we?"

"Dogs and slaves and females!" shouted Jade, twin flags of anger in her creamy cheeks. She turned to her father, challenging. "How would *you* like to be a slave?"

Mr. Lennox began to show more strain and less calm, as he often did at about this stage of things. He regarded the tall slim firebrand he had somehow sired. Her full stiffened skirts of pale pink rose-sprigged chintz suited her about as well as it would her sturdy young brother Matthew—and yet it was hard to say why. She looked like such a sweet young girl, with soft honey-brown ringlets hanging thickly about a slender neck, with long lashes and furtive dimples and a soft round chin—which was now sticking out at him like the vanguard of an army. "How would *you* like it?"

"You can't possibly be serious, Melanie! It's utterly idiotic to make such a comparison! They're *black*. They have nothing whatever in common with us. They're savages, animals, without human sensibilities. And they're far better off here being cared for in a civilized country than they would be in the jungles of Africa."

He turned to leave the drawing room with an air of having settled *that* argument once and for all. He should have known better. Jade defied her mother's warning look and went on arguing. "Who says so?" she demanded of his azure taffeta back. "Do *they* think so? Has anyone asked them?"

"That will *do*, Melanie!" He was exercising far more patience than would most fathers in this year of 1719. This was partly because he hated to whip his children and slaves, and partly because in Melanie's case it never had any effect except to make her more defiant and usually flippant besides. He drew himself up, a towering figure of authority. "You are being both stupid and impudent. It is quite unnecessary to ask further than the Bible. God created Heaven and Earth, and placed all animals and inferior beings under the dominion of Man. Do you call the Bible a lie?" he finished, resorting unfairly to a question with only one possible answer.

Jade gave him the impossible one. "Yes," she said, and produced her small lopsided smile, a typically Jade smile that mocked at herself and taunted the world. In this case, it was a smile that recognized the exact point at which she'd earned herself a whipping—and didn't care.

Except that she did care, of course, searingly. Not so much because of the pain; that was the least of it. But in an age when whipping was common and an inescapable part of growing up, Jade resented the whole concept as instinctively as she did slavery, and for much the same reason. It was an outrage against human dignity. Intolerable that any person should have such rights over another! Abominable to have to stand and submit! . . . And unthinkable that she should try to avoid it, for that would be surrender.

Being Jade, she quite naturally went to the other extreme, went out of her way to invite whippings, and then turned them into a kind of backdoor victory, to prove her own courage, perhaps. Already, now, she could see the baffled expression Father always wore on such occasions. Chin high, as befitted a heroine, she strolled nonchalantly toward Father's study where her punishments always took place, walking with that mysterious controlled grace which puzzled all of Williamsburg except Monsieur Maupin and a slave named Joshua.

"Hurry up, Father," she said cheekily, her smile indicating clearly how little she cared. It was a very effective act. It should have been. She'd had lots of practice.

Mistress Lennox sank limply back into the cushions of her chair, lips quivering. "I *don't* know why you're so naughty, Melanie! Lavinia's *never* like this, thank goodness. And I can't *think* why you go on and on about our slaves that way. We're not at all harsh, and goodness knows you get *far* more beatings than they do."

Jade paused in the doorway to consider this. "Well, so I should," she pointed out fairly. "I deserve them, don't I? But you'd punish a slave worse for doing the same thing." And with a side glance at her father to see how he took this (for Jade was seldom unaware of her effect on her audience) she marched on out of the drawing room and down the wide sunny hall to the study—whence she emerged a little later with dry eyes, a composed face, and a distinct air of insolence.

It was her father, straightening his full-skirted taffeta coat, who looked upset and defeated, as well he might. He had been trying for the whole of her sixteen years to turn her into a Virginia lady, and the result was simply abysmal failure. She was no lady at all. She had no sense of propriety or shame or family dignity; her pride was entirely the wrong sort; even her virtues of courage and honesty were altogether willful and reckless. He couldn't understand her at all.

Jade stared at him for a moment with a straight back and cool dispassionate eyes; then turned to go up the shallow stairs to the schoolroom. Father stopped her with a hand on her smarting shoulder that almost—but not quite—made her wince. It was only a flicker of her eyelids, but Jade could have kicked herself for even such a weakness. She despised weakness! What if Father had noticed?

"The Howes are coming over tomorrow for morning coffee. You'll apologize then, and say you're sorry you loosed William's fox."

"Shan't," said Jade. "I'm not sorry; I'm glad."

"For heaven's sake, Melanie!" cried her angry and harassed father. "What devil is in you? Do you *like* being punished?"

Jade surprised herself. She had always pretended not to care. Now pride was demanding complete honesty. "No," she said, but her chin went higher, just in case he should think she was conceding anything except sheer truth.

"Then why do you make me go on doing it? Why can't you be a well-behaved young lady instead of a little demon?"

"I'm *me!*" she told him passionately, her jade-green eyes darkening. "I *have* to be me; I'm not a rabbit, and I won't turn into a rabbit, whatever you say!"

"I don't want you to be a rabbit," he told her wearily, for they had been over this a hundred times. "I want you to be a lady."

"It's the same thing, to you."

"You know it isn't."

"It is! You want a meek little blob of sweet jelly who'll agree with everything you say! If I were a boy—"

"But you're not a boy. You're a girl. And girls are meant to be docile and biddable."

"And obey men!" Jade sneered spectacularly, lifting one side of her small mouth in a quite splendid snarl.

"Yes!" said her father, relentlessly reasonable. "Of course! What else? My dear child, you have got to accept the fact that you are of the inferior sex—"

"I'm not! We aren't!"

"—and your inability to see the obvious simply proves your inferiority. Good heavens, girl, look at the silly, irrational notions you've just been spouting, for examples of female inanity! Next you'll be saying that slaves should be free and women allowed to own property!"

"Well, I do say it," Jade retorted at once, and while he was still reeling from this, she let loose another shaft. "And it's not fair to make up a rule that anyone who disagrees with you is silly, and then use it to prove itself. I just wish I were Queen of England! I'd—"

"Well, you're not!" Her father's long suffering temper was rising again, and she was saved from another whipping on the spot only by the fact that he didn't feel up to it again so soon. "You're a willful and insolent girl in the Colony of Virginia, and English law says that you shall obey your father until you marry, and after that, your husband, God help him."

"He'll be sorry," threatened Jade, tight-smiled. They glared at each other for a moment with identical eyes, and his hand tightened painfully on her shoulder. Then he controlled himself with a visible effort and let go.

"You'd take another whipping right now rather than give in, wouldn't you?" he discovered, wonderingly.

"Yes," said Jade simply, and went upstairs, victorious.

Matthew and Lavinia were waiting in the schoolroom, and Zelda—with superb timing—was just bringing in a tray of cakes and a pitcher of nice cold tea. She always produced treats when Jade had been punished. She adored Jade; all the slaves did; she was their champion.

Their champion now paused in the doorway, partly for dramatic effect and partly to make perfectly sure she had herself well in hand, because Father had hurt her rather more than usual. Her brother and sister surveyed her with interest. They didn't feel sorry for her, because she always brought it on herself; and they didn't in the least understand her; but they both admired her stoicism, however misplaced.

Jade presented them with her sideways grin, self-mocking. Lavinia, whose blue eyes missed very little, was regarding her searchingly and with disapproval. "I suppose it was about William's fox?" she decided, interpreting the grin with ease.

Jade nodded impenitently, sauntered across the room, and helped herself to a cake. Vinnie, tiny and erect, gave a small ladylike snort. Vinnie was twelve, and it was hard to imagine that sisters could be so alike and still so different. They were both slight, straight-backed, with slender hands, and honey-brown hair, and fine-boned oval faces, and strong wills. But Jade was tall and Lavinia small, Jade's eyes green and Vinnie's bright blue—and Lavinia was as conservative by nature as Jade was radical.

As for nine-year-old Matt, he gave Jade the grin of someone who *does* like things stirred up a little—so long as it doesn't get too serious. Matthew had a well-developed sense of self-preservation.

"I expect Mother's having a megrim," he announced equably. Mother always had a megrim when Jade was wicked. "You *are* awful, Lanie," he added with admiration.

Jade took another cake. "Born to be hanged," she predicted flippantly.

Matt looked alarmed. Lavinia, the realist, considered the remark and found it all too probable. "I dare say you will, too," she agreed darkly. "*And* it'll be all your own fault, you know."

"It always is." Jade never deceived herself on that score, and loathed excuses as a particularly detestable form of weakness. She reached for a third cake. Lavinia snatched the plate away.

"Pig!" she said. "That's mine, and you needn't think a sore back gives you any right to be greedy."

Jade shrugged and instantly regretted it. "Think how many of my share you'll have after I'm hanged," she suggested persuasively; but since her sister seemed disposed to settle for a cake in the hand rather than two in the future, Jade had a drink of tea instead. It was cool and refreshing in the thin handleless cup.

"Well, Miss Melanie?" It was the acid voice of Miss Turner the governess, whose thin, whaleboned figure stood in the doorway wearing a severe expression. "Been beating your head against stone walls again, I hear?" Jade nodded, deliberately cheerful. "When will you learn, you silly girl, that you only bruise your head that way, and don't bother the wall at all." Jade stuck out a truculent chin. "And how often must I tell you that there are ways around and over walls?"

Jade felt like Columbus being told that one could, after all, reach the Indies by sailing eastward. "I don't *want* to go around or over! I want to knock the beastly wall down; it's got no business being there; it's bad and unfair!"

"Which wall?" inquired Matthew, perfectly ready to help knock it down, but uncertain as to where it might be. No one paid any attention.

"And who are you to decide what's bad?" demanded Miss Turner.

Jade just looked at her, and then turned to stare coldly out of the window, over the garden and hedge to the dusty width of Gloucester Street. Miss Turner had *admitted* to her that she thought society was unfair to women; she needn't try to back down now! And Miss Turner, interpreting her silence correctly, sighed and tried a different logic.

"Even supposing the wall does want tearing down, you can't do it that way. It needs a subtle approach, especially from us females, or we only put their backs up. Miss Lavinia understands that. We must wheedle the men, play up their sense of importance and superiority, let them think they're having the ideas, and then admire them for it."

Jade stuck out her lip. Vinnie looked smug. She already had Father wrapped neatly around that slim finger and fully intended to do the same with her husband and sons and sons-in-law.

"That's right," she agreed with a rather malicious glance at her small brother. "Just keep them happy thinking how superior they are, and the poor sillies never guess it's really us."

"It isn't!" cried the outraged Matthew.

Jade sighed. Her high courage and defiance were trickling away now that they were no longer needed, leaving her, as always, sore and empty and depressed. And she didn't even understand why she had to go on beating her head against that wall—except that it was unjust and evil, and so must be attacked. It was no good to go around it, or twist it to your own convenience as Vinnie would always do, or even just kick it now and again in a spirit of fun as Matt did. Matt, to be sure, was better than nothing

—but he was a boy, and of the ruling race and class, and everything was to his advantage as it was. Why should he seriously try to change it?

"Oooh!" said Jade, turning her face from Gloucester Street back to the sunny schoolroom. "I hate men!"

Matt looked hurt. "Even me?"

She pulled his fair hair, forever escaping from its queue to rise like a mane around his face. "Not yet, but I expect I will if you grow up like all the others," she prophesied gloomily.

"Just because your father punished you—" began Miss Turner. Jade looked at her blankly. What had that to do with it?

She lay awake for a long time that night, lying carefully on her front, but otherwise not really noticing that her back smarted. Woe swept over her in waves. What was she, that she must be so lonely and alien? Was she indeed possessed of a devil? In all the world, only four people lived in her heart: her dead grandparents, an eccentric old Frenchman, and a slave. For the rest, she was a mosquito in Williamsburg's ear, and Williamsburg was to her a bed of roses: sickly-pink roses, overperfumed, and very thorny indeed. As for her family—Jade sighed and turned her head away from the shaft of moonlight. Love, yes—but between alien species, who thought in different languages and spoke through a thick glass wall, who were engaged in an endless war waged, as Jade always waged her battles, with no quarter asked or given. What with one thing and another, she couldn't really much like the looks of the future.

CHAPTER TWO

The Fencing Lesson

Jade awoke at the usual early hour, blinked at the pale sky, and wriggled her shoulders experimentally. They at once protested, and she grimaced. It was, as she'd feared, going to handicap her movements for a day or two. Father had been particularly annoyed this time, and of course she never let him know how much he was hurting her.

She considered it without rancor. She never bore him any resentment for punishments; they were a logical consequence of her actions, just as a burn was the logical consequence of touching fire. Nor could one hold it against the fire. This was part of the Code Monsieur Maupin had taught her. Still, it was rather discouraging that in all these years of consequences, she hadn't really got anywhere. Father was as stubborn as she, and so far she had just managed to hold her own.

A cock crowed, and she got up, stuck her head briefly out into the fresh dawn, and curled her lip at the pink roses. (She detested pink, preferring the clean lines and scent of flame-colored tulips.) Then she withdrew her head and went to stand before the long mirror, frowning judiciously. It was Melanie who stared back at her from a soft young face quite out of character for Jade. Melanie Lennox—not as pretty as Lavinia, but with a look of sweet femininity that Jade found quite revolting. Her short round chin ought by rights to be sharp and jutting, her eyebrows severe. That thin little neck looked positively fragile, and as for her arms and legs. . . .

Jade began to grin. Such softly rounded little arms, such slender, shapely legs, giving no hint at all of the trained muscles beneath! And only two people knew. No one else even suspected—how should they?—unless one counted the puzzled glances William Howe had been giving her ever since that day he had tried to kiss her and she knocked him flat and bloodied his nose. . . .

She grinned again and tensed one of those long legs. Like a rock it was, beneath the silken flesh. They were nice looking legs. Jade couldn't for the life of her see why female limbs were considered so shameful. Why was it perfectly proper to show as much bosom as possible, but disgraceful to reveal so much as an inch of ankle? Grown-ups, she decided, not for the first time, were a species bordering on the totally irrational.

Another cock reminded her that she had no time to dawdle. Joshua would be worried. Hastily she dressed, ignoring the steel-and-whalebone horror of stays (a diabolical invention which Jade, abetted by Zelda, usually did ignore), and put on a blue riding habit. Down the wide stairs she ran, with only the slaves about to smile and nod as she went past, out to the stables where Joshua had saddled the horses and stood waiting, as he had waited nearly every morning since Jade was nine. His ebony face had begun to pucker anxiously. Was she too stiff to get up this morning?

A huge, muscular, gentle man, Joshua was more than groom, much more than slave. He was Missy Lanie's closest household friend and ally, her partner in crime. Her blazing rebellion was unawakened in him, who had been born another man's property. But it was there. It took the form of noticing with great sympathy that the lot of white females wasn't, after all, so very different from that of blacks. Neither had rights or property or liberty, both could be bought and sold, for there was the Divorce by Sale law, by which any Englishman could actually sell his wife for cash. Joshua pitied anyone who tried to buy Missy Lanie! He smiled at her, watched carefully as she mounted, not missing the slight caution of her movements.

"Morning, Missy Lanie," was all he said, and they set off, riding as they always did to the end of Duke of Gloucester Street, past William and Mary College, and then along the Richmond Road, all with glowing innocence, just in case Williamsburg should be paying any attention. As a matter of fact, Williamsburg wasn't. It had long ago stopped noticing the daily morning ride, which, after all, was the least of that Lennox minx's idiosyncracies.

A mile or so along the empty road there was a path that led eventually to a white-painted house where lived that old Frenchman commonly known to Williamsburg as Mad Maupin. Many things were whispered of him, at least one of them being true. He was indeed a master of the rapier.

He put a scowling white-peruked head out of the door as Jade dismounted.

"Late," he grumbled. "I ask of myself why I bother with you, bad *enfant*."

"Because I'm the best pupil you ever had," she told him cockily and ran into the house and to the small changing room where knee breeches and a long-sleeved shirt awaited her. This was the best hour of the day; the only hour, in fact, the others being a long bore to be enlivened only by getting into trouble or arguments. Here she was alive and challenged. Here she wasn't merely a female named Melanie, but a human being called Jade. Monsieur Maupin had no use for irrelevant categories such as male and female; he trained her to the top of her considerable talent, demanded still more, and took great pains to conceal his delight in her. She was the pupil every fencing master dreamed of: one with speed and precision, coolness and audacity, subtlety and fire. He had seen the fire at once in the scrawny child brought by her grandfather, and he had trained her for some seven years now, an hour or two every morning, a secret miraculously and assiduously preserved.

"*Bien*," he said when Jade presented herself in the large room. "We work now on defense, a thing at which you are very bad indeed. You wish always to attack, never to defend yourself, *non?*"

Jade grinned. Monsieur Maupin returned it with a frown and tossed his peruke to the watching Joshua. "It is a pride of the most stupid," he told her. "A fencer who does not parry first will never live to riposte, however quick she may think herself to be. Now, I shall attack in any quarter I choose, and you shall complete the parry before riposte, or I skewer you." He scowled ferociously.

Chuckling, Jade went on guard.

Within three minutes the fierce scowl had become a genuine one, and Monsieur Maupin lowered his point.

"Ah, bah! you are today even more bad than yesterday, and as slow as—" He stopped. His eyes narrowed. "It is that you have been wicked again, eh?" he demanded, not without approval. Jules Maupin, rebel and reformer himself, never tried in the least to curb these tendencies in his pupil. "Why do you never tell me when it hurts you to move?"

Jade merely grinned again, derisive.

"*Mais non,* of course you would not," he agreed. "It would not at all fit your role of Amazon." He twinkled a little, for Jade had quite recently discovered Greek drama, and this very much amused him.

Jade frowned. "Well, I don't think much of those Amazons. They gave in too easily, or at least Antiope did. I like Medea better, or Clytemnestra. They fought back."

"*Ma foi!*" He tried to look shocked, failed utterly. "Such murderous ladies! Clytemnestra killed her husband, even. And both came to very much violent ends, you remember."

"Agamemnon deserved it, the beast," said Jade, unrelenting. "And a violent end's a lot better than dying of boredom!" She scowled in vast anger at the lot of young ladies in this modern day. Breakfast, with dull chit-chat, and lectures on behavior. Lessons in dull things like Deportment and Household Management. Embroidery. Backboards. Sedate walks wearing a face mask to protect the delicate white skin essential to well-bred young Ladies. Visits, with incredibly twitter-witted conversation. Silly boys trying to pay silly compliments, and looking as if they feared to have their ears boxed—which they well might, at that. The nearest thing to any kind of mental activity was French, and Jade was already fluent in that language, from her practice with Monsieur Maupin, so the only really interesting bit about French lessons was trying to keep Miss Turner from guessing how much she knew.

The old Frenchman was looking at her thoughtfully, as if reading her mind. But he merely jerked his head, stern again. "*Bien,* to work. We practice the swift footwork, retreat, advance, and lunge, and your back shall tell you if you move your shoulders when you should not."

Jade nodded, brimming with affection for the peppery old man, who paid her the compliment of demanding much and making no concessions. No quarter asked or given was the bond between them, and mutual respect as well. Why couldn't other people be like that?

A moment, and it was already time to go. Jade sighed, mopped her perspiring face, and wished it were tomorrow already. So did her teacher, who hadn't the slightest compunction about deceiving her parents. His conscience, if he had ever had one at all, had long since perished of neglect . . . or almost.

"You are like your grandparents, cherie—both of them. They and I, we defied prejudices; you try to make war against the whole structure of society, I think." He gave her a sharp look. "Society will punish you, *enfin.* You know this? You are prepared to pay a so-high price for going your own way?"

"It's none of society's business what I do," she told him truculently, but he shook his bald head at her.

"But yes, it is very much society's business, when you break its rules and defy its conventions and refuse to respect its values. You are a danger to established order, and society cannot permit that you endanger its existence."

"Pooh," said Jade. She had always defied conventions and done things no lady must do. She laughed. "No quarter asked or given!"

"Ah, bah!" he growled, his own words turned against him. "Impudent child, you challenge the world and the gods, and it is a thing you cannot possibly guess, the revenge they will take. How you will suffer for it! Be prudent! Go away and study to be a lady and never come near me again."

Jade felt herself going scarlet with furious disbelief, felt it glowing hot on her cheeks. How *dare* he ask her to cage herself like that poor fox of William's? Then she laughed. "You don't mean it!" she discovered, relieved.

He laughed too, the moment of conscience gone. "*Parbleu*, if I were a good man, no doubt I should mean it, but I am a wicked old fool who sees that you are bound to be in trouble always in any case, and what use for me to tell you to be someone different?" His clever old face wrinkled with amusement and he gave a very French shrug. "So I abet you. Now go home, or you will be late for breakfast again, and they will punish you by taking away your morning rides."

Joshua spoke unexpectedly, his deep voice amused. "No, they won't. The time they tried it, she wasn't fit to live with and the governess quit and they had a terrible time finding a new one. But you'd best hurry anyway, Missy Lanie. No need to ask for any more trouble quite so soon after yesterday."

Jade chuckled and went to change.

They started down the lane again presently, Jade once again in her riding habit, and somehow (though with difficulty) contriving to ride astride in spite of it. The pale blue sky to the west was piling high with swift ominous thunderheads, and a sudden wind swooped upon them with rain on its back. Jade chortled gleefully and lifted her face to it. She loved storms.

"We'll be soaked," she predicted happily. "Race you to the road!" And digging her heels into Seagull, she was off, around the double curve that hid Monsieur Maupin's house so well from the Richmond road. Rumbling thunder and wind and the pelt of rain blocked out sight and sound, and it was most unfortunate that another rider happened to be racing back to Williamsburg just at that spot and that moment. The two horses nearly collided at the point where path and road met, scaring each other into near hysterics, and for several exciting moments both riders were quite thoroughly occupied in controlling them. Seagull in particular seemed inspired by the spirit of a whirlwind, and Joshua—his own horse calm—hovered nearby, watchful but unalarmed. He knew his Missy Lanie. She'd be furious at any unneeded help. She laughed aloud, intoxicated by the bright storm and the face of danger.

The other rider failed to enjoy the fun. "You little devil, Melanie Lennox!" raged William Howe, who had already had more than enough of her this week. "Just you wait!" And, his horse under control again, he spurred on toward the town, his dignity even further assaulted by the derisive laughter that followed him.

The storm passed as quickly as it came, and Joshua and Jade, soaked but in sunshine, arrived back at the stables. Jade ran lightly up the back stairs, carrying the wet train of her riding habit. At the top of the stairs she met Lavinia and Matthew, fresh and clean and well-groomed, ready for breakfast. They looked at her.

"You're wet," observed Matt, a trifle wistfully. An idea struck him. "I'm nine now; I think I'll go on your morning rides, too."

"You won't!" shouted Jade.

Matt bristled. "I'll ask Father. He'll say I may."

"I don't care if he does! Jade's greenish eyes darkened with anger, and her face looked pinched. She almost hated Matt, or anyone else who threatened the one thing that made life enjoyable. "I'll push you off your horse if you try! It isn't fair! You already get everything because you're a boy. You go to William and Mary school, and learn interesting things like math and history—"

"Yes, and you're always taking my books!" he accused her, indignant.

"—and you have a fencing master, and you're learning to shoot, and you're allowed to climb trees, and ride astride, and you don't have to be ladylike and mind your petticoats and face mask, and—and now you want to spoil the *only* nice thing I'm allowed. Selfish pig!"

Matthew looked startled and crestfallen. He had a good opinion of himself, and didn't at all see that his presence would spoil things. He said so.

Before Jade could answer to that, it was Lavinia's turn. "You'd better go get clean and changed for breakfast, Lanie," she said with a disapproving glance at the sodden blue broadcloth and dark wetness of hair, all out of curl. "Mother's sure to be feeling languid; she always is after a megrim. And Father'll be cross. And anyway, don't forget the Howes are coming to coffee and you're supposed to apologize. You'd best hurry. Zelda's in your room waiting for you this minute." And she swayed her own immaculate small self past Jade and along the hall toward the front stairs.

Jade, irresistibly tempted as always by the sight of conscious virtue, made no effort at all to resist the temptation. She reached out a hand . . .

"Awp!" squeaked Lavinia.

CHAPTER THREE

Challenge

Jade had never liked William Howe, who heartily returned the sentiment. This was largely because William considered himself to be a special gift from a benign God to humanity—or at least to Virginia—and Jade, to put it simply, didn't. Since William's parents had spent most of his life fostering this notion, it was perhaps not fair to blame William entirely. Jade, nothing if not fair, impartially spread her dislike to include them as well.

His parents sat now in the charming green-papered parlor sipping coffee, and William—who always put on a grand show in public—rose to bow with elaborate charm as Jade entered with Lavinia and Matthew in tow. His smile was that of a cat with one paw planted firmly on a mouse's tail, just waiting for the mouse to notice.

Jade ignored the charm and took note of the smile. William was not of a forgiving nature, and this matter of the fox was quite the most infuriating thing she had done to him since punching him in the nose more than a year ago. Meeting his eyes, she gave him a curtsy so deep as to be a mocking parody of a curtsy, which produced several startled glances from the others and an entirely wrong conclusion from her father. Only William understood perfectly. The mouse was going to behave in a very unmouse-like way.

"I think Melanie has something to say to you, William," said Mr. Lennox. Jade turned a surprised head, shook it emphatically. What was Father thinking of? He was frowning now, his eyebrows saying apologize or else. Jade remained silent.

"Very well," he said, his voice tight. "Melanie has chosen, rather than apologize for loosing your fox, to have me tell you publicly that I have whipped her severely for it."

There was a constrained silence. William contrived to look noble and still give Jade a triumphant glance. Lavinia flushed. And Jade, seething and mortified, held her head high and looked altogether impenitent.

Vinnie, fearing lest something even more embarrassing be said, at once asked Mr. Howe in a high sweet voice how his tobacco crop was coming along, and everyone plunged into this subject with almost audible relief. The conversation flowed as if afraid to stop, through all aspects of tobacco: how crops got worse, requiring new land, and prices from England got lower, and the East India Company greedier, so that what with one thing and two or three others, smuggling was as much a necessity here as it was in England. Even piracy was almost respectable and distinctly useful.

"After all, the government's always been quick enough to hire privateers to harass the Spanish and French and Dutch trading ships, and the pirates just do the same thing independently. And keep the profit for themselves, of course."

"Except," Mr. Lennox pointed out disapprovingly, "they don't draw the line at English ships. Pity. London might not have taken such strong action against them last year if they'd restrained themselves. And after all, some of them are upper class and quite socially acceptable, like Paul Raynor and James Brown."

Mr. Howe nodded. Then he frowned. "But then there are the ruffians like Blackbeard, and scum like Calico Jack and that jezebel Anne Bonney—"

The ladies looked shocked, Lavinia pained, Matt deeply interested, and Jade truculent. "I thought you said she came from one of the good families in Charleston," she pointed out. "So why isn't she socially acceptable, too?"

They frowned at her, displeased. "She's a female," said Mr. Howe, falling into the trap.

Jade slanted a derisive smile. "Then good birth makes it all right for a man to be a pirate, but worse for a woman?"

Matt looked suddenly reflective. (Jade had hopes for Matt.) But the others never noticed that the trap had been sprung—or even existed. They nodded, complaisant and complacent. Of course.

Wrath arose in Jade, and for an instant she hated even her own parents and sister.

"Why don't you be honest, and just pass a law against women being braver or cleverer than men?" she demanded, scathing, and received a battery of shocked and affronted stares.

"*Melanie!*"

Jade, not wanting to be sent to her room, subsided. There was a brief silence, not comfortable.

"That was a very sudden storm we had this morning,"

ventured Mrs. Howe in the bright tones of one who is tactfully changing the subject. "Young William says he ran into Melanie out riding early."

Jade chuckled suddenly. "We ran into each other," she amended accurately, and watched, alert, as his eyes brightened with malice.

"Do you always ride astride like that, Melanie?" he inquired with faintly pained courtesy. "It seems—well—a bit odd for a young lady."

"Melanie!" squeaked her mother, "you *weren't!*" And Jade knew that William knew he had scored.

"Yes, I was." She nodded, unchastened. "And a good thing, too, or William would probably have unseated me with that great monstrous horse of his."

Mrs. Howe, sensing a lack of charity toward her William, frowned. Her William at once fired another shaft, not entirely at random. "You shouldn't come galloping out of side lanes like that. And what were you doing at Mad Maupin's, anyway?"

"He's not mad!" blazed Jade incautiously. "At least," she added with belated and rather lame guile, "he wasn't when Grandfather used to take me to visit him." She scowled, hating the indignity of such deceptions. It wasn't at all the sort of thing Antigonë would have done—but then Antigonë had only her life to lose, while Jade had fencing.

"Do you visit him very often, alone like that?" persisted the diabolic William, looking like someone trying not to look shocked.

Mr. Lennox, who believed in keeping skeletons within the family, broke in with a smile. "Oh, Melanie never visits him now; not since my parents died," he said with a smoothness that gave no hint of what he might be thinking—or what he might say to Jade later.

William gave him one pitying glance, instantly covered by a mask of shining good manners. He was a splendid actor, was William, much better than Jade. "Oh, of course sir—er—if you say so." He looked doubtful.

"I *like* Monsieur Maupin," announced Matthew, with a sure instinct that his sister needed rescue.

"He's an incorrigible old eccentric." Mr. Lennox, refusing to be drawn, shook a rueful head at his son.

"In—incorgible eccentric," repeated Matt with satisfaction. "That's what I'm going to be when I get old, too."

Jade spared him a thoughtful glance. He might, at that.

Lavinia spared him a disapproving glance, but only briefly. She was busy concentrating shocked reproach at William. She had high principles, had Vinnie, and William had just violated several of them. He would probably come to a bad end, she decided darkly, and she treated him forever after with a manner of frozen sherbet, sweet but icy.

The visit dragged to an end. Jade admirably concealed a sense of sick apprehension. William studied her face and those of her parents in vain for any clues to how much damage he had done. It would be disappointing never to know. When his parents rose to leave, he hung behind, letting the others go out into the wide entry-hall, ahead of him. Melanie, gratifyingly, hung back as well. William smiled. He was about to find out whether he had scored.

He found out at once. Without preliminaries she picked up a small footstool and hit him with it.

The next few minutes were quite simply appalling. And the period after the outraged Howes had led their bruised son away was even worse. Mother had a severe attack of the vapors requiring the urgent attention of Lavinia; and Jade stood before her grim-faced father, her full taffeta skirts still awry from battle, her chin up. She was in for it now—but if only Father would forget the bit about Monsieur Maupin, she didn't mind.

He spoke at last, looking at her as if she had finally but unsurprisingly sprouted visible horns and forked tail. "Aside from the matter of"—he seemed unable to believe his own voice—"assaulting a guest, I want to know at once whether you went to Maupin's house this morning."

Now Jade had no moral scruples about lying in general. In fact, she considered some lies quite beneficial. But a lie to escape consequences was shaming, loathsome, degrading even if one got away with it, and unthinkably humiliating if one didn't. A whipping was far less damaging to the pride. But the price of truth now was her fencing lessons—and a whipping for Joshua. Jade set her teeth.

"No," she said, and stuck her chin out.

Possibly it was the chin that gave her away. Her father looked at her with withering contempt that brought a hot crimson blush to her cheeks, and then sent a slave to fetch Joshua. Then for a few moments the silence was broken only by Mother's vapors, while Jade stared at the floor, stricken with shame, anger, and despair. Poor Joshua, so transparently truthful by nature, about to be confronted with an impossible choice of loyalties—and without even knowing what had already been said, either!

He arrived, uneasy and apprehensive. "Did you accompany Mistress Melanie to Maupin's house this morning?" demanded his owner brusquely, and watched the slave's stricken eyes turn helplessly to Jade for some clue.

"Leave him alone!" she cried, reckless. "He has to do what I tell him. He's mine; you gave him to me," she added truthfully but not quite accurately. Joshua had indeed been presented to her on her tenth birthday—and taken back five minutes later after she had insisted on trying to free him.

Her father ignored her, kept inexorable eyes on Joshua. "Answer me."

Jade released the slave from his awful dilemma. "If you want to know, we did go there." She paused, nursing the faintest of hopes that the confession might be allowed to stop at that. But Father went on staring at the miserable Joshua.

"What for? Have you gone more than once?"

Jade flung her head back and prudence to the winds. Not for her was back-to-the-wall fighting! Her nature was to attack when cornered. "I fence!" she announced. "I've been learning for years, and I'm good at it, too!"

It really was as if a lightning bolt had torn through the room. Her mother instantly had a fainting fit, Lavinia gave a scandalized squeak, and her father stood still for a moment, staring at her with an expression she couldn't at all decipher. Then he jerked his chin at the door.

"Go to your room and stay until I've decided what to do."

She swaggered out, insufferably nonchalant in order to hide her misery. And she stayed all day in her dainty pink room, hostess to a stream of visitors. First there was Zelda, red-eyed, with a tray of good things from cook and a message of devotion from Joshua. Miss Turner, tight-lipped. An astonished Matt wanted to know more about her fencing lessons. A prim Lavinia who lectured until Jade threatened to box her ears. And finally Mother, weeping and reproachful.

It was a hopeless interview. Mrs. Lennox couldn't in the least understand her changeling daughter and was by now reasonably sure she didn't want to. Jade couldn't understand such determined spinelessness as Mother showed to Father and to convention, and didn't try to hide her contempt. By the time Mother left the room, they were further apart than ever.

And at last the stranger who was her father came and stood staring at her as an unnatural sort of wild animal. Mr. Lennox knew the laws of nature as well as anyone. Boys were meant to be manly, spirited, brave; girls to be feminine, gentle, charming. It was true that his own mother had had rather more spirit than was seemly; in fact the Lennox family had an unfortunate tendency to produce and to marry girls of this sort. He recalled uneasily the tales he had heard of his own mother, and his grandmother, and great-aunts, who did hair-raising things, and of *their* almost mythical grandmother, the Lady Valerie. . . . And here was his own daughter, with the wildness and perversity of all of them combined, apparently dead to all feeling.

And Jade, wretched behind her jutting chin, braced herself. She felt unbearably vulnerable. How could she ever face life without Monsieur Maupin and fencing?

"I don't suppose," her father said heavily, "that it would occur to apologize, or express shame or regret for your behavior?"

It was a novel idea. Jade searched her soul. "I'm sorry I embarrassed you in front of the Howes," she conceded. "And I'm sorry I didn't hit William harder," she added with deep sincerity.

Father reddened, controlled himself. "But not that you lied?" His voice was scathing, and it was Jade's turn to flush.

"Yes!" she said hotly. "I *hated* that; you know I never lie; it's cowardly!" Astonishing that she should have to explain what was so obvious! "But I had to."

He didn't understand, of course. "Are you not even ashamed of your iniquitous behavior, aping men, wearing male clothing like a brazen little hoyden?" His scorn was patent. It should have shriveled her.

It didn't. She wasn't ashamed of any of these things, and it never occurred to her to pretend that she was. She shook her head.

Incomprehension lay between them, thick and unyielding.

"You can't go on like this," he said at last, grimmer than she had ever seen him. "You're making your mother ill, alienating all our friends, disgracing the whole family. And you think punishment just cancels out whatever you've done, leaving you free to go do it again." This was perfectly true, and Jade didn't try to deny it. "Will you promise me never again to see Maupin or touch a sword?" he demanded, inexorable.

"No," said Jade, just as inexorable. Might as well promise not to breathe.

Father must have seen this in her face, for he tightened his lips. "This time there's going to be no compromise, Melanie. I don't want to break your spirit—whatever you may think—but one way or another, I *am* going to curb it. Do you understand?"

Jade grinned defiance. She was just asking to have her ears boxed, knew it, waited for it. But her father just looked at her for a long hard moment and then shrugged.

"Very well, I've no choice but to send you away."

She stared at him, startled and uncertain, the grin gone now.

"When I go to Jamaica at the first of the month, I shall take you to stay with your Aunt Louisa and Uncle Augustus. They've been asking to have you visit ever since your cousin Clarinda died."

"They'll send me right back," predicted Jade, always a realist.

"They saw what you were like when they visited us," her father reminded her, "and are willing to have you anyway. Your uncle trained horses before he moved to Jamaica, he's handled slaves ever since, and I don't see why a niece should be all that different." His face was stony. "In any event, Melanie, they want you at the moment—and I regret that no one in Williamsburg does. I'm sorry if this hurts you, but you've only yourself to blame."

Jade wouldn't for the world have shown how much it hurt. She indicated that she was delighted to be going anywhere at all. And it was true, she reflected desolately after he had stalked out of the room. Woefully true. She didn't want to be alienated from her family, a stranger living among them to their great disturbance or sent away in disgrace. She wanted—she wanted to go adventuring with love and regret. She wanted to be sad at the thought of leaving. She didn't know what she wanted at all.

It was days before she managed to elude Miss Turner and the obligingly short-sighted Zelda, and go back to see Monsieur Maupin, who opened his door quite as if he'd been sitting there expecting her—which he probably had.

"*Enfin.* My wicked jade of a pupil, who has been even more wicked than usual. Come in, and we will have a most ferocious duel, just in case it is our last. Where is Joshua? And have you hit your unfortunate governess over the head in order to escape?"

"No, I only locked her in her room." Jade stepped briskly over the threshold. "And of course I didn't bring Joshua; do you think I want to get him punished?"

Monsieur Maupin regarded her with hooded eyes, half laughing. "And you, *ma petite?*"

Jade shrugged. "I wanted to see you again," she said simply. Monsieur Maupin understood, for it was part of the code he had taught her, that he who calls the tune must pay the piper. Once she understood that, he never questioned her right to call what tunes she chose. "You know I'm going away? Father's been to scold you, I dare say."

Monsieur Maupin straightened his old-fashioned peruke. "*Bien entendu*, and very much the angry father, too. But he found it very much uncomfortable because I kept reminding him of when he was a naughty boy and his father and I used to fish him out of the river and smack his bottom."

Jade giggled irrepressibly and went into the other room to change to her beloved breeches and full-sleeved shirt.

When she came out, they had a splendid battle, no quarter asked or given, which darted all over the large room like a dance of dragonflies: fierce and glorious and swift. The tune was the sibilance of steel on steel, and Jade's occasional peal of joy at a close parry or a skilled feint. There was nothing like it, nothing at all! No score was kept; it just went on until both duelers dropped to the floor in blissful exhaustion. Jade sighed. When again would she know this delight of skilled, precise movement? She caught her breath.

"I can't give it up! I won't!" And she set her lips lest Monsieur Maupin think she was whining at consequences, and despise her.

The old man hid his own bitter dismay at losing the one person in the world he really cared for. "Then demand it of God," he suggested. "Remembering always, *enfin,* that you will sooner or later be presented with the reckoning, and you cannot then change your mind and say the price is too high, you do not wish to pay. *Le Bon Dieu* is not mocked, and I think He does not admire quibblers and whiners."

Jade nodded.

"Swords!" she cried. "Adventure! Freedom! And I'll pay any price!"

Monsieur Maupin regarded her for a long minute with grave eyes. "*Bon.* Remember always to demand more of yourself than anyone else," he warned her. "Otherwise you become merely a tiresome rebellious young girl who wants that the whole world should change to suit her whim. The world is full of such as these; most of them grow up at last, but are not particularly admirable, *enfin.* They are against everything, *for* nothing."

Jade frowned uneasily. Did this apply to her? But the old man was smiling. "You, I think, already fight to a purpose, and soon you will begin to discover what it is and concentrate your energies on that instead of all things at once." He laughed at her puzzled face, arose. "You shall have a going-away gift from this Mad Maupin which your father will permit you to accept—but which no one but you will enough understand. *Regardes-toi.*"

He lifted the lid of a traveling box which stood unobtrusively under the window; a beautifully-made old box of satiny wood. "A most suitable gift, non?" he chuckled, and lifted a totally unexpected false bottom. "So small a space under here, just enough, I think, to contain a rapier laid corner to corner and wrapped in a pair of breeches and a shirt or perhaps two—"

He got no further, for Jade had caught him in a rapturous hug that nearly deposited both of them in the box.

"*Bon,*" he said at last, when they had both recovered their dignity and self-possession and were extremely matter-of-fact just as a precaution. "We say *au revoir* now, and you shall go home and let the poor Miss Turner out of her room and take your punishment and presently sail away. But if you stay too long, *ma petite*, I think I shall then go traveling myself, perhaps to Jamaica, for this place will very much bore me when you are not here to make trouble. *Va-t-en!* Go away, quickly!"

CHAPTER FOUR

The Pearl

The *Pearl* clawed her way southward under reefed topsails, a stiff westerly wind singing in the rigging and laying the little merchant ship over like a toy boat in a pond. She climbed the long rollers diagonally: first the starboard bow rose and tilted, pointing its bowsprit at the sky. Up and up, until with a twisting lurch at the crest she began rolling massively over the other way, pitching dizzily as the wave passed under the stern, the bow nosing down and over until Jade—delightedly clinging to the fo'c'sle rail—stared almost straight down into the foaming sea. The lovely thing was that it was never done. One corkscrew complete, another swell started it all over again.

"Cor, you shouldn't be up here, Mistress Lennox!" It was Tom Deane, nicest of all the crew, staring at her with wondering eyes. "The quarterdeck's for officers and passengers." He waved a tanned hand at the raised and railed deck at the stern, "Fo'c'sle's for us common sailors."

Jade turned and looked at him pertly, liking the cleft chin, peaked eyebrows, fair hair streaked and bleached to pale gilt by the sun, and smooth-muscled arms—and especially his air of astonished admiration. Jade had never before been admired by a young man. The boys in Williamsburg had a number of emotions toward her, but esteem was not one of them. This was a novel sensation—and pleasant.

"I like it here in front," she told him simply. "I mean, in the bow. On the fo'c'sle." She frowned slightly over all these new nautical terms, in which port was left and starboard right, and abaft behind and abeam to the side. . . . "Tell me if I've got it right," she commanded Tom. "That part of the deck down there—I mean between the fo'c'sle and quarterdeck—is the waist; and there's the foremast in front and the mainmast amidships and the mizzenmast in the stern; and those crossbars up there that the sails hang on are the yards; and the ropes that hold it all up are the rigging; and those nets you climb up are the shrouds; only the ropes going across—the ones you stand on—are the ratlines . . . and . . . Oh yes, the helm is the steering bit, and the hatches are the openings to the hold, where we stow cargo. What else?"

Tom laughed and twinkled down at her from his very blue eyes. "What about motions and directions?" he suggested, swaying easily to the slanted deck.

Jade moved away from the rail a bit, to prove she could balance as well as anyone. "Rolling's from side to side like a cradle, and pitching's front and back like a bounding dolphin, and the quarter is between abeam and astern, and we've got the wind on our starboard beam now, and windward is toward the wind and lee is away from it, and you must never spit to windward or get blown onto a lee shore." She smirked at him, openly pleased with herself. "Now teach me the sails."

The *Pearl* swooped again, over a particularly large

roller. Jade, giggling, had to grab the rail to keep from falling right across the deck, and even Tom staggered slightly. Spray lashed over them. "You sure you wouldn't be more comfortable on the quarterdeck?" Tom repeated, concerned.

Jade cast a wickedly amused eye astern, where her father was altogether failing to enjoy the heaving of the ship. In fact, he was invisible in his cabin, with Joshua attending him. Jade strongly suspected that he was doing some heaving of his own, and she felt a most unfilial sense of triumph. Mere inferior female, was she? She giggled at Tom Deane.

"There's only one place I'd rather be than here," she told him with truth, and lifted her face to stare longingly aloft, where the great pyramids of sails reached up, up, sweeping wide circles against the blue sky, and where the nimble shape of a sailor climbed the shrouds toward the topgallant masthead. How she longed to put on her breeches and follow!

"You wouldn't!" said Tom, staring at her.

"I would! Why wouldn't I? Don't *you* like it up there?"

"Yes, well enough I suppose." He looked faintly surprised at the notion. "Unless the ship's too lively, of course, or a blizzard's blowing. Only—one doesn't expect a girl— But then, I dare say any girl who actually enjoys *this* sort of thing, when any respectable landlubber loses his dinner and wishes he'd stayed home—" He chuckled.

Jade chortled back and gave another unsympathetic glance at the quarterdeck. "I just wish we'd have a storm," she declared, trying to imagine waves like mountains coming at them.

"Oh, do you, now?" It was the harsh, satiric voice of

one Rory MacDonald, the second mate. He towered above her, balanced easily to the lurching of the ship, sneering down at her with those unpleasantly ringed and slanted blue eyes of his, so different from Tom's mild and friendly ones. "Daft female! You'd change your mind quickly enough," he went on with obvious relish at the idea. "I can see you now, green and tossing your biscuits and bawling for land!"

Jade turned to face him, her back firmly against the rail as the *Pearl* shoved her bow into the air once more and hung there quivering before the downward heave and corkscrew. It would be most embarrassing to lose her balance in front of this arrogant and ill-tempered boor, whose face looked as if it had been carved in a hurry with a blunt knife. And she felt herself rather at a disadvantage, anyway, because he had been through storms at sea and she hadn't. She surveyed his crooked and oversized nose, the thatch of black hair and eyebrows, with an air of lofty disdain while she considered how best to counterattack. Defense wouldn't do here; she knew that instinctively. All very well for fencing, but in argument it merely weakened one's position immeasurably, besides being undignified. No, she needed a scathing, crushing retort, something that would instantly puncture his arrogance. . . .

"Your hair needs cutting," she said.

It was not one of her better efforts. He looked disgusted and Jade couldn't honestly blame him. Even Tom seemed uncomfortable—but this was probably because he would have liked to come to Jade's defense, and didn't dare. To oppose one's superior at sea was mutiny, punishable by hanging from the yardarm should the captain choose—and Captain Narramore was a very severe disciplinarian.

Not that Jade would have wanted Tom to fight her battles, of course, but this was no comfort to Tom. He stood looking at her miserably, while Jade tried to recover her lost ground by arranging her face into an expression something between hauteur and tolerant amusement.

MacDonald looked at her—infuriatingly—as if she were a bellicose mouse. "No use sticking your chin out at me," he told her. "For one thing it's the wrong shape, and for another, it makes you look ridiculous. All those airs for a scrawny, impudent wee wretch of a lass who needs spanking even more than most—and I never yet knew a female worth talking to except my grandmother. . . . She was a witch," he added reflectively.

"That," said Jade scaldingly, "explains a great deal! And nobody asked you to come up here and make a nuisance of yourself talking to me, so why don't you go away and make us both happy?"

That was better! His swarthy, angular face flickered with surprise and annoyance. "Go sound the well, Deane," he commanded Tom, who turned reluctantly and left. "As for you, miss, get back to the quarterdeck where you belong."

"Shan't!" said Jade, still seething.

MacDonald looked very much as if he'd like to knock her right over the rail and into the sea—now surging just below as the ship's bow leaned into the trough between swells. Balancing herself against the dizzy tilt, Jade laughed in his face, loving the thrill of danger. For a long moment he stared, brooding and menacing; then he spat over the lee rail, turned with a contemptuous swing of wide shoulders, leaped down to the waist, and made his arrogant way aft to the helm.

Jade turned her back on him and her attention to the sea just a fraction too late to be really effective. She couldn't feel that she had really won this encounter, and she was almost as deeply annoyed with herself as with the second mate. How she'd love to continue the argument with that small hard footstool from the parlor back home! With very little effort, she felt, she could hate that Rory MacDonald even more than William Howe.

"You all right, Missy Lanie?" Joshua's massive figure loomed worriedly. No knowing what devilment his young mistress might get into while he was busy tending his master's illness. From the first day out, she'd tended to stare at the shrouds and rigging with a longing and speculative eye that stood Joshua's hair on end. And Minnie, the dull-witted bond slave supposed to act as lady's maid, was hopelessly prostrate in the tiny cubbyhole allotted her, and no help at all.

"You all right?" he repeated, falling against the rail as the *Pearl* started downhill, and clinging there with his eyes fixed suspiciously on her face. "You look like you're fixing to throw someone overboard. You don't want to get in any more trouble *yet*, do you, Missy Lanie?" he pleaded, with the air of a man who would love to egg her on, but thought it much more comfortable for them both if he didn't.

Jade's grin took on that familiar tilt, self-mocking. "Don't worry, Joshua, I'll be good until it's too late for Father to take you back to Williamsburg with him." Joshua looked relieved. "All the same, I *would* love to throw someone overboard! And cut off his horrid beak of a nose first."

Joshua followed her glance and identified the nose in

question without difficulty, since it was aimed disrespectfully in Jade's direction. Joshua didn't at all care for its owner. A rough, common young man with fierce eyes and tongue and a blazing contempt for both slaves and females.

"Don't you have anything to do with him, Missy Lanie," Joshua advised strongly.

But Jade had already dropped him out of her mind and turned back to her new love, the sea. Her uptilted nose sniffed the salty air with rapture, her vagrant dimples were showing. The sea! Who'd live on land when there was the sea, lonely and ever-changing; menace, mystery, and challenge? Why couldn't girls be sailors? It wasn't fair! She chalked up another bitter score in her account against society.

And she sighed. The future lurking over that southern horizon, depressed with the memory of vague, fluttery Aunt Louisa and an Uncle Augustus who ruled her with benevolent pomposity and who could train—or was it tame?—any horse, slave, or female. Well, he wouldn't tame Jade! But the process of proving this to him promised to be a long and unpleasant one, and she wondered with a sense of panic how long she could go on fighting the whole world. What if it broke her at last, so that she wasn't Jade any more, but only an empty shell named Melanie? She shivered in the hot sun, lonely as the sea itself, but much more vulnerable.

A patch of yellow sargasso weed tossed past. A school of dolphin scalloped up to the ship and, smiling, began to play games with it. Joshua laughed down at them, one brown eye fixed uneasily on his small mistress. But Jade couldn't talk about this to Joshua, who'd been defeated before he was born. And Monsieur Maupin was far away, and Grandfather and Grandmother dead, and there wasn't anyone else. She squared her shoulders, and turned to Joshua.

"There's Father out on deck," she observed, glancing toward the stern. "I dare say we ought to go see how he feels." And with a lilt of something very near to malice in voice and step, she led the way down to the waist and aft to the quarterdeck.

Father stood listening to Captain Narramore, a lean man with an aristocratic-looking face, a choleric temper, and the strong conviction that if he wasn't actually God, he was the nearest thing to it that mortal man would ever see. For that matter, on his ship he *was* God, and an Old Testament one, at that. Passengers and crew alike were expected to listen with reverence to every word he uttered. And Mr. Lennox was at once too polite and too weakened from his recent indisposition to put up any struggle at all.

"—usually run the Middle Passage," the captain was saying as Jade mounted the steps and returned her father's somewhat wan smile with one of pointed well-being. Captain Narramore spared a nod of godly affability and went on with his monologue. "Liverpool to West Africa with cotton goods, then to the West Indies, and back to Liverpool with sugar, coffee, fruit, cocoa, ginger, indigo—the lot. I just did this little extra run to the mainland and back to Jamaica—"

He interrupted himself before Jade could ask what the Middle Passage might be, and whirled around to glare at the helm with the air of Jehovah about to hurl thunderbolts. "Port that helm, MacDonald! Can't you feel the wind shifting, you blazing landlubber?"

MacDonald, already in the act of helping the novice helmsman port it, glanced at the captain over his own right shoulder. His voice became dark syrup with just a drop of corrosive acid. "Aye aye, sir."

Captain Narramore stared, scowled, couldn't quite put his finger on it. "Young Beelzebub," he muttered uncertainly. "If he ever gets out of line with me, I'll have him flogged."

Jade privately thought that a splendid idea, but unlikely. MacDonald—who shot her a knowing and sardonic glance even as she looked at him—was far too clever to provide an excuse. All the same, his tail *did* want cropping, the arrogant fellow! She smiled suddenly, lifted her voice to carry, fluting, over to the helm.

"He looks the sort of fellow," she observed brightly, "who'd have a witch for a grandmother."

The fellow shot her a look of pure poison, and Captain Narramore (the sort of man who'd instantly burn any such grandmother at the stake) nodded darkly. "Shouldn't be surprised." He looked at MacDonald with suspicion. "If he hadn't such a good sea eye—"

He was interrupted by a shout from above. "Deck there! Sail off the starboard bow. Looks Spanish."

Militant preparation at once swept the ship. Sailors ran up and down the rigging, nine-pounder brass guns were run out, and the course veered to port. It was clear even to Jade's novice eyes that the *Pearl*'s best defense was her speed rather than her little pop-guns—and also that this strange sail on the horizon had the weather gauge on them. Her heart beating with pleasurable excitement, she pranced like a child around the quarterdeck, and finally waylaid Tom Deane on his way to the mizzen shrouds.

"What's all the fuss about? Would a Spanish ship really attack us? Aren't we at peace?"

Tom shrugged, the cleft appearing in his tanned cheeks, and his teeth white. "On paper and in Europe," he agreed. "Surely you know that, Mistress Lennox! Out here, Spain still thinks she has Divine Right to the whole western hemisphere; and whenever she likes the odds, her ships act more like pirates than the pirates do. Much more," he added, rubbing his sun-bleached head ruefully. "At least most pirates are English, and they say—" He changed his mind about finishing that thought. "But you mustn't worry, Mistress; you'll be safe any road," he added belatedly and with far more good will than conviction.

Jade at once bristled. "Stop treating me like a half-witted butterfly! If *you* think *I* think anybody's going to tell his bullets and cannon balls to be sure to stay away from the passengers—"

"Get aloft, there, Deane!" Tom at once fled up the shrouds, and the second mate came over and glared down at Jade, contemptuous. "And you stop flirting with the crew, you silly minx!"

Jade, for once speechless, felt herself turning scarlet, and he observed this with clear satisfaction.

"Deck there!" bawled the masthead. "Dutch flag. Veering to parallel course."

There was a general impression of relief and things returned to normal with a slightly sheepish air of having been just practicing, anyway. Rory MacDonald grinned offensively at Jade.

"You *are* a half-witted butterfly, you know. Do you really pretend that you don't expect special treatment because you're a young lady? Liar!" And he strode away in the most cowardly fashion before Jade could rally her wits for a riposte. She had never in her life been so taken-aback. *No* one, not even William, had ever accused her of being a whiner, a liar, or a flirt—or even, for that matter, a lady! The injustice of it seared. How she longed to make him take it back, admit he was wrong—preferably at rapier-point! It wasn't fair! Why should women be denied the right to demand satisfaction in a duel? Men's rules!

Loathing the entire breed, she gazed with embittered eyes on her father, who chose that moment to pay serious attention to his daughter for the first time since succumbing to the motion of the ship. His own gaze could not possibly have been mistaken for approval.

"Melanie!" he realized, staring with startled discovery upon her sunburned face. "Where's your face-mask? Your sun shade? What will your aunt say? Your complexion is ruined!"

Jade smiled, unrepentant.

CHAPTER FIVE

"*Dear Little Melanie!*"

Jamaica, as even the unpoetic Jade was ready to admit, was an emerald set in blue enamel. And Port Royal, atip a long spit of land guarding the bay, was still a pretty place, despite the earthquake that had all but destroyed it a generation ago.

"The coming town will be Kingstown across on the north side of the bay," volunteered the first mate as they started to round the point. "Tops'l sheets! Tops'l clew lines! Helm a lee!" he added in a bellow not at all meant for Jade. She didn't mind. She stared with quick interest at the activity aloft, at the ships all turned to the tide in the mirror of the harbor, and, right at the point on the starboard, the massive and lofty tower of Fort St. Jago de la Vega, with a narrow mole running around its outer wall. She might have paid more attention had she guessed she was destined to know it much better; but as she didn't her eyes turned quickly to the blaze of green beyond, and a number of trees bearing highly unlikely scarlet or purple blossoms. A wave of warm fragrance was suddenly blotted out by another smell: an overpowering fetid stench that caused Mr. Lennox's eyebrows to rise inquiringly and his daughter to turn a startled face. The first mate had vanished, and it was the ubiquitous MacDonald who slanted a disrespectful eyebrow.

"Slave ship," he remarked laconically, one ringed blue eye fixed on the jib. Jade made a strangled sound, and he glanced at her cynically. "Pack 'em in like spoons, on their sides 'tween-decks. Lots die, of course, but that's cheaper than cutting numbers to start with. Unless there's a storm, of course. . . . Avast there! 'Vast hauling!" He leaped down to the waist. Jade sped him a look of passionate hate, and her father looked pained.

"Not at all the thing," he said, but in tones that seemed to deplore the conversation more than the fact. Doubtless he had always known how slaves were shipped, and thought it all most unfortunate, but one of the facts of life and business. Almost everyone thought that way. Jade, hating him for his silent acquiescence, didn't ask. She hated everyone. How dare God let such things go on, and unpunished? Her peeling face was pulled into a sullen scowl while a message was sent ashore for Uncle Augustus, and the slave ship at the far end of the quay proceeded to unload some of its cargo.

The hatches were opened, a mournful wailing carried over the shining water, and a string of naked, gaunt captives appeared, crawling and staggering over the deck and to the quay. Mr. Lennox turned away, his sense of decency and fastidiousness deeply offended, and his sense of propriety, as well. Young girls shouldn't witness such things!

"Come over to this other rail at once, Melanie!" he ordered sharply.

Jade paid no attention. Shaking with outrage, she teetered on the verge of the most enormous scene she had ever perpetrated. Then Joshua was there, thrusting a parasol into her hands, staring down at her with pleading eyes. "Don't, Missy Lanie!"

She glared at him, hating his slavishness, her eyes flashing green in a way that nearly unnerved him. He was staring at her rather as a pagan might look at a very black thunder cloud, she thought furiously, as if he very much hoped the goddess could be placated this time—but strongly doubted it. Unfairly, she turned her fury on him.

"Don't look at *me!*" she spat. "Look at *them!* Your own parents had that done to them!" How could he be so spineless? "Don't you *care?*"

"Yes, Missy Lanie," he said humbly, but it was clear that his anxiety was more for her than the unfortunate wretches across the harbor. After all, his only tie with them was that of race and bondage; there was affection between him and Jade. She glared at him, knowing this, and knowing too that he was looking deliberately humble, his most effective weapon over her.

"Melanie! Did you hear me?"

She stalked across to the other side of the quarterdeck—but as far from her father as she could get. He at once came to her side, his long face stern and angry.

"I expect instant obedience from you, Melanie; you know that. And anyone who claims to be distressed over slavery ought to begin at home by treating her own slave with a little kindness. What have you said to poor Joshua?"

Jade nearly committed violence. She was accidentally saved from it by MacDonald, who strode past just then, arrogantly unconscious of her insignificant existence, and diverting the stream of her wrath.

"If you'd let me free Joshua, he wouldn't *be* a slave," she muttered accusingly. "And I don't care what you say, or what the Bible says, either; it's *wicked!*" And she whisked herself off to her tiny sleeping cabin to sulk.

Uncle Augustus, arriving in due course with carriage and liveried slaves, was brilliantly clad for the occasion in saffron waistcoat, mauve knee breeches, and a great deal of lace at cuffs and cravat. He looked much too warm for the heat that clamped down wherever the trade winds didn't touch—and yet he also gave Jade the vague impression of a large pale frog, white and clammy, although he was neither.

A massive man was Uncle Augustus, with a large face, round pink cheeks, pale blue eyes, and a mouth like a kindly steel trap. He patted Jade's cheek with a benevolent and self-satisfied palm that was moist only with the heat.

"Well well, the little Melanie. What a pretty young lady you are growing to be, *Liebchen.* Your aunt and I will be very pleased to have you stay with us. I am sorry to hear that you are sometimes very naughty, but we will change all that, *nein?*"

Jade gave him her crooked little smile and declined to commit herself. She didn't much like her mother's sister's Prussian husband, at best.

They drove up the seven-mile finger of peninsula and into the plantation country behind, brilliant green. Here and there were patches of fascinating jungle, a blaze of huge flowers, a whirr of bright tropical wings, and behind it all the rise of the Blue Mountains. It was beautiful country—with a slight air of menace lurking beneath the beauty. Jade's spirits rose to the novelty and sense of adventure in spite of her sulks.

Through vast sugar canes of that violent green they rode, and then up a drive to a large airy house with shaded verandas, set in glowing garden and lawns. Inside, large fans hung from every ceiling, worked by small slave children tugging at the pulleys in slow rhythm, and Aunt Louisa waited, moist-eyed and sentimental and clad in a tight-laced full gown of a pink that set Jade's teeth on edge.

"Dear little Melanie! Poor dear Thomas!" she cried, enveloping them both with solicitude and damp kisses. "Was it a terrible trip? Were you dreadfully seasick? Poor dears, you must be tired! You can go right up to your rooms and lie down for a nice rest before the dinner tonight; we're having guests, and it was so nice you could get here in time, although I suppose you couldn't know, could you? And in any case I quite understand that ships arrive whenever they please, although I do think captains could do better if they'd only put their minds to it. . . . Dear Melanie, you're choking! Poor child! Have you caught a horrible rheum? I'm sure I shouldn't be surprised, with all that sea air about! Now you go right upstairs with Fidelia and lie down for a while, so you'll feel like meeting dear Dr. Hughes, and Governor Lawes and his wife and sister-in-law, and the Quayles—Dear Chester is just the right age for you—and—" Her soft face clouded a little. "—and Mr. Chidley Bayard, whom dear Augustus says is quite respectable, and who visits all the best people, but whom I must admit I can't altogether like." She looked apologetically at her husband, who patted her hand, tolerant.

"Now now, Louisa. You mustn't hold it against him that

he speaks with a Cockney accent. After all, he is now a very successful businessman with a great deal of power, and offices in Spanish Cuba and French Hispaniola and the Bahamas."

His wife looked muddled. "But dear Augustus, I was sure you told me once that he was a very wicked man, and did business with all the pirates, and brought that dreadful female one to the governor's ball, where I remember distinctly she hit Mistress Tyson and knocked her down, just because Mistress Tyson said she wasn't fit to associate with, which was quite true, you know. . . . Oh dear, I've shocked poor dear Melanie," she added remorsefully and quite inaccurately. Jade was perfectly fascinated.

"What female pirate?" she demanded. "You mean Anne Bonney? Have you really seen her?"

"*Ja,* Anne Bonney," agreed her uncle, frowning. "That was when Mr. Bayard had his main office on that island of New Providence, when it was a pirate republic, and it is true he brought the pirate jezebel to that ball. Some of the men found her very attractive," he told Father disapprovingly. "And the ladies naturally didn't at all like it."

"What happened?" breathed Jade, entranced. If Jamaica was a place where wicked female pirates could come to governor's balls, she felt there might be much merit in it.

"The governor's sister-in-law spoke very frankly," said Uncle Augustus, clearly on the side of propriety. "It was true she was not very polite, but she is a lady accustomed to saying what she thinks, and the Bonney woman should not have been there." He paused, thoughtful. Jade fairly wriggled with impatient curiosity, and her father looked as if he much regretted this whole conversation.

"Was that when Anne Bonney knocked her down?" demanded Jade.

"*Ja.* And Bayard had to rush her on to one of his ships and use all his influence to save her from being arrested. Governor Lawes swears he will hang her one day." He looked at Jade's delighted face with disapproval. "She is one of Satan's minions. You should take warning, *Liebchen.*"

"I'm way ahead of her," Jade boasted, unimpressed. "I hit guests over the head with footstools."

"*Melanie!*" thundered her father.

"*Dear* Melanie!" bleated her aunt.

Uncle Augustus, not believing a word of it, pretended she hadn't said it. "As for Chidley Bayard, he now hates the Bonney woman even more than Governor Lawes does, and repents ever associating with such scum, and has made Port Royal his main office, and is now quite respectable. "Besides—" Virtue slipped slightly into practical expediency. "—he is now so wealthy and powerful that not even Governor Lawes wishes to offend him."

Jade's cynical smile fell off her face altogether.

Hypocrisy! They'd justify anything that was to their self-interest—and they'd never forgive anything that damaged their self-importance or their pockets! It was a vicious, brutal, horrible world; Jade would never compromise with it; she loathed them all! And she looked at her elders with the air of a small garter snake wishing it were a cobra.

"Mercy me," said her aunt, entirely misinterpreting Jade's expression. "I'm sure this isn't at *all* good for poor dear Melanie to hear! Run upstairs with Fidelia, love, and have a nice rest until time to dress for dinner."

And Jade, her feelings much too strong to put into words, anyway, allowed herself to be led upstairs to a cool blue and white bedchamber, dim and venetian-blinded and mosquito-netted. There was a high blue-canopied four-poster in the center, and tall jars of water in a corner. Fidelia, with flat eyes and expressionless face, skilfully mixed water and scent in a large basin while Jade tried in vain to make friends.

It was no use. Fidelia had apparently decided that a slave couldn't afford to be a person as well. She was efficient—far more efficient than the sulky Minnie, now consigned to general tasks about the house—but that was all. Efficiently she bathed Jade, unpacked her box, wrapped her in a loose silk robe, and took a brush to the untidy curls.

"Missy got pretty hair," she observed with remote politeness, arranging the thick ringlets that clustered to Jade's shoulders in a style all the fashion just now but decidedly hot. "Turn gold on top, where sun hits."

Jade, mildly surprised, peered into the mirror. Sure enough, the honey-brown hair was now a distinct shade nearer honey-gold, and very becoming, she felt, to her ruined complexion. She eyed her sweet-young-girl reflection critically.

"Let's put my hair on top of my head, Fidelia. It would be much cooler that way."

Fidelia looked frightened. "Not done for young missies," she protested, and produced something Mother had packed in Jade's box, and Jade had shoved to the very depths, just above the innocent looking false bottom.

"Missy's stays," pronounced Fidelia.

"Well, you can put them right back again," Jade told

her firmly, "because I shan't wear them." Fidelia looked shocked. Young ladies always wore stays, surely? "I never wear them," Jade explained. "Why should I? Look how skinny I am. Besides, I'll wear a *contouche* most of the time, and that's just a loose dress without a waist at all, so how can anyone know if I'm wearing stays or not? And if Aunt Louisa finds out, I'll take all the blame."

Fidelia gave in at last, reluctant but faced with adamantine. Jade appeared for the dinner party dressed in shift, petticoats, and her prettiest contouche, a loose-fitting overdress of pale daffodil silk over a vine-embroidered petticoat stiffened with strips of whalebone.

"Dear Melanie!" said her aunt fondly. "Isn't she sweet!"

Jade could instantly sympathize with Aunt Louisa's dislike of Chidley Bayard. With his thin, sharp-featured face, he looked like a prosperous ferret wearing a wig; and the elegant peach satin breeches and stiff, full-skirted coat of apple green looked all wrong on him. His very expression was furtive, suspicious, cruel, and Jade couldn't but hold a very low opinion of any woman—pirate or not—who would go anywhere at all with such a mean, cold little man. Her opinion of the intrepid Anne Bonney dropped perceptibly.

On the other hand, she could admire anyone—pirate or not—who punched the governor's sister-in-law in the teeth. Detestable woman! Much worse than Governor Lawes, who at least was intriguing. A florid, portly man, he spoke in clichés, bounced when he got excited, and gloried in self-importance. He was unabashedly vindictive, too—but Jade found his very candor rather engaging; a welcome change from hypocrisy. He had a certain wit, as well, which was more than could be said for his visiting nephew, Chester Quayles.

Jade flickered a critical and distinctly bored green eye at Chester, an amiable young man prepared to admire and be admired. It was unfortunate that Jade was not. Affable young men—even Tom Deane—were so tiresome!

"You aren't listening!" discovered Chester, astonished and offended.

"No," agreed Jade rudely. "You're saying such silly things. I don't care about your new horse or your three slaves of your own; and I'm not in the least like a lily or a rose, and it's stupid to say I am. And of *course* I know I have long lashes; I look in the mirror every day, don't I?"

"Then there's no point in my paying you compliments, is there?" said Chester, justifiably peeved.

"No," agreed Jade.

Conversation languished, and she turned a far more interested ear to the other end of the dinner table, where her father was being brought up to date on recent events in the West Indies.

Dr. Hughes, a lean, gray-wigged man who seemed both kindly and sensible, was speaking.

"You knew, of course, that England sent Captain Woodes Rogers to New Providence last July as the new governor of the Bahamas?"

"I'd heard of it," said Mr. Lennox. "He's been cleaning up piracy, hasn't he?"

"Yes. He offered a free pardon to any pirate giving himself up by the end of September, and they say he's turning New Providence into a respectable, law-abiding place."

Jade broke into adult conversation with a want of manners that caused her father to redden and give her an ominous glance. "You mean all the pirates are reformed now?" she asked, vaguely disappointed.

At once they forgot her manners, and began talking all at once. Not all, they said. Not by any means. And they waved their arms. Look at Bartholomew Roberts, they said. And Charles Vane! Not to mention Calico Jack Rackam and the Bonney female, who, it was said, was really captain of his ship.

And at the mention of Anne Bonney, Chidley Bayard quite literally snarled. Jade stared, fascinated. It was the first time she had ever heard such a sound come from a human being. It was also the first time she had ever felt such a wave of hatred; and she stopped eating suddenly, to eye him with cold revulsion.

Governor Lawes had turned beet-color. "Just wait!" he said, bouncing. "She'll pay for her sins! I'll hang her if it's the last thing I do! I'll break her to pieces with my own two hands!" He looked delighted with the prospect.

Jade remembered the woodcut she had seen of the notorious pirate: a hefty Amazon like those beefy women Rubens painted, much more likely to break the squabby little governor in pieces. She giggled, causing his small blue eyes to fix themselves on her narrowly.

"What if she accepts the pardon?" asked Father, probably trying to divert attention.

Mr. Bayard turned a most unhealthy color and seemed unable to find words. Governor Lawes didn't mind; he liked doing the talking.

"She can't," he gloated. "She's wanted on other charges. A woman of Satan, she is! Burned down her own father's house!"

"Why?" demanded Jade, erupting again into the conversation in a manner that caused her father to look despairing, her aunt shocked, and her uncle suddenly determined. The guests all regarded her with the kindly tolerance one paid to such inferiors as the feeble-minded, children, and females.

"Because she's wicked," they told her patiently, and Jade bristled at such stupidity.

"That's silly! Even wicked people don't do things for no reason! Why didn't she burn down someone else's house instead? What did he do—" She caught her father's menacing eye and subsided into smouldering silence, while they all told her she was being irrelevant, and Aunt Louisa got up rather hastily to announce that the ladies would now retire and leave the men to their port and conversation.

"And that's another thing," muttered Jade subversively. "Why shouldn't *we* stay for port, too?"

"*Melanie!*" said her goaded father. But Governor Lawes —detestable man!—laughed. Comical little thing, wasn't she? he asked as if she weren't there. More fun than a kitten. She could hear his laughter all the way to the parlor.

CHAPTER SIX

Domino

"But Dear Thomas, I left her right here on the veranda, with the loveliest bit of embroidery to do; she *must* be here. Melanie? Dear Melanie, where are you? Perhaps she's strolling in the garden. *Melanie?*"

The red and blue parrot flew away. Jade said a rude word under her breath, and looked down at the grown-ups from her perch on a modestly low branch of the tree. "You've scared it off," she told them reproachfully.

They looked at her. Her contouche was torn, her hair quite out of curl, and she had an altogether indecent expanse of petticoat and bare leg showing. "*Dear* Melanie!" squeaked Aunt Louisa, horrified.

"Melanie!" echoed her father, while Uncle Augustus averted embarrassed eyes. "Come down here at once!"

Jade wriggled her bare toes, rejoicing in their freedom, and slithered off the branch—displaying the rest of her petticoat. They were a distinct handicap, petticoats. If only she dared wear those hidden breeches, in which she had conquered most of the trees near Monsieur Maupin's house.

"Dear Melanie!" cried Aunt Louisa again, enfolding her

niece to her soft bosom and seeming hardly to believe that she was unbroken. "So dangerous, love, and unladylike, too! You mustn't do it again! Besides, what if a snake should get you? And anyway, your dear uncle has asked your dear father to go into town with him to look at some very special slaves Mr. Bottlesford is saving for special customers, and he wondered if you'd like to go, too; and although *dear* Thomas said he didn't think you would, I thought it would be nice to ask you."

Jade flinched away from the very idea. Which, of course, was the precise reason she had to go. "Yes," she said, glowering.

Her father stared. He never *would* understand her! "Very well, then, go have Fidelia make you presentable. But we'll not have any scenes when we get there, young lady; remember that!"

The carriage stopped before a shabby building, square and Spanish-looking, with an eccentric red-tile roof looking as if it had never been repaired since the earthquake. Dust lay thick in the road, and the slave stench poured over Jade as she stepped out of the carriage. She instantly shuttered her face, and stood there like a very young sphinx with extremely green eyes, while the men got out.

Mr. Lennox paused uneasily at the entrance, glanced at his daughter, murmured something to Uncle Augustus, who looked startled and amused.

"*Himmel,* next you will want us to clothe the pigs and cows before she is allowed to see them," he commented; but spoke good-naturedly to the scrawny, gray-headed Mr. Bottlesford, who blinked, stared, nodded, and went back inside. Presently he appeared again, and they all went in. Jade's fists were clenched in the folds of her skirts, and her chin was high, and she wished she were somewhere else.

The fifteen or so slaves in the small hot courtyard had been hastily and skimpily clothed in assorted loincloths and shifts. They wore chains as well, for these were the pick of the lot, and therefore stronger and more inclined to violence. They didn't look much inclined to it just now. They were gaunt with the ordeal of the slave ship, and their eyes dulled with shock and hopeless misery. They could easily become like Fidelia, Jade decided, hoping she wasn't going to be sick here and now and all over the floor.

"Hardest to tame, these are," murmured Uncle Augustus, feeling muscles and examining teeth and eyes with a practiced air. "But rather good specimens, all the same. Here, take a look at this fellow, Thomas. What do you think?"

Mr. Lennox glanced sideways at his stone-faced daughter, wishing he hadn't let her come. "They don't really mind, you know," he muttered, almost as if he were convincing himself as well as her. "No more than horses do. They're only Blacks."

Jade looked at him, coldly accusing. Of course they minded! How could he lie like that? They minded just as wild horses minded, and William's fox, and any other free creature in captivity—before their spirits were broken. She saw herself in all of them. She hated everybody!

At her expression, her father tightened his lips and turned away to join his brother-in-law, leaving Jade to stand there near the door, poised to leave and determined *not* to be a coward.

And then she saw the girl, standing with the four other women, but infinitely aloof, dwarfing them in size and spirit. She held herself like a queen: ignoring chains, ragged shift, her own bare satin flesh, and everyone in the courtyard. Her face was swollen from a blow—but beneath the swelling was great beauty. A slender black column of throat rose proudly to meet the curve of a long delicate jaw; the head was beautifully shaped; and between high cheekbones and a strong lovely arch of brow were clear intelligent eyes—eyes like William's fox: proud and angry and unyielding. Except for those eyes, the face was a mask of composed indifference.

Jade stood transfixed, her own eyes wide with shocked recognition. She knew that look! It was her very own after-a-whipping expression, and for a moment she had the dizzy sensation of meeting herself in someone else's skin. Or meeting someone else in her own? Suddenly she was sharing the searing humiliation of being discussed and marketed like a farm animal . . . the savage desire to kill her captors, or foil them by killing herself . . . and the pride that kept her calm as a statue because the final degradation would be to show that she cared. . . .

With a jolt she was alone in her own skin again, staring a startled question into the brown eyes in the mask. Had *she* felt it, too? Such a thing couldn't be one-sided—could it? But there was not a flicker of the black lashes.

Jade found her voice, tugged distractedly at her father's fullskirted ochre coat. "Father!" Her voice was oddly hoarse. "This one. Father, I want her."

He stared. "Are you out of your mind, Melanie? What are you talking about? You can't have a wild slave out of Africa!"

"I want her," repeated Jade as if she hadn't heard him. It was most peculiar behavior for her, who—for all her other faults—never asked for presents. She could see amazement on her father's face and then thoughtfulness. She didn't care what he thought—so long as she had her way.

"I'll buy you a nice, docile, well-trained handmaid before I go back home," he suggested. "You're old enough to have one of your own."

Jade shook an intractable head. "This one." Her eyes glittered. Her father's mouth set in a line very similar to her own, and he turned his shoulder away.

"Impossible."

Jade did what she had thought she'd never do. She used Lavinia's tactics. "Please, Father, *please!* I could train her myself. *Please!*" She wasn't very good at wheedling, being unable to imitate Vinnie's melting smile or beguiling ways, and looking rather more like a desperately earnest young witch. But it was so extraordinary for her to plead at all that her father stared uncertainly.

And then, surprisingly, Uncle Augustus came to her support. "*Ach*, why not? Let her try. We can make sure of her safety, and it will be good experience. If she fails, I put the slave to work in the fields. Quite probably you *will* fail, Melanie *Liebchen*, for I have seen this sort before, such stubborn mules, ungrateful for food and bed. Sometimes I think they die on purpose rather than obey, just to spite their owners."

Jade refrained from saying that she didn't blame them. She turned beseeching eyes to her father, instead. "I'll never ask you for anything else," she promised, more truly than she dreamed.

He hesitated, while Uncle Augustus made encouraging faces indicating that this was the best way to cure her of all that nonsense about slavery. Father, less optimistic, frowned at her. "There'll be no nonsense about trying to free her, as you did with Joshua, you know."

"No." Jade lowered her eyes so he wouldn't see her anger—at herself for stooping to wheedle, at him for making her. She did intend to free the girl, too, if ever she could figure out how to do it; and she had no scruples at all about the lie she was telling.

"Well, if you think so, Augustus—Let's see if we can get a reasonable price. We'll call it an early Christmas gift, Melanie."

And finding Mr. Bottlesford, the men began haggling.

Jade's Christmas gift was duly delivered that afternoon, still in chains, and put for safe-keeping in the slaves' punishment hut behind the kitchen garden. "We must get her cleaned and de-loused first," Uncle Augustus explained kindly. "Then we probably will need to starve her for a while to make her more tractable, and grateful to you when you bring her some food. Remember, she is only a savage, and you must handle her as you would a wild horse or dog, not expecting intelligence. You will also have to teach her English, remember."

Jade maintained a deceitful silence, causing her father and uncle to suppose quite mistakenly that the acquiring of property had already given her an entirely new outlook on things. They exchanged looks of great satisfaction, which Jade didn't fail to notice. Within an hour she had coaxed some food from the good-natured cook and was out in the gold of late afternoon: through the kitchen gardens and to the bolted door of that small prison shack —where she paused. Unexpectedly her heart was pounding at her ribs, and the shack seemed to be throbbing, too, with silence.

It was bolted on the outside; not, thank goodness, padlocked. After all, who would want to break *in?* Jade looked at it for a moment, savoring her own half-fear. Then she went in.

Sunlight striped the dark in narrow slices, and a trenchant stillness lurked in the far corner. It didn't move while Jade leaned against the door waiting to be able to see in the dimness; didn't move even after it had materialized into the tall darkness of the African girl. Jade waited for a moment, trying to recapture that earlier contact. But it was gone, and the space between them filled with wrath.

It made it very difficult, not to be able to talk. Jade crossed the space, smiled up at the set face. "Food," she said simply and produced it.

There was no response whatever. "Food!" repeated Jade coaxingly, and held it closer. "Aren't you hungry? You must be!" She regarded her offering anxiously. A bit of cold chicken and ham, some bread, one of those yellow tropical fruits that Aunt Louisa had called papaya, or perhaps banana: Jade hadn't got them straight yet. "Food," she said a third time, and stopped, afflicted with the stupidity of her conversation. Savage or not, the slave wasn't a total idiot: she knew it was food. And she was hungry. And she was having none of it.

Jade finally left, defeated. She didn't even dare leave all of the food behind for Uncle Augustus to find: only the smallest bit of bread. The eyes glittered at her as she left.

They glittered again the next morning. The girl had been well scrubbed and presumably de-loused now, and was dressed in a clean shift and the same expression of remote disdain. But the bread was nowhere to be seen.

"Oh, you have eaten it?" cried Jade, delighted. "More food!" She held out her new offering—and found herself confronted with yesterday's bread, untouched. With it there was a glimpse of white teeth in what looked suspiciously like a malicious smile, vanished so quickly that Jade couldn't be at all sure. She stared at her property, baffled and exasperated.

"Oh, don't be like that! Can't you see I want to be your friend? I'm on your side! We—" But the brown eyes refused even to look at her, stared with impassive hostility at nothing at all. Jade stamped out this time feeling considerably less sympathetic and charitable than she had.

But she was back as soon as Jamaica had settled down for its afternoon siesta, under a sun that beat hot fists on her bare head. How unfair to be angry, when she'd probably be acting the same way, herself. . . . At least she hoped she would. It was not a small thing to refuse food if you were hungry.

The striped dark this time tended to spin a bit giddily with the effect of the sun. Jade was forced to close her eyes for a moment and brace herself against the door while she got her vision back. Just for an instant she thought she caught a wave of longing and misery—but doubtless it was her own. She'd never break through! The girl was going to starve herself to death, refusing all friendship.

"Oh please!" she begged, forgetting the language difficulty. "Please let me try to help! You might at least try! I do know how you feel; I want to be friends; you could always starve later, if—" She had started toward the girl, but the shack hadn't stopped whirling, and Jade found herself forced to stop and sway, reaching into emptiness for something to hold on to. She'd been warned about midday sun! She—

Something at once soft and powerful scooped her from the middle of nothing and seated her gently against the wall of the shack. When the dizziness subsided a little and she opened her eyes, it was to see a heart-shaped black face glaring into hers with a look of concern, and annoyance, and a kind of wry amusement. Jade needing help had at last penetrated the slave's pride, as Jade the benefactor could never have done.

Dimly sensing this, Jade smiled rather shakily. "Thank you," she mumbled, trying to sit straight, and subsiding without much of a struggle when that strong shapely arm pushed her firmly back again. "Food?" she suggested, remembering her mission.

The girl unexpectedly gave a small chuckle—and then looked amazed at herself. "Food," she agreed in a husky voice that probably had not been used for some time. And she helped herself to a chicken leg, politely offering the wing to Jade.

The slim wrist was raw where chains had cut it, and Jade caught her breath sharply with new anger. The girl paused, her eyes searching.

"Well of course I care!" Jade answered the unspoken remark with hot passion, and then sat absorbing several things while the slave applied herself to the food. She had courteously offered Jade some, though she must be ravenous; and she was eating with firmly controlled dignity, not gobbling. No savage acted that way! Moreover—it occurred to Jade that the girl must have hidden that bread the other day with shrewd foresight, knowing that no one else must see it.

The food finished, they looked at each other with appraising eyes, quite used now to the dim light. Jade felt that she was being invited to communicate.

"Jade," she volunteered, touching her chest.

The slave stared hard, brows level. Then she nodded, pointed at herself. "D'hom'no," she said, with a combination of sounds that never happens in English.

Jade did her best. "Domino?" It didn't sound the same.

The girl chuckled again, more easily. "Domino," she agreed, tolerant of this unfortunate race's linguistic handicaps. Then she leaned back against her own hands and tilted her head, studying Jade. "Melanie?" she suggested at last, looking puzzled.

Jade gaped. "What? But how— Oh, you must have heard Fa—" She stopped the useless one-sided conversation with a sigh of frustration. "Melanie," she conceded. She would explain later, when Domino could speak English, that Jade was a kind of secret name.

"Two name?"

Jade's mouth flew open and her head jerked around to stare at Domino, whose eyes glinted with mischief.

"Learn little," she confessed, having evidently decided to give Jade her full trust. "Come man my city, teach. Not speak *them!*" And her gesture indicated the entire world of slavers and Jamaica. Her lip curled in a near snarl.

"No," Jade agreed instantly. "Not tell *them* anything."

Their hands met. Domino took a whole new look at life. It was not the look of someone who had been tamed by kindness . . . or anything else.

"Not slave!" she hissed.

Once Jade had—with appalling difficulty—persuaded Domino to pretend to be a slave temporarily and in public, it was a perfect conspiracy between them. With others around, she was grudgingly submissive (though with a spark in her eye that strongly reminded the nervous Aunt Louisa of a half-trained tiger she had once seen). Alone together, the two girls were equals without question. Or if there was a question, it sometimes seemed to be whether Jade was Domino's equal, being merely a pink-skin. As for Joshua, Domino clearly had her doubts about anyone who would submit to slavery for some thirty odd years.

The grown-ups were delighted. Jade was far too busy conspiring with Domino to have much time left over for rebellion or mischief, and they mistakenly put this down to her new status as slave-owner. Splendid idea, that was, they told each other contentedly. Made a new child of her. Responsibility, that was it. Mr. Lennox sailed back to Virginia some six weeks later a deluded but happy man.

And as a matter of fact, trouble didn't start for some weeks after he left.

"Why does your Domino not obey your aunt?" demanded Uncle Augustus one hot autumn evening when an order of Aunt Louisa's had been received with a hostile blank wall of a face.

There was a very simple answer to this, but it was not one that could be given to Uncle Augustus in terms that would be even slightly acceptable. Jade, who was perforce becoming rather good at lies for other people, invented one on the spot.

"She doesn't understand," she explained hastily, thankful for the dimness of the candles that flickered in the breeze from the slave-worked fans above. A careful look at Domino's expression would instantly have disproved her words. But no one looked closely, and for the moment this explanation seemed reasonable to her aunt and uncle.

But the problem was only postponed, of course. She faced that fact later that evening, when Fidelia had been dismissed and Domino was theoretically preparing Jade for bed. In practice, any help that Domino gave was purely nominal and because she felt so moved. She felt moved now to help Jade slip out of her voluminous contouche and to pin up the heavy hot curls, while Jade grumbled that Domino was far more comfortable in her single garment and cropped hair. Then they sat together on the window seat, staring out through the netted window at the silvered garden below, hotly fragrant in the tropical night.

Domino broached the subject herself. "He beat me soon; I kill him," she announced, not in the least backward about assessing the situation.

"I'll help!" cried Jade, carried away for the moment. Then she came back down to earth. "He *will* beat you, too, if you ever refuse to obey him," she realized slowly and helplessly.

Domino's magnificent body stiffened; she lifted her small shapely head even higher. "I not his," she pointed out with a masterly grasp of essentials. "I belong *me!*"

"*I* know that, but *they* don't!" cried Jade for the twentieth time. "And you know I've promised to free you somehow the very minute I can. But I can't now. They just wouldn't pay any attention. And Uncle Augustus expects you to obey him even more than me, because he's a man, and in charge of me, and—"

Domino interrupted with smouldering eyes. "Pink man, pah! Pink women slaves too. You belong your men, your property belong your men, not?"

Really, for someone just learning English she was remarkably pithy and effective! And astute, as well. There was no denying this succinct analysis, and Jade didn't even try.

"Yes, it is like that!" She scowled, and knew that Domino was scorning her for submitting to it. It was a novel and disagreeable sensation to be scorned for spinelessness. Jade could have thought of a number of trenchant things to say if self-justification hadn't been against her code. She jutted her chin instead.

"Anyway, you can't kill Uncle Augustus, because they'd just kill you," she said sternly. "And don't say you'd rather die, because I already know it. But that's only as a last resort, and there are lots of other things to try first."

The beautiful head turned slowly, dim in the pale light, challenge slitting the heavy-lashed eyes. "Hmmm?" drawled Domino. "What try first?"

Jade racked her brains. "Well—there's Cockpit Country. That's over in the west corner of Jamaica, and Uncle Augustus says it's a refuge for escaped slaves and Indians. And nobody has ever been able to conquer them, because they defend themselves so well, and the country is so wild and terrible and filled with snakes and yellow fever and things. . . ."

Domino curled her full lips, clearly not much taken with the prospect. Jade saw her point. She sighed. "We'll think of something. And if Uncle Augustus beats you, he'll have to end up beating me too, and we might just as well grin and bear it, because it really isn't at all practical to try to kill him."

"Mmm," said Domino, deeply shocked at the way pink men beat their children, and not promising anything.

It was characteristic of them both that the thought of Domino obeying Uncle Augustus never entered either head.

CHAPTER SEVEN

The Stays

Jade let her horse amble between the cane fields, Joshua dutifully behind her, and wondered how it could really be November. Jamaica was as fiercely green as ever, sun-drenched, ablaze with the scarlet of flower and flamingo—and swollen with slave labor. Everywhere there were swarms, rivers of chained slaves, toiling in the fields under the snap of whips. And not the little riding crops such as fathers used on rebellious children, either, but great long horse whips, cracking savagely. Jade winced at the thought.

She had been preoccupied with Domino for too long. Now that she began to look around at Jamaica, the sick hatred rose again in her, far stronger than ever. Virginia had never been anything like this! Sometimes she really wanted to kill every slave-owner in the world, even her own family!

She turned to say as much to Joshua, and was startled at the hunted look on his face, almost as if he were afraid of being snatched away and put to work with the field slaves. "What's the matter?" she asked anxiously.

Joshua glanced over his shoulder uneasily, and then

shrugged. "Too much," he mumbled obscurely. "This country hates man, Missy Lanie."

Jade looked at him with sudden keenness. "You hate it, too, don't you?" she discovered.

He nodded with another sideways glance into the hot damp green, from where came sounds of slaves at hard labor. "Masters here treat field slaves worse than animals," he pointed out. "They're cheaper, you see. It's better business just to work them to death and buy new ones than to treat them decent. It's—" He stopped and then started again. "I can understand men killing for hate, Missy Lanie; this is just not caring, and not even knowing there's anything to care about. That scares me."

It scared Jade, too. She shivered in the hot morning air, and felt the familiar hot urge to strike out with violence at something established and orderly and smug and impervious. She kicked at her horse—who was not without those same qualities, come to think of it—and raced along the track, Joshua behind her, until she was stopped perforce by a group of shambling, sullen slaves. Feeling more ferocious than ever, she turned again, bolted towards the shore, up the hill until she stopped on the top, breathing the clean salty wind of the sea, refreshing her eyes with the far reach of ocean before her and the graceful swoop of a large merchant ship, wings outspread, heading for Port Royal.

"I feel in a mood to be simply *horribly* wicked!" she told the apprehensive Joshua, and set her aggrieved horse at a full gallop for her uncle's plantation.

She began her wickedness by charging past Dr. Hughes as he rode up the drive, and leaving him trying to control his rearing horse. Then, leaving her own horse and Joshua in the stables, she went stalking into the house looking for more trouble.

Nor had she far to look. When she reached her bedchamber, there sat Aunt Louisa, looking stricken and accusing, Jade's unworn stays in her lap. A tearful Fidelia and impassive Domino stood near.

"Dear Melanie!" The outrage in her voice sounded almost like Mother's. "I've made Poor Fidelia tell me! Dear wicked Melanie—*are* you wearing stays?"

Jade could never resist a chance to be disconcerting. "If Fidelia's told you, you needn't ask me," she pointed out practically. "And if you can't tell, what difference does it make?"

Her aunt, not unnaturally, took this for plain impudence. "It makes a great deal of difference, dear Melanie," she said, boxing Jade's ears with a decisiveness that was very surprising indeed. "Now you're going to put them on at once, dear, and don't ever let me hear of your leaving them off again. I do hope God will forgive your immodesty, but I shall particularly ask Him in my prayers this evening, in case He doesn't understand. I'm not at all sure that I understand, myself," she confessed as a rather plaintive afterthought. "But I don't think you'd better try to explain, dear Melanie," she added hastily, as Jade opened her mouth to point out the simple truth that the beastly things were hot and hurt her ribs. "I really think I'd far rather not hear it. The devil might have a hand in this, and if he does, I don't want to know anything about it. You just put them on, dear, and we won't mention it again; and then you can come on down and have coffee with me. Your dear uncle is in his study having his with

Dr. Hughes." And she left the room to Jade, the two slaves, and the stays.

Jade looked at the hateful things. Then she looked at Domino, who wore the expression of someone deciding that her newly-acquired English must be at fault. Surely not even pink-skins would wear a thing like that? Unless— Perhaps as an odd form of punishment? She regarded Jade with deep interest, waiting to see what she'd do next.

Jade opened her neglected sewing box and took out the shears. Then she proceeded to cut the offensive garment into separate strips of whalebone and steel, while the terrified Fidelia watched with small moans of dismay.

"Don't be such a coward," Jade told her impatiently. She had no use at all for weakness. "No one's going to blame you, for goodness sake!" And with a reckless laugh she marched downstairs and presented her aunt with the remains.

Aunt Louisa eyed the strips in blank silence. Domino (who wouldn't have missed this for worlds) watched with deep interest, and Fidelia stood quaking. Jade waited with a bland face and just the tiniest sensation of danger fluttering pleasantly between her lungs. After all, Aunt Louisa had surprised her once today.

"Dear Melanie, that was very silly," she said plaintively. "I quite remember, of course, that your poor father warned us about your wicked behavior, but I should have thought that climbing trees and being rude to our guests and frightening Poor Dr. Hughes' horse and being difficult about your slave were quite enough for just the short time you've been with us; and in any case, I've left out a number of other wickednesses. My poor dear Clarinda never behaved like that in all her life, and she was very pretty, besides. And now, dear Melanie, you'll just have to go up and stay in your bedchamber until you've remade your stays."

"I can't," Jade said simply and truthfully. Sewing was not her strong point at best, and a set of stays was quite beyond her.

Her aunt considered this point, accepted it. "Well, then, you'll have to stay there and make slave dresses while someone else remakes the stays."

This was fair and reasonable, and also unexpected. Jade had been prepared for almost anything from her twitter-pated aunt, from hysterics to thumb-screws—except this. But there was one point that had to be made.

"I still won't wear the stays, so it's a waste of some-body's time remaking them."

Aunt Louisa looked flustered. "But dear Melanie, it isn't decent not to wear them. Besides, you wouldn't be able to receive callers, like dear Chester Quayles," she added with a cunning that was altogether misplaced. Jade grinned like a fiend.

"Good," she said. "He's a bore. Anyway, I don't expect him to call again, because I told him not to and stamped on his toes the last time he came."

"Melanie!" bleated her outraged aunt, backing up a step and regarding her with growing dislike. Jade felt a pang of regret. She usually managed to make people dislike her, even when she didn't want to. She couldn't seem to help it: it was her demon that drove her. Aunt Louisa really was rather sweet, in a way— But she unquestioningly ac-cepted all the loathsome things people did to one another, so long as it was her race and class that did it. Jade hardened her heart.

"You can send the sewing up to me," she said curtly, and went straight-backed up the stairs, followed by a puzzled Domino, who planted herself in the middle of the room with furrowed brow.

"Why?" she demanded. "Why sew? Why not fight?"

Jade, her code second nature by now, found trouble explaining it in simple words. It was so clear and obvious to her: when the tune was played and the piper came to collect, one paid without quibbling. But how to explain it to the angry-eyed Domino, who clearly considered this a spineless surrender?

"I do fight," she objected, "but there are–rules." It sounded lame even to her. Domino, whose only rule was no holds barred, looked as if she thought Jade afflicted with sunstroke again. Inspired, Jade appealed to the pride that possessed them both. "You didn't fight in the slave market, did you? And you won't fight if Uncle Augustus beats you. You're too proud!"

"Oh," said Domino uncertainly, and retired into baffled silence to figure out the connection.

Jade turned to stare out the window with a small sideways smile. There was a connection; she knew that. But she'd have been hard put to explain it. Let Domino puzzle over it; it would do her good.

The jacaranda trees stood brooding over the drive, the garden was vivid with butterflies and humming birds and improbable blossoms, the parrots screamed. On the hill two palms swayed, and beyond them was the sea. Wild restlessness seized Jade. It was unbearable to be cooped up like this! How many weeks since she had worn her breeches, held a rapier, climbed a tree? And when would she do these things again?

A hard-ridden horse tore up the drive, and a servant tumbled off and raced inside for Dr. Hughes. This had happened once before when he was visiting. Someone was ill, and Jade's mind leaped to the thing most feared in the tropics: more than hurricane or earthquake, pirates or fire, or even malaria. Yellow fever! It could sweep whole cities, killing thousands. It could quite literally wipe out an entire ship's crew, leaving the empty hulk to drift aimlessly over the seas or rot deserted in some far-off harbor.

"Yellow jack," she predicted morbidly, not wanting it to be true, but in an odd way relishing the prospect of any excitement whatever. The three tall masts of that merchant ship, sails reefed, could just be seen where it was now anchored in harbor. "That ship's docked with it on board, and they've come running for Dr. Hughes. And we'll have to go home to Virginia, because Father made Uncle Augustus promise faithfully to send me straight home if there were even one case . . ." She grinned wryly. "And they can't stand me there—and they'll find you even more unbearable—so I wonder where we'll be sent next? Domino, you aren't even listening!"

"No," agreed Domino, who felt no more obligation to listen than to serve or obey. She was squatting beside Jade's box, looking at the unusual thickness of the bottom with alert and curious eyes. Now she looked up, a question forming on her lips.

Jade's eyes widened. Why not? She leaped across the room, bolted the door, flew to the box. Presently she was teaching the fascinated African girl the rudiments of swordsmanship. It wasn't a workout with Monsieur Maupin, but it was better than nothing; and Domino showed great promise and enthusiasm.

At the end of the lesson, Jade let her feelings and muscles loose with a wild attack against a certain offensive spot on the blue wallpaper. And at last she sprang to the bed, killed the bedpost with one neat thrust at its oaken heart, tangled herself completely in the hangings, and collapsed giggling, her hair a hot mass about her neck.

"Someone come up," Domino announced coolly, and bestirred herself to help hurl sword and breeches back into the box and unbolt the door again. When Aunt Louisa opened the door, both girls stood demurely by the window, Jade in a shocking state of undress.

"Oh, dear Melanie, a terrible thing!" she cried distractedly. "Whatever have you been doing, child? Do make yourself decent, dear; I have such shocking news!" She sank into a chair and began fanning herself.

Jade's eyes widened. Good gracious, *was* it the dreaded yellow jack, then? She hadn't for a moment *believed* her own fiction.

"Do you remember poor dear Mr. Bayard? Only I shouldn't call him dear, I suppose, should I? Because I never did like him, you know, and although one mustn't speak ill of the dead, I have never quite understood why being dead changed anything about what folk were like when they were alive, and I find that I can't like him a bit better now than I did yesterday. But *poor* Mr. Bayard, anyway."

"Is he dead, then?" asked Jade, coming to the heart of the matter with some slight effort. "Good. He was a horrible man. Oh, and that means it couldn't be the ship, then," she added, infected for the moment by her aunt's speech habits.

"What?" Aunt Louisa looked confused. "Why, it was his ship that caused it, of course, but I can't think how you knew, dear Melanie."

"I didn't! I don't!" Jade was now more than a little confused, herself. "Do please tell me what happened!" She made an impatient face.

"You see, that's his merchant ship the *Royal Trader* that's just docked, only it wasn't supposed to be here at all, you see. Well, not alone, I mean. It was coming down from New York, and it was supposed to be met by his very largest ship, the *Queen Royal*, which is really quite as big and well-armed as a warship, Mr. Bayard says—or at least I mean he *said*, poor man, when he was alive to say it. . . ." She fell into reflection over the strange ways of life and death.

"Well, what happened?" begged Jade.

"Oh, yes." Aunt Louisa began fanning again, agitatedly. "Yes, the *Queen Royal* should have met the *Royal Trader* and escorted her here safely, because of all that pirate-infested sea, you understand." (She clearly had a mental picture of a sea swarming with pirate craft from horizon to horizon.) "And she did meet it, just as planned. But—" Aunt Louisa's eyes were circular. "Dear Melanie, do you know what happened?"

"No!" said Jade with considerable restraint.

"The *Queen Royal* was a *pirate* ship! I mean, she is! She's been captured somehow by that dreadful Calico Jack and the Brazen Female, and they stole all the cargo from the *Royal Trader* as well, and eight of her crew even joined them, and then the pirates sent the rest of the crew on to Jamaica in the looted ship to tell poor Mr. Bayard."

Jade giggled, totally unsympathetic.

"Oh, you wicked girl, it isn't at all funny!" cried her aunt, outraged. "And when he heard the news, Poor Mr. Bayard foamed at the mouth and fell down dead of an apoplexy!" She tried to look grief-stricken, or at least suitably distressed.

"I'm not a bit sorry," said Jade heartlessly. "I think the world is a whole lot better off without him, and so do you, really, so why pretend?"

Aunt Louisa looked doubtful—not so much of what her niece had said, but of the propriety of saying it. "You mustn't say such things, dear Melanie," she murmured. "And anyway, we ought not to rejoice in the triumph of wickedness; and you know those terrible pirates are a great deal more wicked than Poor Mr. Bayard ever was. Governor Lawes is perfectly furious: you know how he hates the Bonney creature; and he's sending out a man-of-war to capture the *Queen Royal* back again, and bring them all back and hang them . . ." Her voice trailed away ever more dubiously. Jade had the distinct impression that her aunt entertained some doubts about the probable success of this militant venture.

She was right, too. The man-of-war returned sheepishly after a while saying that it hadn't seen the *Queen Royal* at all. This was undoubtedly perfectly true. But rumor in Jamaica had it that the warship had been very careful indeed not to go anywhere near the area where that unusually large and well-armed pirate ship was known to be cruising. And Jade smiled cynically.

CHAPTER EIGHT

"Lovely and Cool!"

The stays remade, Jade put them in her box and went on not wearing them; and Aunt Louisa (recognizing implacable obduracy when she saw it) was careful not to ask. It was Uncle Augustus who finally did that.

"Are you wearing your stays as your aunt told you?" he demanded one morning over his breakfast of eggs, steak, and onions.

Aunt Louisa glanced up from her own dish of fruit, and if ever a grown-up appealed to a young person to lie, Aunt Louisa did then. Jade did no such thing, of course. She stuck out that deceptively soft round chin, smiled, and shook her head.

Pale blue eyes and jade-green ones fixed themselves upon each other like a clash of swords. "I will not have disobedience in this house," said Uncle Augustus. "Not even from your aunt, much less from you. You will go up and put on this garment, and then come down and be gracious and polite to Dr. Hughes, who comes for morning coffee." He saw the defiance on her face, and added a warning. "Otherwise I have the slaves hold you and put it on by force, and we leave it on day and night."

Jade paused for reflection. He could do it. And she wouldn't be able to get it off by herself, and if Domino helped, it would precipitate all sorts of awful possibilities. At best the whole thing would be atrociously mortifying, and at worst an inglorious defeat. She narrowed her eyes at him, seething and considering.

"Moreover," said her uncle, pushing his luck, "I do not like your hair all up on top of your head so. It is not becoming a young girl, even though the French do it." He clearly thought little of the French. "You will hereafter wear it as before, in the curls on your shoulders. You have finished your banana? Go then upstairs and obey me. Dr. Hughes will be here presently."

Jade obeyed the bit about going upstairs, Domino appearing en route from the hall where she had been shamelessly listening. Once in the bedchamber, they looked at each other, silently speculative. Domino—who knew her own courage but had grave doubts about Jade—fixed expectant eyes on her.

"What you do now?" she challenged.

Jade chuckled suddenly. Surrender was not in her. She was going to earn a whipping: she couldn't help herself. And she felt in a mood to enjoy the process. Moreover, Domino was looking just faintly startled and impressed at the chuckle.

"What you do?" she repeated hopefully.

"Something he doesn't expect." She concentrated. This clash had been inevitable from the first, and she must make it a telling one. Goodness knew how it would end. "Like going downstairs wearing nothing at all. Or cutting off all my hair. . . ."

Her eyes lighted. She hauled out her sewing box, produced the shears that had been so useful before, and—with the enthusiastic help of Domino—cropped off all her hair to within a ragged inch or so of her head.

"Lovely and cool!" she said with satisfaction, and went downstairs to confront her relations and their guest.

Aunt Louisa screamed and had an attack of the vapours on the spot. Dr. Hughes gaped. Uncle Augustus looked stupefied. No one had ever defied him like this before, and he couldn't believe his eyes.

Jade watched him closely behind her mask of bland serenity, and her heart was beating rather quickly. He was an unknown quantity still, for they had never crossed swords before. She knew it was no quarter—but what she didn't know was just how formidable an opponent he might be. Recklessly, she compounded her felony. "I'm not wearing stays, either," she announced, brazen.

Her uncle—now a rich beet red—found his voice. "Up!" It had an oddly thick quality, barely controlled. "To your room! I come later."

He was a long time coming, and it wasn't very pleasant waiting. But she had to keep up appearances, of course, especially with Domino there, looking superior. Jade made a great show of throwing away the shorn mane of hair and then strutted over to the mirror to survey the result.

Her eyes rounded. So did those of the girl in the mirror; otherwise Jade might almost have thought it someone else. Domino came and grinned over her shoulder as she stared. The soft, oval, feminine face of Melanie, no longer framed by all that hair, had changed its shape, become pointed, all mouth and eyes and ears and cheek bones: not in the least soft or feminine or even pretty. It was now distinctly a Jade-face, and its owner stared in shocked silence for a moment, not at all sure she liked it now that she had it.

"You grow again?" suggested Domino slyly, reading her feelings with diabolic ease.

Stung, Jade shook her head with more vigor than she really felt, still eying her reflection as a stranger. Then she began to laugh.

"Mother'll have fits! And however hard Uncle Augustus beats me, he can't have his slaves hold me down and stick it on again."

"Come now," Domino predicted, listening to the sound of Dr. Hughes' horse departing, and heavy footsteps up the stairs.

Jade braced herself. And her uncle stormed in flourishing his riding crop, with which he administered discipline after a fashion that earned him no respect at all. Father could do better than that! Jade had expected something far worse from this stern martinet.

But the martinet, as it happened, was quite unnerved both by Jade's apparent frailty and her disconcerting silence. His daughter had been a large hefty girl who always yelled and wept lustily on such occasions.

Presently he could bear it no longer. He stopped, moved around to peer at her tearless and apparently unmoved face. "*Himmel!*" he said, almost plaintive. "Don't I even hurt you, *meine Nichte?*"

Jade treated him to her lopsided grin. "Yes," she said, scorning to deny it—and also guessing shrewdly that this would baffle him more than ever. His rules admitted only two reactions to pain: one either cried and carried on, or one refused to admit that the thing hurt at all. The first was for females and cowards, the second for men. To have a fragile girl show a man's courage and then casually admit that it hurt threw him quite off his stride.

He finished the beating half-heartedly. She had somehow got the upper hand, and he couldn't figure out how or why. Disgruntled, he ordered her to stay in her chamber until further orders, and left the room.

There was silence. Domino was watching. Jade strolled over to the window and glanced out, looking bored. Domino shrugged. "Very small beating," she observed, unimpressed.

Small or not, it hurt quite enough. Irritated, Jade turned. "That," she predicted, "was only the beginning. Just wait!" And her spirits sank as she realized the truth of the remark and the depressing future ahead. All very well, now and then, to establish a moral victory this way, but as a steady diet it was poison. Why did she go on fighting, with no weapons but her own stubbornness? It was stupid, hopeless, probably suicidal in one way or another. But she couldn't help it. She couldn't imagine giving in, any more than could Domino.

At least there was Domino! Jade gave her a sudden brilliant smile as the door opened and a distraught Aunt Louisa came in, scolding and commiserating and armed with an ointment that was, as Jade pointed out, totally unnecessary.

"Better save it for next time," she suggested realistically, and produced such a storm of emotion that she had to give in and submit to treatment just to make her aunt feel better.

That over, the day dragged out, enlivened only when

Domino unexpectedly slapped her on the arm. Jade stared, too astonished even to slap back.

"Kill he," said Domino with satisfaction, and displayed the corpse of a mosquito.

Jade giggled. The militant Domino's fear of mosquitoes was so incongruous. "Don't you have them in Africa?" she asked. "I do think you believe they're evil spirits or something."

Domino nodded. "Yes. You think silly, but not. Bad devils. Make sick."

"Sick?" Jade shook her cropped head. It felt so *light!* "Nonsense. They only itch a little."

Domino glared. "Sometimes make sick. Very sick. Make die. Yellow-eye sickness."

"Yellow-eye? You don't mean yellow fever? Yellow jack?"

Domino indicated impatiently that she didn't know or care what pink-faces might call it. "First very hot, hurt in head and back," she explained. "Then not hurt, eyes yellow, get cold, soon die."

It was a perfect description of yellow jack. "Well, but it hasn't got anything to do with mosquitoes, silly," said Jade, intrigued by such superstition. Really, the ideas people had!

"They bring," said Domino firmly. "Bad devils ride on tooths. Bite sick people, get devils. Bite well people, devils jump off, make well people sick. My people know . . . knew." Her face darkened as she remembered the small African city where she had grown up—now wiped out forever by a massive raid. Its arts and developing sciences were vanished, its streets and buildings and central square already being swallowed by an insatiable jungle, so that in a few years no trace would remain of a proud little civilization. A hundred years of slave-trading was already plunging Africa back into savagery; in another hundred . . .

Jade saw her slave's lips tighten, and she guessed at something of the unspoken misery. But she couldn't show pity, for Domino defied pity. She wasn't pitiable. Her husky voice was cool and matter-of-fact when she went on.

"My people knew this thing, killed devil-bugs. No devil-sickness except when monkeys come, bring many new devil-bugs."

Jade firmly subdued another giggle. "And what do the devils look like?" she challenged.

"Not know. Very small devils, not can see." And that was that. Domino narrowed her beautiful eyes, daring Jade to mock. "You not believe. All right, but kill devil-bug anyway," she advised with forthright practicality. "Believing not matter if not get yellow-eye."

"All right," agreed Jade, this seeming fair enough.

But Jade slept poorly that night. It occurred to her that sooner or later Uncle Augustus would discover a perfect weapon against her—a simple, convenient weapon that would be most effective indeed. All he need do was punish Joshua and Domino for her sins—and Jade would become tractable. She'd have to! Lying rigid in her bed, she realized to the full how much easier it was to be brave for one's self than for someone else, and how terribly vulnerable it made one, to feel responsible for another. What was she going to *do?*

She spent nearly a week in her room—much of it trying

to teach Domino swordplay without being heard below. Then her uncle came and announced magnanimously that he had decided to let her resume her morning rides for her health. Jade, suspecting Dr. Hughes' hand in this, merely smiled obliquely.

"Perhaps also I let you come down to meals and for Christmas day," he added, grudgingly. "But not if visitors come. You are not fit to be seen, with that ugly cut-off hair, so unfeminine; and also you are not fit to associate with my guests, who are civilized people."

Jade had been holding her tongue with what seemed masterly prudence and self-control. This was too much. "Like Mr. Bayard?" she jeered, and at once lost her dinner privileges for another week.

And by the time she was allowed out again (except when visitors came) Jade felt that she perfectly understood at least one reason why Anne Bonney might have burned down her father's house.

Still, the worst hadn't happened. Uncle Augustus hadn't —yet—thought to make Domino and Josh hostage for her behavior. As a matter of fact, he never would have thought of it, as he couldn't conceive of anyone caring that much about a mere slave. But Jade didn't know this.

Life was not genial at the plantation as Christmas neared. Jade, constrained to unwilling prudence by her fears for Joshua and Domino, agreed to wear stays with tight-waisted gowns and in public. It meant little enough practically, since she was still incommunicado and always wore a contouche, but in principle it was distinctly a retreat. In consequence, she went around with an air of a leashed demon that made everyone uneasy. Domino sulked, making it perfectly clear what she thought of weak-spined pink-skinned girls who lowered their banners under threat. And Uncle Augustus—who had also been forced to compromise, and for the first time in his adult life—was quite awful. His blue eyes were cold, and his steel-trap mouth no longer amiable, and he took it out on everyone—including the overseers, who in turn passed it on to the hapless slaves. It was a temporary armistice in which no one could take any satisfaction, for pride smarted on both sides.

And sooner or later Domino would receive a direct order from him, and then it would be all-out war.

A tense Christmas passed, jovial without being happy.

And then Dr. Hughes rode up the drive one morning with an oddly abstracted expression, and closeted himself at once with Uncle Augustus. When he had gone again—not even waiting for coffee—Jade and her aunt were summoned to the study.

"Dr. Hughes has just diagnosed a case of yellow fever," said Uncle Augustus. Aunt Louisa gasped and put a hand to her throat, and Jade felt her own eyes widen. "It will be a fortnight before there is another case," he went on, expressionless. "That is the peculiar thing about this disease; it always behaves so. Dr. Hughes has a theory that this is significant, but—" He shrugged massively. "Now it is the time to send Melanie home, at once, before news leaks out and ships will refuse to carry passengers from here."

He looked like a man trying not to look relieved. Jade had a notion that if yellow jack hadn't provided an excuse to send her home, Uncle Augustus would have had to invent one. Aunt Louisa, too, looked singularly resigned.

"Oh, yes; we mustn't keep dear Melanie in danger a

moment longer! Fidelia will help Domino with your packing, dear."

Jade jutted her jaw at them both. Not that she was heartbroken, herself: far from it. But she was beginning to feel like a hot potato, never knowing where or when she'd be tossed next. To Father's Lennox cousins in England? The prospect failed to appeal. She quirked her mouth wryly and said nothing.

"We cannot go with you, *Liebchen*, you understand." He was looking almost his old affable self, genuinely concerned for her welfare. "But you have two strong and loyal slaves to protect you, and your father will much prefer that I send you with them instead of letting you stay here in danger of infection. And it is very fortunate that the *Pearl* is back in Port Royal, for I can entrust you to the captain, and he will return you safely."

Jade would have preferred a different ship, just for the sake of novelty. But this was no time to quibble. "Yes, Uncle Augustus," she said with astonishing meekness.

His large pink face looked puzzled. "Very well, then, I go now to speak to the captain and tell him to take you on board as soon as you are ready. You will now go up and pack."

"Yes, Uncle Augustus," repeated Jade, and flew upstairs.

CHAPTER NINE

The Storm

The *Pearl* sailed with the early tide two mornings later. Jade, hardly believing the suddenness of the thing, stood on deck waving to her aunt and uncle with sudden mild affection (doubtless brought on by the fact that she was safely out from their authority) while Captain Narramore warped the ship away from the quay to catch the land breeze and head out of the harbor. The water between ship and shore widened. Jade drew a long breath and heard it echoed by Josh and Domino. Horrible place! Brutalized by slavery, owners as well as owned. . . . The stench of the slave market was still in her nostrils, seeming to fill the harbor whether there was actually a slaver in port or not. But she was leaving!

She chortled with pleasure, tilting her head back to see the crew swarm among the rigging, working all along the yards to set sail, at a dizzying height above deck and sea. Joshua, reading her thoughts easily, put a restraining hand on her arm, just in case. And Jade, reading his worry as easily, laughed—to the mystification of the only other passengers, an elderly Mr. and Mrs. Plomley, on their way back to England. The couple raised their eyebrows.

Out of the harbor now: "Helm hard over!" roared the captain; and the *Pearl* came around. Past Drunken Cay and South Cay they moved, and then eastward as the land breeze filled the sails, billowing them and causing the choleric captain to bellow more orders.

Jade gave one more rapturous look around, and then bolted for her tiny cabin in order to remove the stiffened petticoat and detestable stays. "Come on, Domino," she laughed, staggering happily up the tilting deck. Domino came–slowly and sullenly.

"There!" sighed Jade when she was able at last to breathe freely. "Now let's throw them overboard."

No response from Domino. Jade eyed her sharply. "What's the matter?"

The *Pearl* heeled over as she came about on a northeasterly tack. Jade let her knees give to it, chortling with delight. Domino staggered against the bulkhead and looked at her with sick reproach, her superiority quenched.

"Good heavens," said Jade, astonished. "You're not seasick, are you?" But another look convinced her that Domino was indeed seasick–and perhaps it was no wonder, considering that her only previous experience at sea had been the ghastly one of lying on her side amid a tight-squeezed row of other captives in the stinking 'tween-decks of a slave ship.

Jade, all tender solicitude, didn't say a word about the natural inferiority or otherwise of pink-faces. She tucked Domino into her own bed–though what Captain Narramore might have said was an interesting question–and she wiped her suffering brow. And then, there being nothing more Domino wanted but solitude and perhaps a quick death, Jade went back on deck.

The trade winds forever blew toward the west here among these islands, through the narrow funnel between Cuba and Hispaniola, giving it its name of Windward Passage. It took a good deal of tacking to sail against it, and it also involved a good deal of rolling on some of the tacks. Jade swayed with the ship, watching alternately the activity above and the dolphins below with a joy that not even Domino's state of misery could quench.

"Hullo, Mistress Melanie!" It was Tom Deane, pausing in pleased recognition. "Glad you're aboard again. Have you been ill?" He saw Jade's bewilderment and touched a finger to the short feathery hair—a full two inches long—standing on end in the wind. "Your face looks thinner, and your hair's cut. I didn't know you at first."

Jade giggled. "No, I just cut it off myself to be wicked and because it was too hot," she told him unrepentantly, and then wrinkled her nose as a sudden whiff of foul air struck it. "That awful slaveship smell is still with us! All the way from Jamaica!"

Tom shook his sun-gilded head. "Not from Jamaica, Miss Melanie. Didn't you know? The *Pearl*'s a slave ship more often than not. We've got a load from Africa now. Sorry the smell disturbs you, but you won't get much of it on the quarterdeck. And—short hair becomes you, Mistress." Smiling appreciatively, he made his way forward, quite oblivious to Jade's stricken rigidity.

She stared after him, hating him. He didn't even see anything wrong—except the inconvenience to the nose!

No one did! Was she out of her senses, after all, and the rest of the world sane? Panic shook her. It seemed all too likely. But if that were so— Then how could there be a God at all? Or divine justice? It must be that Satan ruled the world, and Christianity was just a horrible practical joke he invented for his own amusement. The world was black and ugly and wicked, and she hated everyone!

As if to complete the picture, Rory MacDonald stalked past, his face uglier than ever with a savage scowl that matched her own. He didn't recognize her at first, with her altered appearance under the shorn head; when he did, he just increased the scowl slightly.

"I see you've collected another fine slave," he sneered. "Mate for the other? Fresh from Africa? You wait until you see our new lot stowed below!" And he was gone again before Jade could collect her wits and figure out what he was talking about. The words had been plain enough—but the meaning quite baffled her. She began to wonder if MacDonald was missing some of his wits in addition to having a witch for a grandmother.

There was the hatch in the middle of the deck just in front of the mizzenmast, suddenly grim and significant. From below Jade could feel hundreds of invisible eyes fixed on her in mute reproach. If *she* cared, why didn't *she* do something?

And there was nothing she could do. It was true that the hatch was fastened only with ropes and a bolt, impossible to break through from beneath but easy to open from above. But— Her eyes fixed themselves smouldering on the bolt. What good would it do even if she opened the hatch? Out at sea there was no escape but the sea itself; in any port they would be quickly recaptured. It was hopeless.

Moreover– Down in Jade's cabin lay Domino. Presently she would be over her seasickness and out on deck, and then she'd find out what kind of cargo they were carrying, and then– Jade couldn't feel that Domino's reaction would really improve matters. She went down to her cabin, peeped inside at the prostrate black head, and firmly locked the door. Then she went back up to the quarterdeck and stared out at the flying fish skimming away in panic, furrowing the silken surface of the sea, while a tuna hurled itself high out of the water. They had all lost some of their enchantment, and an ominous-looking shark fin was much more to her mood just now.

Joshua, one watchful brown eye always on her, kept his distance. She was in a vile temper, her chin out and her back stiff and her eyes stormily on the horizon. He sighed, not at all astonished. He knew what the cargo was, too.

"You're going to have your wish, Landlubber."

It was the familiar rough voice, getting to be almost a habit. Jade tilted her wind-tumbled head toward its owner with the air of an aristocrat being kindly but patronizing toward the lower classes.

"There's a storm coming," he informed her, his slanted eyes gleaming blue. "We'll just be seeing how you like it."

Jade regarded him with suspicion. She looked at the blue sky, the smooth swell of the sea, the bright sun. "Where's the storm?"

He grinned with profound disrespect, showing sharp wolfish teeth in a pointed jaw, white against swarthy skin. He sniffed the air with his crooked nose, fixed those weird eyes on her again, and made it perfectly clear that he was picturing her in the complete indignity of terror and seasickness. "It'll come; you'll see."

Jade, scowling ferociously, glared after his vanishing back—he never gave her a chance to think of a scathing retort—and sniffed the wind herself. She could imagine, now he'd put the idea in her head, that there was something heavy in the feel of it. And perhaps those swells were oddly smooth? She went and watched the helmsman, who had one eye on the wheel and the other on the captain; and he, in turn, had one eye on the sails and the other on a jut of land to the north.

"Cuba," he said brusquely in answer to Jade's question. His fiery temper seemed permanently on edge this trip. The wind was becoming erratic now. The sails flapped suddenly, and he swore. They could not, it seemed, weather Point Maysi on this tack, which meant that they must turn and make a long beat back toward Hispaniola before they could tack back again and be out of the Winward Passage.

"Prepare to come about, Helm!" Captain Narramore sounded as if it were all the helmsman's fault. Jade pitied any sailor who fell afoul of his wrath. Even more, she pitied the poor slaves packed under the hatches in prolonged misery. She looked at the captain with loathing which he entirely failed to perceive, mistaking it for admiration or perhaps anxiety.

"Plagued with bad luck this trip," he grumbled, to Mr. Plomley rather than Jade, young females not being worth talking to. "Looks as if weather's brewing, and I've got perishable cargo below. A bad storm could wipe out half, or even three-fourths, and put me out of pocket at a dead loss. That's the trouble with live cargo," the captain added.

Mr. Plomley nodded, rather indifferent, so long as he and his wife got safely back to Liverpool. But Jade looked the captain squarely in the eye.

"I hope pirates get you!" she told him earnestly, and left him staring at her with a puzzled face for just an instant before he decided he couldn't have heard her right, and turned back to more important matters of wind and sail and profits.

They weathered Point Maysi on the next tack, in growing yellowish dusk, and left Cuba behind. The storm was visible now, with sulphurous clouds low in the sky and an ominous feel in wind and swell. The *Pearl* was lurching in a most peculiar way, irregular and exciting. Jade, loving it, stayed clinging to the taffrail (with an expostulating Joshua beside her) until MacDonald came by and ordered her to her cabin. Using most offensive language, he gave her to understand that her loss overboard would be a small loss, if any, but the captain might find it awkward and blame the crew.

"You're just annoyed because I *am* liking the storm!" Jade accused him, jerking her arm away from his rude grasp, and clinging to the taffrail as the *Pearl* lurched again and showed every indication of burying her port side in the dark wetness swelling below.

"This isn't even the storm yet, daft idiot!" he retorted, showing his teeth again. "It's hardly a taste. You go below, and no nonsense. We'll be shipping green any minute."

Infuriatingly, Joshua sided with him. Even more infuriating, Jade strongly suspected that they were right. With a great show of reluctance she staggered across the wildly tilting deck and down to her cabin, where Domino roused herself long enough to demand indignantly why she'd been locked in.

"Because if any idiot looks in and sees you in my bed there could be a lot of silly nonsense about it," Jade retorted—truthfully, even if it wasn't the main reason. "Do you want any dinner?"

Domino made a sound of utter revulsion and buried her head.

All night the wind increased, and by morning the storm was fully upon them. The Plomleys remained in their cabin, Domino remained in Jade's bed (Jade had slept in her cubbyhole), and even the intrepid Joshua looked worried.

Jade was wild with excitement. She loved it! It was true she was scared. The *Pearl* might easily go down, and her heart thudded when she thought of it—but this only added to the thrill of howling wind and the extravagant leaping of the ship. Decks and bulkheads creaked and groaned, and there was a weird vibration from the taut standing rigging and masts, and it was quite impossible to stand up in any normal sense of the word on a deck that tipped insanely first in one direction and then in another. Her box went sliding across the cabin floor, came up with a bang against the wall, and at once zoomed off in another direction. Domino had braced herself in a corner of the bunk and was staring at Jade, who clung to the door handle, laughing. It was crazy to laugh, she knew. Quite possibly they were all about to drown. But the laughter bubbled out of her throat of its own accord, not caring about anything but the wild idiot joy of the storm.

"I have to go out on deck!" she shouted, and did so.

The wind seized her, shrieking, the instant she opened the door, and she had to clutch the handle while her full skirts tried to turn into sails. She considered going back and unearthing her breeches, but decided against it, and let the gale blow her forward to the main mast. There she wound her hands in the ropes and hung on with all her might, breathless, scared, and giggling. The wind now pinned her against the mast, wrapping her skirts around it. A huge wave appeared astern, hovered over the poop for a moment, plunged across the deck, nearly knee-deep. Jade's fencing-hardened muscles gripped fiercely against the tug, but she began to wonder how she would get back to her cabin.

Another larger wave loomed. She braced herself. And then a hard ungentle arm clamped itself painfully around her back pinning her to the mast more effectively than the wind, nearly squeezing out what little breath she had left. The wave raged over, deeper than before. And MacDonald's harsh voice swore at her with perfectly awesome inventiveness. Still swearing, he whipped out a loose end of rope and tied Jade firmly to the mast.

"You like it so much, you can just bide here until we get into harbor," he snarled, the wind whipping the words into her ear.

"Harbor?" she shouted back. "What harbor? Can we?"

"Over yon." He jerked his black head toward a bright green shape glimpsed between waves and flying spray. "One of the Bahamas. Captain knows a good cove on the sheltered side, and we'll heave to until it's over." He gave her his irreverent, wolfish grin. "This isn't a bad storm, you understand. We'd be riding it out but for the cargo. You stay there, daft female; if you go over, no one will even try to get you back." And he fought his way aft again in the teeth of the gale.

It took a masterly bit of seamanship to work the ship into the lee of the little island and then beat her upwind into the small cove. Inexperienced as she was in seamanship, Jade could have only the dimmest notion of how masterly it was, quite impossible had there been any reefs here.

The air was quieter now, almost silent by comparison, while the storm went roaring past above. Half sorry and half relieved, Jade took a deep breath and twisted around to untie her bonds and go find out how Joshua and Domino had fared. The after-hatch was being opened as she went past, and someone starting down to inspect the cargo.

And it was then that the idea came. A small uninhabited island—and the ship hove to until the storm abated, which would be at least until morning—and a dark noisy night—and a tired crew. . . .

She opened her cabin door very thoughtfully indeed.

CHAPTER TEN

Escaped Cargo

Domino was very much affronted when Jade bundled her ruthlessly out of bed that evening and into the tiny dark cubbyhole that was hers. "I want to sleep in my own bed for a change," Jade said cold-heartedly, and closing the door, locked it.

There was a moment of astounded silence, a rattle of the latch, and a flood of what must have been simply dire cursing in several African dialects. Jade set her chin and turned away. She couldn't explain anything to Domino, or Joshua either. They must be completely innocent, whatever happened.

Joshua was trickier because he knew her better. When she finally turned the key on his cubbyhole door, it was in breathless silence, to snores within, long after he believed her to be safely in bed and asleep, herself.

Then she tiptoed back to her own cabin and set about removing the false bottom from her box by the pale light of a slush lamp (bare candles being too dangerous aboard ship). The black breeches slipped on easily, free and comfortable. The dull blue shirt—unworn even in her practice sessions in Jamaica—was wrinkled and damp, but a good color for blending into darkness. Then she frowned at her rapier. A good sharp knife would have been better, in case she needed to cut any of the ropes, but as she hadn't a knife, the rapier must do. She buckled the scabbard to her belt and felt very bold and adventurous. Sharp excitement hammered her heart pleasantly, and she found herself grinning. Clearly she was becoming positively addicted to danger.

And there *was* danger: Jade didn't deceive herself about that. The captain had absolute power aboard his ship, and he was merciless. And a law that hanged children of eight or nine for the theft of a shilling was not likely to intervene on behalf of a great girl of sixteen who, in effect, stole a whole cargo of slaves. The knowledge distinctly added spice to the adventure.

She blew out the lamp, slipped out of her cabin, and crept up the narrow passage to the deck, where she stood getting the feel of the night. The storm was abating overhead, but there was still a fair amount of noise in the air. Somewhere behind the driven mass of cloud was a half moon, so that things were slightly less than pitch black. After a moment Jade could see a jagged line between jungle and sky, and then the line between ship and water. There was no binnacle light tonight, there being no need for compass or helmsman. Nor was there any sign of a watch.

The after-hatch slowly became visible as a square of a different shade of dark on the deck. Jade stared at it, suddenly assaulted with misgivings. She hadn't planned well enough! What if the padlock were fastened? What if she couldn't move the cover at all? What if the slaves were chained? How was she to make them understand, and what if they understood too quickly and all swarmed out in a riotous mass?

But it never occurred to her to go back to bed and forget the whole thing. She had to try. Taking a deep breath, she moved forward over the black deck, stumbled slightly when her foot hit the corner of the hatch, and crouched in tense silence as the slight sound almost seemed to be echoed. But nothing stirred, and after a moment her fingers began moving slowly around the edge of the cover. If the bolt was locked . . .

But it wasn't. Someone had obligingly left it secured with only a pin through the staple, and with the wedges already loosened. All she need do was open the bolt, shove back the cover, and—And what? Call down for them to come out now? She smiled rather grimly, facing the fact that she would have to go down there herself. Another imagined movement made her freeze again; then she put her strong young shoulder to the cover.

It held firm—gave a little—moved back with an atrocious grating noise which she could only hope was drowned out by the surrounding storm noises. One more heave, and a foul-smelling oblong of black space spread itself uninvitingly beneath her, filled with small moaning. Jade's stomach lurched. If only they'd come up themselves! But it was no use hoping for anything so unlikely; she had to go in.

The ladder stretched down and down, darker than imagination could realize, so that colors invented themselves within Jade's eyes. Down and down, following the stench and the moaning that seemed to fill the hatchway, to the wide 'tween-decks just below the waterline. And there it was, the presence of many people, breathing in heavy fear of whatever it was creeping down upon them in the dark. Then new sounds, scuffling sounds; coming from above? She looked upward in alarm for the comforting pale strip of open hatch, and for an awful moment she couldn't find it. Then it was there again, and the scuffling was probably rats or the slaves. She must *not* give way to fear!

With a mental nudge, she applied herself to the problem of communication with the invisible and doubtless terrified cargo. "Go!" she whispered uselessly. "I mean, come!"

Silence. Despairingly she left the ladder and began to grope her way along the deck—felt a bony arm that at once jerked in fear. She patted it comfortingly, then gave a gentle tug. "Come!"

A new shuffling sound very near. A sense of motion unseen. A small muted babble of other tongues, and a whimper picked up by a score of voices.

"Shhh!" Jade hissed urgently, and found that this seemed to be the same in Africa, for the whimpering died away, and one voice whispered, and the arm she held suddenly consented to her tugging.

The smell was perfectly horrible. Gagging, Jade pulled the arm and its owner toward the ladder, hoping that the idea was getting across and others would follow. She couldn't just send the poor creature on ahead: she had to take him, possibly even push him overboard. At least he was docile enough, as a whipped dog is docile, submitting to whatever might happen next. Or perhaps the obvious secrecy of her visit had given them some inkling of what was afoot? Other whispers and scuffles echoed themselves up the shaft, and surely there were other captives coming behind?

The slit of sky loomed larger; now she was through it and on deck again, glancing around quickly in what seemed almost bright daylight by contrast. She could see the masts and rigging, the line of the bulwarks on the port side—the shore side—and not the sign of a human being.

Silently she urged the slave up from the hatch, silently led him across the deck and pointed at the black mass of jungly land. She found the mizzen chains—and the African finally realized what she intended. No need to explain further. He made one small odd sound, grasped the mizzen chains, and was gone over the side. Jade, hoping profoundly that he could swim, turned back to guide the next emerging dark shape.

The second—a woman—was over, and the third, and then the news spread back down the hatch and there was no need for urging or explaining, but a rush that grew less and less silent. Everything was falling apart. Someone was apparently trying to bring order— And then everything went to pieces at once. Splashes. A warning shout from alerted crew, somewhere forward a panicky scramble for the bulwarks nearly sweeping Jade off her feet. Then she was in a complete chaos of milling humans, some shouting "Slaves loose!" and others just trying to win their way overboard. A gun went off. A hand grabbed at her, found and lost her ear, slithered off, feeling for her shoulder.

Jade whipped out her rapier as she leaped backward, crashed against someone else, twisted away in the dark, and faced another dark shape—not so dark now that a lantern was waving its orange way toward the melee. She had to get back to her cabin before that light arrived! The man was barring her way with a cutlass.

Jade's rapier felt its swift way under the blade and jabbed into the arm holding it just as a sharp stab of pain knifed through her own left arm just below the shoulder.

"Got one!" yelled a jubilant voice. "Bring the glim!"

But Jade wasn't waiting for it. She was already eeling a silent path back across the deck, groping down the stairs and along the narrow corridor and finally inside her door with a gasp of relief. Bolting the door, she sank down panting in the dark. Her mind was spinning, her arm hurting abominably—but triumph held her. How many had got away? She had no idea, but some! It was worth it, then! She found herself grinning widely. There was no question about it: she *liked* this sort of thing! She was only sorry they hadn't all got free—and also that she had got wounded, she added to herself, wincing.

The voices on deck had risen now, topped by the infuriated bellow of Captain Narramore, who had apparently just arrived on the scene. More purposeful sounds began, and Jade came back to practical reality. Blood was soaking her shirt sleeve. She must get Domino to do something about it in the morning, but just now it would be enough to bind it tightly and stop the bleeding. It couldn't be very deep or serious, for she could flex her arm, and even manage to strike the flint and steel and relight the slush lamp.

She was just starting the tricky business of wrapping a silk scarf tightly around her own upper arm—one end caught between her teeth—when there came a banging at the door.

She stopped breathing in the middle of a breath, staring at the unoffending door as if it had deliberately betrayed her. Again the banging, and the first mate's voice.

"Mistress Lennox! Wake up, Mistress Lennox! Demme, she *can't* be sleeping through all this!"

Jade took up her cue. "Wha– What is it?" she called, making her voice sound small and alarmed with very little trouble. "What's happening out there?"

"No danger, Mistress. But someone's let some of the slaves loose. Captain wants to talk to everybody on board."

That was predictable enough; of course he would. But no one could possibly think of suspecting her. It would be quite beyond imagination, so long as she hadn't actually been caught in the act. Feeling quite comfortably safe, she breathed again and played for time.

"Slaves loose!" she squeaked. "Well, I'm certainly not coming out there, then! Not until you get every one of them put right back again!" She fumbled with the scarf, clumsy in her hurry, pulling it so tightly that the bleeding must stop, even if her fingers went numb. And she tied it somehow with right hand and teeth while the idiotic conversation went on.

"I tell you there's no danger, Mistress. But the captain wants to see everybody. The chap wot loosed them is on board somewhere, and he might've got into your cabin," he added cunningly.

"Well, he didn't!" snapped Jade in splendidly convincing indignation. "And I'm not going out there in the middle of the night like this; it's not decent; and besides, I've got my night-rail on, and my slave is locked in her cubbyhole, so I can't get dressed." She tied the final knot. The pain of the cut had become something far away and irrelevant, something her body felt but her attention couldn't be bothered with. The mate was still waiting in baffled silence outside the door.

"Well, couldn't you just put on something by yourself, Mistress?" he suggested finally in a diffident and embarrassed voice. "Captain's wild, Mistress; I don't know wot he'll say if I tell him you won't."

Jade at once perceived that this would be a great mistake. "Well, then, I'll try," she agreed reasonably. "But you'll have to give me a few minutes, you know." And she hurried to her chest to find the most voluminous garment she owned. No time to change from her breeches; she must just put something over them. The rose red contouche would be best, in case blood seeped through the scarf, she decided with a coolness that quite pleased her. The color wouldn't show, and also it had full, deep-cuffed sleeves reaching below the elbow.

She rolled the blue shirt-sleeves as high as she could, and slipped the contouche over her head. It hung full and waistless, hiding any bulge of bandage or breeches. A glance in the tiny mirror showed a few smudges on her face, easily wiped off, and no more pallor than could be easily explained by alarm. She took a deep breath and felt ready to face the world, the crew, and even the captain in his wrath.

The deck was now lit with a dozen or more lanterns, the hatch was an empty black hole down which the captain was staring, the crew swarmed everywhere, and Mr. and Mrs. Plomley stood bewildered and disapproving near the stairs leading up to the quarterdeck. Jade at once went and looked bewildered and disapproving with them.

The squeak and splash of oars below suggested a small-boat returning from a hunt for swimming slaves, and a shout presently verified this. "Caught two, sir!"

Jade gritted her teeth and thought of all the swear words she knew, which was very few indeed. She kept her face carefully blank—a mistake which might well have betrayed her had anyone been in the least suspicious, but they weren't. Captain Narramore was promising a flogging for the culprit when he should be found, and no one else was paying any attention to the passengers except for the conscientious mate, who regarded them anxiously.

"Did any of you hear anything?" he asked the three passengers. The Plomleys shook their heads. Jade tossed hers.

"I should think I did!" she pronounced with as much indignation as she could manage with the distraction of her throbbing arm, coupled with a sad lack of any real dramatic ability. "I've never heard so much racket; and all that banging on my door; it isn't *nice.*" It sounded just like Aunt Louisa, she decided, flickering her lashes in what was intended to be roguish reproach, but which caused the mate to wonder if she was subject to fits.

A few feet away the bos'n was standing up to the captain with the boldness of conviction. "I tell yer, I got the fellow! Blooded me dagger, I did. On 'is arm, I fink, sir. Couldn't see, what wiv it being dark and all, but 'is left arm I fink. 'Ave a look at everyone's arms, and you'll find ve blighter wot let 'em loose."

Jade's heart leaped and then calmed down. It was just conceivable that they might look at Mr. Plomley's arm, but certainly she and Mrs. Plomley would be passed over without question. Ladies simply did not run around turning slaves loose at midnight, and with swords, at that. Unthinkable.

Sure enough, the search was made then and there, every sailor and officer pulling off his shirt if he was wearing one, to prove that he hadn't a wound from the waist up—except for the fellow that Jade had pinked, and he could prove he'd been below with the others until the alarm.

Jade leaned against the bulkhead as she watched, partly to prove to herself and everyone else how relaxed and unconcerned she was, and partly because her throbbing arm was making her feel just the tiniest bit odd. No one was paying her the slightest attention, and she could enjoy the whole scene as much as her wound would permit. The captain was becoming more and more livid—first with the loss of the slaves, and now with the impossible fact that no one had apparently done the thing.

"It was a slave you stabbed," he muttered furiously at the bos'n, his lean face suffused. But the bos'n shook a stubborn head, waved his stained dagger, and maintained that the chap he got was wearing a shirt, which none of the slaves wasn't.

At last the captain turned his enraged eyes on Mr. Plomley. "I'll see you as well, sir," he growled, quite beyond any consideration of courtesy to passengers. "And what about your personal slaves, all of you?" Ignoring Mr. Plomley's indignant sputtering, he swung around to Jade with a sudden thought. "What about your slave, Mistress? That big black fellow—"

"He's locked in the cubicle!" she retorted in brief panic. "I always lock them in! You can see for yourself!" And she blinked, because the ship seemed unaccountably to be swaying in a way that it had *never* done before.

Mr. Plomley's pale offended torso was gleaming now, unmarked. Captain Narramore turned away again as the gaunt figure of the second mate emerged from the hatch to report on the number of slaves missing. His harsh voice and unemotional face tended to fade out. So, for that matter, did the deck. Jade shook her head, screwing her eyes to make things come back to normal. There was a dark hollow sickness in her middle, and a swarm of bees buzzing invisibly.

"Wot's the matter with Mistress Lennox?" It was the anxious voice of the first mate. "I think she's fainting, sir!"

Jade could see the captain turn—a long distance away, and very slowly. There was surprise in his face, and no wonder. What nonsense! She *never* fainted, never in her life! She— A wave of grayness came between her and the world. She shoved her back hard against the bulkhead and tried to tell them that she never fainted.

"Here, Missy, look out!" And the captain reached out and grabbed her firmly by the arms.

Red-hot pain shocked Jade out of any thought of fainting. Caught completely unprepared, she stiffened with a hissing gasp—swayed in his grip—and when she could breathe again through bared teeth and shutter her face, it was far too late to dissemble. His fingers had felt the bulk of the scarf and the warm dampness seeping through. The captain's weathered face wore a look of idiotic incredulity. Behind him, a half circle of blank eyes, and one slanted pair that gleamed ferocious.

The milk being irretrievably spilled, Jade was seized by the old danger-madness that so baffled her family. Her sudden laughter was derisive, triumphant, altogether reckless; it shocked her audience to their very souls, and gave

Jade a most tremendous satisfaction. She laughed again.

Unbelieving voices babbled around her, one hysterically soprano and the rest outraged and masculine. A girl! Impossible! The sleeve of her contouche was ripped open, revealing blue shirt and reddened scarf as damning, incredible proof. The captain turned a face pitiless with anger.

"I swore I'd flog the guilty party, and so help me, I shall!"

They were watching to see her flinch. But Jade was still somewhere apart from reality, in a state of near-intoxication, so that his words slid past her like a sword unable to pierce her guard. She heard appalled exclamations and a small scream from Mrs. Plomley, but she knew her own face remained unmoved. She even managed one of her small crooked smiles, aimed right at Rory MacDonald. He was definitely not looking down his nose at her now.

It was a brief moment of glory—which Captain Narramore refused to pause and admire. "Lock her in her cabin until morning," he ordered curtly. "The storm's abating, and I want to sail with the next tide if the sea isn't too heavy. I'll deal with her after that. Did you hear me, Lawton? That's an order!"

The punishment for disobedience at sea was hanging. Clearly reluctant, the first mate obeyed, leading the unresisting Jade to her cabin and then staring down at her dumbly. Jade stared back, still exalted, but uncomfortably aware that reality was waiting to break through. And being the heroine of a Greek tragedy had probably been very unsatisfying indeed for the real Antigonë. Still, so far she was still on stage, and meant to make the most of it. Besides, there was a practical matter to be seen to.

"Will you do something for me?" she asked, carefully calm.

He swallowed, properly impressed. "If I can."

"Look after my slaves, please—and don't let anyone let them out until it's over. Please! They'd be wild. And try not to give the girl any orders; she's not used to them. Here, I'll give you the keys to their cubbyholes."

And her hand, she was pleased to see, was perfectly steady.

CHAPTER ELEVEN

Nightmare

She lay on her bunk in her boy's clothes, watching the tiny patch of sky visible through the window as it turned gray and mauve and blue; and she wished she were dead. Her battle-courage had all ebbed away, and she was in the grip of a smothering black fear such as she had never before dreamed of. It churned and lurched in her stomach, and made her pulse pound in her ears and her hands clammy. And with it was the humiliating discovery that she was not, after all, the stuff from which Greek heroines were made.

She had thought she was brave and strong, had despised weaklings. Now, with her courage about to be really tested, she knew herself a shameful coward who longed to undo the whole thing, put the escaped slaves back below the hatch, go back to yesterday and pretend she had never thought of it. It was a mean, despicable wish—and she wished it with all her heart!

She lay perfectly still, arm throbbing and fists clenched, not crying because tears were wholly inadequate. She tried to tell herself that it would just be like one of Father's beatings—only worse, of course—but her body knew better, for her heart twisted painfully at the mere thought, and the tiny room was so filled with her own dread that she could hardly breathe.

It was of no use to remember her code. That didn't tell what to do if a consequence was too much for her untried courage, and broke it. The thought of herself screaming and crying under the lash was in a way as great a fear as the lash itself. Perhaps greater. If only she could *know* she wouldn't break. . . .

But she couldn't run away. She had to face it—and with at least an imitation of bravery, if that was the best she could do. And while she could keep it up, would it be pretense at all? Wasn't that what courage was: facing the thing you feared and pretending not to fear it?

It was light now, and the ship was coming to life. The sails were being spread; she heeled over into the brisk wind; came about, creaking, as the tide ebbed.

Jade shivered, already exhausted. She was cold with fear, and numb, and her arm hurt more and more. The *Pearl* must be out of the lee of the island now, into the strong wind that remained from the storm. And presently the first mate, hangdog, came for her.

A sense of unreality possessed her now. She forced herself to look around, squinting into the hard bright sunlight at the sullen crew, and Tom's pale distraction, and MacDonald's ferocious ringed eyes. The Plomleys were conspicuously absent, and Captain Narramore's mouth was a thin slit in a thin face. Jade put her shoulders back and her chin up, propelled as much by habit as will. Her legs were weak and her mouth dry, but she stared back at him, astonished that her craven animal fear seemed to show so little.

"Well, Mistress Lennox?"

Nothing was left now of principles or code: only the warring passions of pride and terror that caused her stomach to twist and gripe until the fear of being sick came to add itself to the others.

"Have you anything to say?"

She shook her head, not daring to trust her voice. An attempt at a smile stuck halfway, but she could feel that by some miracle her pretense was holding up . . . so far. . . .

"Right." He gave an inaudible order. Reluctant rough hands began to propel Jade across the deck, and the sick terror swept down on her again, almost blotting out sun and sky. And then MacDonald's voice cut in, harsher and sharper than usual, like a jagged saw.

"Don't be a fool, sir! How could a puny wench like this possibly loosen the wedges, even if she had a key to the padlock? . . . Matter of fact, I did it myself."

No one took it in for a moment. Jade stared with suddenly clear eyes, shocked for the moment right out of terror and nausea. "Liar!" she said with conviction, her voice a thin croak.

"Liar!" echoed the captain, but he looked slightly shaken. "She's admitted it," he pointed out unanswerably. "And look at the wound on her arm—and her clothes—and the blooded rapier in her cabin. Are you sweet on her or something, MacDonald?"

At this calumny they both forgot the crisis for an instant and turned furious eyes upon him. Rory MacDonald fairly spat. "How in blazes d'you think she got the hatch open, you flaming imbecile? And who d'you think prodded the poor devils into moving?"

Jade gaped, remembering certain odd sounds and

shapes in the dark of that few moments. Captain Narramore was looking like a man receiving a third kick in the pit of the stomach.

"A conspiracy!" he breathed.

"It wasn't!" yelped Jade, quite irrational.

"Mutiny!" added the captain. "That'll hang you, MacDonald—*after* I flog you both. What are you waiting for?" he snarled at the first mate. And the two criminals—hating each other almost as much as the captain—were marched off to punishment.

After that, things became mercifully blurred, for the black fear and unreality flooded over her again. There was a long, nearly-unbearable wait . . . and the hideous sound of a whip coming down on someone else's back . . . and then in sharp focus Rory MacDonald's masked face and a bright glance of derisive challenge. If it was intended to quench her, it had the opposite effect, for she rose to it. If he could stand it, she could! And he wasn't making a sound. New courage surged through her, in a confused rush.

Then raw fire seared across her own back, shocking the air from her lungs with the unexpected savagery of it. She heard her own gasp—felt an instant of not caring whether she were brave or not—and then came a wave of obstinate pride that wiped out everything but itself. If it wasn't courage, it made a good substitute.

Time measured itself in streaks of lightning, and then someone was yelling. It wasn't Jade; she was sure of that. It seemed to be everyone else. Then the lightning stopped and there was a most astonishing eruption of noise: a medley of shouts and shooting, of running feet and strident swords, and crashes and crunches, and then, to her great relief, nothing.

Jade came slowly up from a deep dark place shot through with lurid bits of light. Probably a well, she decided foggily. There was someone hurting, too, but she didn't much care, because she was busy with the effort of rising out of the well, and also with the problem of breathing. It was stuffy down here, and the murmur of voices echoed hollow and faint.

Lights grew stronger presently from the other side of her closed eyes, and she was no longer sure she wanted to come up at all. She had a nasty suspicion that it wasn't going to be pleasant, and that the person hurting so badly might even turn out to be herself.

It was, too. She had just a moment to notice that she was face-down on a huge bed, and to receive a brief impression of a tall man bending over her. She could see no more than a glimpse of velvet breeches and a narrow strip of silk shirt, and then the pain attacked, no longer dull, but flaming red and orange, shot with streaks of murky yellow. Jade drew one sharp breath (which made it worse) and the figure at once bent over her.

"Awake?" it asked. "Can you hear me?" It was certainly not the bloodless voice of Captain Narramore.

Jade made a small grunting sound intended to indicate that she was and could.

"Hurt?" asked the figure.

Jade's grunt this time was thick with derision. What a stupid question! As if anyone couldn't tell, for goodness sake!

"I'm sorry you're awake," said the voice, sounding sincere.

Jade considered this, frowning into the sheet that was hampering her breathing. She herself felt very regretful to be awake, because it was so much more uncomfortable than not to be awake. But why should the Velvet Breeches be sorry? It sounded ominous, somehow.

"Why?" she croaked suspiciously.

Velvet Breeches seemed not to hear. "Brace yourself," he commanded.

"Why?" Jade croaked again, vainly trying to roll her eyes far enough sideways to see the face atop the silk shirt.

"Because I'm going to put something on your back, and it will hurt like murder," replied the voice simply.

It seemed an eminently reasonable answer to Jade. "Oh," she said, satisfied, and braced herself. The voice chuckled. Then fire touched her back, spread over it, shooting the pain up the scale out of red and into yellow-orange and gold and saffron. Presently she fell back down the well again, thankfully.

When she slowly rose to consciousness once more, it was night and she was alone in pain that seemed to beat her down into the bed. She felt much better. Whatever else had happened, she had passed her own test; she was sure of that. Now it just remained to come to terms with the pain. It was no use fighting against it: that made it worse. The trick, she had begun to discover when she was quite small, was to accept it, absorb it unresistingly—and relax. Perhaps this didn't actually make it hurt less, but it did make it much more bearable.

Jade set her teeth once, and then began the business of relaxing. Jaws—fingers—hands— She could do it! She was beginning to feel almost her old cocky self again! . . . Well, almost. . . .

She slept at last, and awoke to morning and the same tall figure, still only a section of shirt and breeches. "Thirsty?" asked the same voice. Jade, able now to take some interest in things outside her own body, was positive she had never heard it before. Who was it, then, and where was she? At sea, certainly: that was clear from the movement of the ship, but—

Deeply puzzled, she grunted assent and tried to roll over.

"Careful! Here—" And a hand lifted her from the bed just enough so that she could drink the cool water proffered by a matching hand. Jade drank avidly, and then paused, staring at the hand. A small strong hand, with slender tanned fingers and wrist. Jade frowned, thought backwards and listened in her memory to the voice that went with it. Then she twisted her head and eyes once more in a determined effort to see more.

"You're a girl!" she discovered, accusing, and was rewarded with a rich low chuckle.

"I know," agreed the voice affably.

Jade wriggled in impatient but injudicious curiosity, caught her breath with pain, and found her voice again. "But who are you? And where are we and how did I get here and what's happened to Domino and Joshua and that Rory MacDonald, and where's Captain Narramore?"

The Velvet Breeches chuckled again and obligingly propped Jade slightly sideways with pillows, so that she could see that she was in a blue silken cavern formed by the hangings of the four-poster bed. Just in front of her eyes was a tall and rather beautiful young woman with a mane of blazing red hair, who was looking amused.

"The young man's in about the same condition you are," she remarked. "And you're both on a pirate ship, if you want to know—and a lucky thing for you we came along when we did."

Jade thought back to the recent nightmare, and the confusion and noise at the end of it. That was it, then! A pirate attack.

"Well, it would have been a great deal luckier if you'd come a little sooner," she pointed out in a voice of deep reproach that drew another chuckle from the red-head. "Please tell me what happened to Joshua and Domino! My slaves! They were locked up in their cubbyholes."

The lovely face grinned. "Oh, those! Banging and yelling like furies, they were. They're all right. Locked up to keep them from killing the *Pearl*'s crew, and still banging and yelling by all accounts."

"Well, let them out at once," Jade commanded faintly. (It was astonishing how exhausted she had already become!)

The red eyebrows went up. "You're very despotic for a completely helpless captive," she observed.

"I want to see them," whimpered Jade, closing her eyes against a rush of weak tears.

"Oh, all right," the young woman agreed with tolerant good-nature. "If you'll stop fretting and get well, so I can ask you questions. You fill me with vast curiosity, girl. And by the way, did you still want to know who I am?"

Jade roused herself enough to consider the matter, and

found that she already knew. "I dare say you're Anne Bonney," she observed without surprise, and went to sleep.

This time she was restless and hungry when she awoke, and might even have considered herself nearly well had it not been perfectly clear that she must be suffering delirium. For beyond the bed-hangings she seemed to see a queen's chamber. It was *obviously* a queen's chamber! What other kind of room would have distracting carved mahogany woodwork inlaid with gold and silver and mother-of-pearl? Or walls composed of equal parts tapestry and gold-framed paintings and mirrors? Or a high-backed throne? Or rich fabrics and jewels and gold plate scattered carelessly around?

On the other hand, what queen's chamber would contain a bit of jungle? Or what jungle would contain a chamber concert? For a monkey chattered above her head, and parrots shrieked and jabbered, nearly blanketing the sweet high notes of a flute somewhere.

And palace and jungle and concert all rocked gently to the long roll of the sea.

"Rmff!" said Jade incredulously, and waited to lapse back into unconsciousness.

Instead, the flute stopped, the parrots squawked anew, and there was an eager movement just beyond her range of vision. She rolled over a trifle—and saw the patient figures of Joshua and Domino, sitting side by side, watching her with the fixed expectancy of two infants waiting for an Easter egg to hatch. They looked comically out of place amid the piled wealth of the queen's chamber. Jade giggled feebly, and then winced.

Everything in her delirium answered at once. The monkey chittered, the parrots swore and flapped around the room in a frenzy of bright feathers, the ship heaved itself over a particularly large roller, the blue hangings were swept completely aside, and the two dark faces stared down at her with boundless reproach.

"Risking your life that way!" scolded Joshua. "You ought to be spanked, Missy Lanie!"

Jade grinned wryly. "I was," she reminded him.

Domino glared, vanished briefly, and reappeared with a bowl which she held like a weapon. "You lock me in!" she stormed and shoved a spoonful of turtle soup into Jade's mouth. "Not let me help!"

Jade swallowed the soup and eyed Domino impenitently. "That was *my* adventure," she said tartly. "If you— Oh! I didn't even think of asking you if you wanted to escape with them," she realized, chagrined. "Did you? I'm sorry, Domino!"

Domino relented slightly, regarding Jade with a respect that was new. "No escape; free now," she announced, eyes gleaming, and watched with subdued glee while Jade tried to puzzle it out. Nothing at all seemed to make much sense just now.

The red-and-blue parrot flew across the room, lighting on the back of the throne. The green-and-yellow parrot screeched. A huge yellow cat leaped up on the bed, sniffed doubtfully at Jade, and condescended to curl up beside her. And the flute bounded lightly into the room and halted at the bedside, held by a willowy man of uncertain age, who crowed elatedly at the sight of her.

"*Tiens*, you wake yourself at last," he twittered. "I shall myself tell *chère* Anne, but at once!" And he vanished.

Jade, blinking at the spot where he had been, considered the theory of delirium again.

"That was Pierre," said Joshua reassuringly and not altogether with approval. "He's a pirate, and also a hairdresser, tailor, cook, actor, stage-designer, and flute-player. And stop laughing, Missy Lanie; it can't be good for you."

"It isn't. It feels terrible," Jade admitted, hiccupping painfully, and falling straight from mirth into fretful weakness. "I do wish you'd *tell* me things," she chafed. "Was that really Anne Bonney with the red hair? How can Domino be free if we're all pirate captives? What happened to the *Pearl*—and Tom Deane—and the captain? You're being horrid on purpose!"

"*Pearl* sink; Captain him dead," Domino reported with relish. "Me not kill," she added regretfully.

Joshua took up the tale with a quelling glance at the blood-thirsty Domino. "Mr. MacDonald's getting better, and Mr. Deane and most of the crew have joined the pirates," he told Jade with obvious pleasure. "They aren't a bad lot at all, you know, Missy Lanie. They set the rest of those poor slaves free right away, on the Cuban coast. There's plenty of wild jungle there, and they'll settle down and make a new life." He scowled at her, reproving. "So you see you just wasted your effort and the skin off your back, pulling a mad trick like you did."

His words plunged Jade briefly back into those hours of anguished fear, and she closed her eyes for an instant, not at all ready to remember that. Later, but not yet.

"What about the others, and the Plomleys?" she whispered, more to change the subject than from any deep concern.

"Them put on ship go England," Domino broke in, ebullient.

And at that moment the parrots began screaming and a small monkey leaped unexpectedly across the bed and into the arms of Anne Bonney, who materialized there quite suddenly with Pierre beaming behind her. The whole improbable setting was beginning to seem so normal that Jade wasn't at all surprised to see that warlike and ferocious pirate now dressed in a rich flowing gown of turquoise satin, studded with pearls and amethysts. "How are you feeling, Prize Prisoner?" she asked conversationally.

Jade rolled over another inch or two. "Am I?" she demanded, fascinated. "What will you do with me?"

"That depends," retorted Anne, looming. She was built just like Domino: as tall as a man, slender, full-breasted, junoesque—and distinctly formidable. She narrowed hazel eyes and suddenly looked what she was: a pirate, who had committed theft, assault, arson, and murder. "Don't you think you ought to be just a trifle alarmed?" she suggested, menacing.

"No," said Jade with sure instinct.

Pierre clapped delighted hands, the cat lifted its head and yawned, and Anne laughed. "So much for my reputation as a female ogre! And as for your Domino—"

"Belong me!" spat Domino, looking ready to dispute it with violence. "Free now."

Jade looked at Anne. "Is she?"

"That's up to you, surely," said Anne, surprised.

"Is it really?" demanded Jade excitedly. "I've never been allowed. And I've been trying to free Joshua ever since I was ten."

"Well, who's to stop you now?" Anne laughed again. "That's one advantage of being outlaws. We make our own laws—and fairer ones, usually, than the ones we left behind."

"Well, thank goodness!" said Jade, sighing deeply. "That's settled, then."

Joshua looked dazed; Domino, pleased but neither astonished nor grateful. Why should she be grateful for what she had considered to be her natural and inalienable right all along?

"All of you out!" Anne commanded suddenly and masterfully. "I'm going to take a look at your back, young Melanie, and then go look in on your friend Rory. Let's see. . . . Mmmm, yes, you're healing very well indeed. You'll always have scars, I suppose you know? In a minute you can go back to sleep."

"But I want to get up," protested Jade, more from principle than conviction.

"Liar!" retorted Anne. "Hold still, I'm going to hurt you again." And by the time she had finished, Jade was glad enough to lie still and rest, and do a great deal of thinking.

There was a great deal to think about. The world had turned upside down, and she with it. In her weakened state she had so far accepted it all as a small child does, without surprise, because all things are equally new and astonishing. But now she felt like a ship, battered and driven wildly off course by a storm. And she must stop drifting and try to start navigating again.

But it was hard not to let her thoughts go on drifting, in unison with the long soothing pitch of the ship. The jeering hawk-face of Rory MacDonald floated before her closed eyes, unbidden, unwanted, baffling. Why had he behaved in that extraordinary way? He, with his blatant scorn for slaves and girls. It was equally crazy that he should have tried to free the slaves, and that he should have accused himself in that idiotic way when it was suicidal to do so, and no help to anyone, even if Rory MacDonald had wanted to help anyone—which seemed highly unlikely from all she had seen of him.

Finding no answer at all to the puzzle, her thoughts gave up the struggle and drifted her right into sleep.

CHAPTER TWELVE

Queen Royal

On a brilliant day, with fresh trade winds, and a school of dolphins cavorting and frolicking alongside the *Queen Royal,* two invalids appeared on deck. Clad in sailcloth breeches and very loose shirts, they looked pale, interesting, composed, self-conscious—and strongly determined not to move too abruptly or back into anything. They met on the quarterdeck, and regarded each other with what could only be interpreted as hostility.

Jade at once opened the attack. "You! Why did you do such an idiotish thing?"

Rory MacDonald, his face bonier than ever, grinned ferociously. "And you weren't a blithering cork-brain?"

Jade blinked, recovered. "Yes, but I— You didn't *do* anything, or if you did it wasn't worth mentioning. I was the one who let them out."

"Aye, and you mucked it up nicely, didn't you?" He mocked her expression. "I'd have got the whole lot away, and no wounds to give me away afterwards, either. Little fool!"

"Fool yourself," Jade returned inadequately. "And anyway, that doesn't explain why you made that silly melodramatic confession that nearly got you hanged and didn't help me a bit."

His eyes flickered, either because she had touched a vulnerable point, or possibly because he guessed he had helped her, quite accidentally, just by being a challenge. He used all his unfair height to look down on her.

"Didn't do it to help you," he informed her laconically. "Why should I?"

They were leaning on the taffrail now, staring down at the wake of this huge ship and at the curveting dolphins. Jade looked up sharply, freed by this remark from the suspicion of a hateful obligation. "Thank goodness for that!" she exclaimed with a relief that nearly shed her dislike. "But why did you, then?"

"None of your business!" He looked almost embarrassed, scowling at the empty horizon with his black brows almost touching. "Did it for me," he added with deep reluctance, and sneered down at her. "You wouldn't understand."

But Jade, staring at him with perfectly circular eyes, didn't notice the sneer. Was it possible that he had a code, too? Unable to believe her own conclusions, she tilted a mocking smile at him.

"Well, I never did suppose you were the chivalrous sort."

"No!" He curled his lip. "Rotten stuff! If you want to help a friend, that's one thing. Or someone who's helpless and can't help himself. But why should anyone be babied and pampered just because she happens to be a girl? A human's a human. Ought to be treated that way. No whining, no special treatment, no—" He seemed to be groping for words, scowling heavily still, belligerent. "Any female with a grain of self-respect—like my grandmother—would stand on her own feet and drink her own brew and not ask any favors. The way you did," he conceded grudgingly and with an air of astonishment.

Jade was gazing at him enthralled. "Go on!" she urged. "Why didn't you ever say things like this before, instead of being nasty and horrible? We could have let the slaves—" She stopped as something struck her. "But— If you feel that way, why do you despise slaves? And if you despise them, why were you freeing them? You don't make sense!"

Rory made a sudden movement of his shoulders and stopped at once, not quite wincing. "Makes perfect sense," he growled. "Can't stand slavery, but I can't stand spinelessness, either. They don't have to submit to slavery. Nobody has to submit to anything. You can always die. You can usually fight first. If they all did that, slavery would die too, and what's left of Africa could be saved."

He stared bleakly out over the dark-blue sea, where the wind was blowing spindrift off the tops of the waves in a shimmer of rainbow foam. His face was as ugly and craggy as ever, the nose as big and crooked, the eyebrows as shaggy. His wide mouth was thin with disillusioned idealism, and stubbornly uncompromising. It was a wonderful face! Jade sighed, filled with companionship. Why, he was part of herself: banging at the same walls; filled with the same anger; damning the world's eyes, and bursting with pity for the wretched and oppressed, and hating the weakness that made them submit.

"If only everyone were like Domino," she mused, her thoughtful gaze on one particularly cheeky dolphin, who was unmistakably putting on an act for their benefit, rolling a merry eye up at them now and then to see if they were properly impressed. Her own ordeal came back to her sickeningly. "Or like us," she added without false modesty. "But I suppose–" She hesitated, tentatively offered her radical new idea fresh from trial. "Perhaps some people can't help not being brave?"

But Rory wasn't having any of that. "Then they ought to learn. That's what life is, a school for courage. The only defeat is surrender," he proclaimed with the air of discovering this for the first time in the history of mankind.

"Oh, yes!" breathed Jade, brushing aside the fleeting thought that there might be one or two other desirable virtues besides courage.

"The Iroquois tribes are like that," brooded Rory, clearly getting a great deal out of his system. "Brave and honorable and fair; much more than we are, for all we call them savages. They respect human dignity–women's as well as men's–and they keep their promises." He looked murderously at the acrobatic dolphin. "That's why we'll wipe them all out in the end. *We* have no honor or scruples or humanity."

His anger pierced Jade. She stared at his sharp profile, sick with the inevitability she caught in his words. He glowered into her green eyes, looking slightly astonished at himself, and fell back into his usual tough jeering manner. "Do I shock you?"

She shook her shaggy-growing head vigorously. "I think you're talking with my mouth!" she marveled. "I hate even to think of going back: it's like a November in my head."

"Back!" he echoed, looking stunned. "You can't go back, Mel– Mis–" He floundered over her name.

"My grandparents called me Jade," she suggested. "And I think they must have been a little like your grandmother, only not witches."

He grinned. "Jade. Suits you. Gran was called Kelpie; that's a kind of Scottish water witch. You've got her kind of grit."

Jade looked sideways at him, pleased. It was the first acceptable compliment a young man had ever paid her, the more acceptable because it was clearly his highest tribute. "I nearly didn't," she confessed with fierce honesty.

"Aye." He nodded matter-of-factly. "Me too. But surely you'll sign on with the pirates now? There's no place for you back on shore. You'd hate it."

She stared unseeing across the cobalt waves, Rory watching her with a not-unsympathetic blue eye. "Your family?" he guessed. "They'll think the *Pearl* went down in the storm, you know. With the Plomleys and mate off to England, and the crew here, there's no one to know different. They'll be thinking you drowned."

Jade winced, visualizing it.

"The point is," Rory went on inexorably, "which is going to give them more grief in the long run: you sadly but safely dead, or you returned from the grave after their worst mourning is over, to drive them daft for the rest of your life? And don't say you won't, because I saw you doing it to your father the whole of the trip out. You can't go back, Jade."

It was true, of course, and quite unanswerable. Moreover, Rory's use of her private name seemed to set a seal on the past and push it irrevocably behind her. Or had that happened earlier? Already her family seemed to her like people she had once met in passing, remote in time and space. She stared straight down at the surging wake, ashamed of the tear that hung on the end of her lashes and presently dropped off to join the other salt water below.

"Of course," Rory added with elaborate unconcern, "if you do turn pirate, you'll no doubt hang with the rest of us some day."

This threat caused Jade to recover at once. With that strange perversity she couldn't understand, she quickened to danger as Vinnie did to horses and Matt to the notion of travel. "Better hang than be bored to death," she returned with spirit, thinking of the unbearable dreariness of being a lady in Williamsburg. "Will they take me?"

Rory grinned wolfishly. "Bartholomew Roberts wouldn't. He has strict rules about females on *his* ship. But this crew's got used to Anne being the best man of them all, for all she won't be twenty until March; and they've sworn Domino in already. Aye, they'll have you. Won't you, Mark?" He turned to a short, beardless young man who had just swung down from the mizzen shrouds (which Jade eyed speculatively).

Surprisingly, Mark nodded at once. "Unless everyone from the *Pearl* is a liar, and Joshua's a worse one. . . . I tried to talk Tom Deane out of it," he added, looking puzzled at himself.

Tom Deane! Jade hadn't thought of him once since that last glimpse of his distraught face. But how on earth had this Mark Read sensed so quickly that Tom lacked toughness? For it was true.

"You want to join, then?" Mark was asking.

There was really no choice. She could no more have deliberately chosen to go back than she could have deliberately jumped overboard. Even if the price *was* the gallows. Invisible chains fell off. Elation filled her, as the blue world of sea and sky became her world. Her laughter was a peal of joy.

"I'm already *very* good with the rapier," she informed them with intolerable complacence. "Now I suppose I'd better start practicing the cutlass and pistol as well."

Life as a pirate turned out to be surprising in several ways. To begin with, Jade had vaguely supposed pirates to be fierce, brutal, lawless, and bloodthirsty like the notorious late Blackbeard; wicked by the very look of them, spending their days and nights in looting, fighting, and other deeds of horrid violence. In fact, most of them were nothing of the sort, and the *Queen Royal* sailed day after peaceful day committing no piracy whatever because the empty seas showed them nothing to pirate.

And Jade felt more at home than she had ever felt anywhere. They didn't *seem* wicked, these pirates—except for a few, like Barton, who liked brutality and killing, who had won a dozen duels and was always looking for another and rather had his eye on the inexperienced Tom Deane. Or there was Rafferty who liked stirring up trouble. Or Calico Jack Rackam who didn't like anyone at all—including himself, said Rory shrewdly. Most of the others were victims of fate or men, refugees from terrible things like bond-slavery, injustice, poverty, and cruelty. And a rough, tough, uncouth, rum-guzzling lot they were, too, with even less reason than Jade to love society, for it had treated them far worse.

They were also, on the whole, kind, loyal, fun-loving, sentimental, musical, and nothing if not democratic. They made and enforced their own laws, elected their own captains, had their code of honor, and maintained justice much more successfully, they said smugly, than did the outside world. Moreover, if they became dissatisfied with a captain, they simply deposed him and elected another the next time they set foot ashore for fresh supplies of water and turtles.

"We voted Charlie Vane out that way a year ago," explained little Sam Clarke, dwarf and self-styled clown. "Elected Jack instead. Figured he'd make a good figurehead (he hadn't gone to pieces then) and Anne'd really run things."

"You kill Vane?" asked Domino bloodthirstily.

Sam looked shocked. "Of course not! Gave him a boat and food; him and them as wanted to stick with him. He's got another ship now; we see him now and then."

"Well, why do you have to do it on land?" asked Jade, intrigued by this rather odd set of ethics. "Depose him, I mean."

Sam looked even more shocked. "Well, we couldn't do it at sea, could we? That'd be mutiny. Besides, it's one of our rules."

They were standing outside Anne's cabin in the aftercastle, which was, in effect, the general lounge for the entire nothing-if-not-democratic crew (except, ironically, the captain himself, who was no longer welcome). Mark was at the helm; and one-eyed Cory Dickson, the star gunner, was up in the fo'c'sle teaching a fascinated Joshua the rudiments of the art. Amidships a trio of trumpet, fife, and drum played a rollicking hornpipe, and a dozen pairs of large horny bare feet flapped out the complicated steps. Domino, unable to bear it any longer, joined in with a dance of her own which she said was the same thing only better.

By now there were half a dozen pirates outside the cabin door, watching with great amusement. Domino and nimble-footed Toby Harris were each determinedly trying to outdance the other in what could equally well be contest or double dancing-lesson. Pierre fetched his flute and joined the orchestra. Other pirates dropped their delicate scrimshaw carving and joined in.

Jade began to laugh. "If they could only see us, those people who scream about pirates being awful, wicked, ferocious, murderous criminals!"

"Oh, we are," Anne assured her blandly. "We've our reputations to keep up, you know; and we pirates would have to kill people for principle alone, even if they didn't fight us."

Jade turned a sunburned nose over her own shoulder and squinted at Anne, trying to make out how much—if at all—she was joking. "Then you *are* murderous criminals?" she suggested, doubtfully.

Anne at once reversed her argument. "No more than the authorities who call us that!" she blazed. "Lawton's a pompous, grasping, vindictive thief who steals under cover of the law, and Chidley is—was—twenty times worse. What's more, that sort prey on the helpless and poor. We may be thieves, but at least we steal with no more protection than our own arms and courage, and we steal from the rich."

Rory grinned cynically. "Just like Robin Hood," he purred.

"If you like," Anne retorted, her famous temper rising slightly. "We don't harm the helpless, and we've little enough mercy on the rich and powerful–and ship's officers who offend us . . ." She smiled grimly at Rory. "You didn't count as an officer of the *Pearl*, considering the condition we found you in. That may have saved your life, my lad."

It was a sobering thought. On the other hand, Anne might well be joking. Most ships, said Mark, surrendered without a fight. And Pierre's description of pirate raids sounded far more like comic farce than serious business. Jade put it out of her mind and concentrated on the business of recovering her strength and preparing herself for the life of piracy . . . and learning to climb the rigging without letting anyone guess how terrifying it was the first few times. She'd never been so high in a tree. Moreover, trees didn't hurl themselves wildly through the air the way a masthead did in a heavy swell.

"How do you like it?" Anne asked her as they clung to the foremast crosstrees, swinging dizzily above deck, sea, deck, sea– She looked with a grin at Jade's rather sickly face.

Jade swallowed heavily and stuck out her chin. "Wonderful!" she said, only half lying. After which she went back up again and again until she was no longer scared at all–and was half sorry she wasn't.

She was up on the fo'c'sle resting from rapier practice and savoring the galloping of the ship one morning when Calico Jack loomed beside her, his handsome face dissolute with drink and his breath reeking of it. Jade had scarcely seen him before, for it seemed that he had created a kind of private tavern for himself in the hold, and seldom left it. Anne was indeed captain in all but name—and Jade found herself wishing that Anne were here now, or Jack somewhere else. She looked at him with revulsion, having no use at all for anyone so lost to self-respect as to get drunk. Not from any moral scruples: she had none, in the ordinary sense. She merely considered that to get drunk—to lose control of one's own behavior—was a disgusting sin against one's own dignity and pride, almost more degrading and contemptible than cowardice. Her lip curled.

Jack squinted down at her, swaying. "Where'd a pretty li'l thing like you come from?" he asked, pleased. His puffed and bloodshot eyes were clearly trying to flash romantically. His finely penciled mustache needed trimming and his wavy black hair was uncombed. His waistcoat failed dismally to meet at what had once been a narrow waist. And he still fancied himself to be an irresistible swashbuckling fellow. Confidently, he reached for her.

Jade eluded him with ease, but her heart was thudding as she ducked neatly around the capstan. She felt that even a touch from that revolting creature would cause her to lose her breakfast at once.

"Wait a minute," Calico Jack called, plaintively reasonable. "All I want's a li'l kiss."

Jade exploded into fury. How dare he! She turned,

drew, flickered her rapier a menacing three inches from Jack's dismayed nose. "Any kiss you get from me will be with this," she announced trenchantly. The smile on her face might well have caused a hurricane to veer off and choose another course.

By this time a dozen pirates had seen what was happening and were gathering on the fo'c'sle, laughing but watchful, cheering both Jade and Jack on. Jade wasn't in the least sure what to make of them, and she much preferred fighting her own battles in any case, so she continued to let her rapier point dance waspishly around Calico Jack's unhappy face. To her increased contempt, he began to back away, wheedling and whining and blustering. A coward, then, as well as a drunk! Jade exchanged an expressive glance with Rory, who had draped himself very casually indeed against the rail some five feet away, amused and mocking and with his hand not far from his own sword. Jade was greatly pleased with him.

And at this point Anne arrived upon the scene and instantly took over the starring role. After just one quick glance, she rounded on Jack like an enraged Medea. "You ever lay one finger on Jade, or Domino either, and you'll hang from your own yardarm," she informed him pithily.

Jack roused himself to the fury of the weak and the drunk. "Who's captain of this ship, you flaming doxy? Threaten me, will you? 'S mutiny! I'll have you hanged, yourself . . . Or strung up by the thumbs! Seize her!" he ordered the crew.

No one moved. Anne laughed at him. "You may be captain, but not even the captain can break ship's law, Jack Rackam! No woman on this ship will ever be touched against her will, by you or anyone else; you signed that yourself, in our ship's articles. Do you remember what happened to Cordon?"

Jack apparently did. His bravado collapsed like a sail in a sudden calm, and he slunk back below to the consolation of his rum.

Anne turned to Jade. "No need to worry about that sort of thing on the *Queen Royal.*"

"I wasn't," said Jade briefly, sheathing her sword. Actually, she'd rather enjoyed it—after that first moment of revulsion, anyway. "Who's Cordon?" she asked interestedly as Anne chuckled.

"Was," Anne corrected her significantly. "He kept bothering me—so I challenged him to a duel and killed him. Come on back to my cabin, young Jade; Pierre wants to make you some clothes." And she led the way aft, leaving Jade to ponder several small points as she followed.

Pierre, who enjoyed a close but quite unromantic friendship with Anne, was like Jezebel the monkey in a new banana tree. He had rich fabrics (looted from pirated ships, of course) spread over the cabin, while he reveled in the joy of two new women for whom to create clothes. Having concentrated his genius on the willing Domino while Jade recovered, he now turned to the intriguing problem of green eyes and tanned face and sun-bleached short hair.

"A *petite* jewel," he told Anne happily. "Not magnificent like you and Domino, *c'est vrai*, but with great *piquance*. See how she is all green and brown and gold!" He stood back and pondered. "*Oui.* See how I have genius! I give to Anne black velvet breeches and white shirts, or cream and fawn and ivory and such subtle shades to set off her hair, and it is not my fault that she sometimes wears bright colors instead. To Domino I give the rich hues—crimson and purple and saffron and magenta, like jungle flowers, which she very much loves. But you—"

"Not pink or pale blue!" Jade warned him belligerently, stooping to stroke Morgan the cat—named for that famous privateer of sixty years ago. "I won't wear—"

"*Mais non!* Never!" Pierre looked deeply wounded. "For you, all the colors of the sea: coral and salmon and shrimp, and the so-many shades of sea-green, and brown-gold of sargasso weed, and amber to match your hair. And you shall have a petticoat of—"

"Petticoat!" Jade literally squawked at him, causing Morgan to bolt under the bed as if the parrots were attacking him. "Oh no, I shan't! I've had enough of petticoats; I'm *never* going to wear them again! Next you'll be wanting to make me stays! I'm always going to dress in breeches from now on."

Pierre looked crestfallen. "*Mais* for parties—for the evening—*Chère* Anne has some beautiful rich gowns that I have created for her, and Domino *aussi*. To wear in this so-splendid room?" He glanced around the so-splendid room, very grand indeed now that it was no longer a sick-room, and Jade was with Domino in the small aftercabin next to it. His dark eyes twinkled and wheedled, his mouth puckered in a distressed moue. "*Voyons*, I have made velvet breeches and silken shirts to be the trademark of the so-famous Anne Bonney. If I make for you also the trademark of breeches and flame-colored shirt, will you let me to create just one gown for you? Or perhaps two?"

Jade relented: she couldn't help it. "Well, I still think canvas breeches and cotton shirts are more practical," she muttered, but more from principle than conviction. It might be rather nice to have one rich and sophisticated and totally unsuitable gown . . . and she would love a flame-colored silken shirt. She stood with astounding patience while Pierre measured and muttered, and then blinked when he shoved her abruptly down onto a low stool and flourished a pair of shears in her face much as she had flourished her rapier at Calico Jack.

"What are you doing?" she demanded.

"Something about your *pauvre* hairs!" he retorted. "For all these days I can hardly to keep my hands off! I ask myself was it chewed off by drunken mice or hacked by a near-sighted monkey with a machête?" And he glanced at the innocent Jezebel pointedly as she swung by her tail from the canopy of the bed. "*Voilà*, I trim and shape it properly, so it frame your pointed face just so," he announced, and proceeded to do so at once, singing softly to himself a song of an *artiste* at work.

CHAPTER THIRTEEN

Pirate Raid

"Touché!" panted Anne, looking astonished. She lowered her rapier and stared at the grinning Jade. "You young devil, you *are* good!"

"I know," said Jade coolly. "Well, I ought to be, after all that training. But now I wish I'd studied the cutlass and pistol, too," she added, dissatisfied at being second-best in anything.

"You'll shape up." Anne took off the bright kerchief which most pirates wore around their heads as protection from the blazing sun. Morgan sauntered purring to the very center of the quarterdeck—just where they'd been practicing—and settled down for a nap. From the gangway came the twitter of Pierre's flute. The wind hummed softly in the rigging. For the first time in her life, Jade wasn't at war with her surroundings, and she hardly knew what to make of the laughter that kept bubbling up for no reason at all. It bubbled now.

Anne laughed too, and tossed her red mane. "I'll have Mark work with you on the cutlass," she promised. "His style will suit you. And we'll—"

"Sail off the port beam!"

There was an instant rush of bare feet for the shrouds. Morgan at once fell into hysterics and fled, swearing horribly, while the crew swarmed up the rigging. Jade, clinging like the rest, while the mast swung a great oval in the air, wondered how she could have been so scared aloft such a short time ago. It was glorious, like flying! She laughed at Tom, who had still not got over his air of shocked admiration, and peered at the horizon, where the two masts and square sails of a brig could just be seen.

"French lines and rigging," muttered Rory, squinting. He had been unusually sour of late, but now he was coming to life again.

"She's low in the water," called the knowledgeable Mark presently, and there was a cheer. This meant she was heavy-laden with possible loot, and also that she would be slow and sluggish in action. A pity she wasn't Spanish as well, said the pirates cheerfully. They'd rather fight Spaniards than anyone. However, they added, swinging purposefully down to the deck, this ship would do very well indeed.

As if she had heard, the French ship altered course and veered off nervously on the other tack, the sails narrowing as she turned.

"Give chase!" yelled Anne joyously, and took a short cut to the deck by sliding down the backstays. Jade, not to be outdone, followed at a rash speed that blistered both palms. "Prepare for action!" Anne was bawling unnecessarily. "Sam, go below and see if Jack's sober enough to come up for the fun. Toby, see if there's any turtle blood. We'll put on our best show for you newcomers: it usually scares and confuses the enemy so badly they forget to fight."

The *Queen Royal* at once turned into a comic romp. Men were either dressing up in wild and brilliant costumes or smearing their bare torsos with the livid crimson of turtle blood. Pierre dragged out a battered tailor's dummy, stained with previous use and set it up in the bow with a bucket of turtle blood ready beside it. The scarlet pirate flag was made ready to hoist at just the right moment.

Jade and Domino, Rory and Joshua stared, looked at one another wonderingly, shook their heads, chortled, and fell happily into the spirit of the thing. Jade felt a slight sense of relief, almost as if she had been dreading a real battle without even knowing it. Only Domino tended to grunt with renewed scorn for pink-skinned beings.

Piles of astonishing weapons were appearing. Every broad canvas waistband now bristled with pistols, cutlasses, and machêtes. Long wicked pikes and boarding axes flourished dangerously—particularly when Domino got hold of one. Chief armorer Peter Mazer clucked lovingly over a pile of peculiar looking flasks and jars, which, he explained to the fascinated Jade, were his inventions.

"Them flasks 'ave a fuse sticking out, you see, an' we lights that and flings it at the enemy and it goes off bang. Sometimes," he added sorrowfully, "it goes off bang too soon. Poor Will Potter lost 'is arm that way just afore Christmas." He cheered up. "The jars is stinkpots. Filled with sulphur, they is. Makes an 'orrible stench when we throws 'em. And I'm working on a new gun, wot—"

But the demonstration was cut short by Anne grabbing Jade's hand and tugging her aft to the cabins. Jade came, bouncing with excitement, and strongly inclined to giggle as she looked about her.

Here came Calico Jack, strutting up from below as if he really thought he commanded the whole operation. There was Joshua, in whom freedom had suddenly unleashed a brand new mettlesome personality, armed to the teeth. Rory stood deep in conversation with Mark, over the wheel, a garish red kerchief around his head. And an entire band of musical instruments had now materialized in the waist, and was drumming, strumming, tootling and trumpeting at least three different tunes at once—if not more, decided Jade with another giggle as Anne dragged her into the big cabin.

"We've got to get dressed," she explained. "Shall I wear my yellow shirt or none at all?" And she laughed at Jade's dropped jaw. "Pirates shouldn't shock so easily," she jeered, and put on the saffron shirt, leaving Jade not in the least certain she'd been joking.

In her cabin, Jade looked over her own shirts. It seemed that one dressed to scare the enemy rather than fight them; otherwise the oldest and least colorful costume would be best. As it was—she chose her new flame-colored shirt, hoping no one would get any of that turtle-blood on it, and put on a waistband as Anne had showed her. Two pistols went in it for effect, and perhaps a cutlass as well. Armed like an arsenal, she strutted out on deck.

The French ship was close enough now for Jade to read the name *Belle Marie* and see the scared-looking faces over the bulwarks. *Queen Royal*'s scarlet flag was up; and the dummy was a gory sight, Pierre prancing dramatically around it with a machête in one hand while he tried to play his flute with the other. *Belle Marie* came about in a panicky attempt to escape.

It was just what Mark had wanted. Over came the

helm, and presently *Queen Royal* was closing in from behind, undeterred by an occasional shot from the stern chasers.

"Showing more fight than most," said Sam, as *Belle Marie* tried to come around and bring her heavy starboard guns to bear. "Most ships just haul down their colors at this point in the game."

Jade swallowed, gripping the shrouds where she was now perched with fully half the crew. Those guns looked extremely menacing! But Mark, skilled tiller-artist that he was, swung around to head terrifyingly directly into the broadside.

"Less target!" bawled Sam, wincing slightly as two or three cannon balls actually tore through the rigging and killed one pirate on the spot. Jade stared unbelievingly as his comrades dumped the body callously overboard and turned at once to repair the damage to shrouds and sheets. The farce was suddenly a farce no more.

Now *Queen Royal* was back at *Belle Marie*'s stern again, and closing with her. The crew was swarming into the fo'c'sle and the bow rigging, and Jade could clearly see the French faces staring in horror at the gruesome dummy and the bloodthirsty-looking pirates. Now Dickson with his single eye took his place at the small bow-chaser gun and silenced *Belle Marie*'s stern guns with half a dozen shots, one of which took away half the taffrail and another the mizzen backstays.

And now, with nothing but musket-fire to stop him, nimble Toby Harris was crawling out on the bowsprit, a mallet and wedge hanging around his waist . . . had swung himself right onto the enemy aftercastle, scrambled down, and neatly driven the wedge between rudder and sternpost . . . and the *Belle Marie* was crippled.

Jade's heart was pounding. What a dangerous thing to do! She yearned to learn it herself! She almost forgot what was happening for an instant. Then the scene leaped into her eyes again: the gory dummy and the terrified eyes on the other ship, torches flying toward *Belle Marie*'s sails and stinkbombs bursting on her deck. Drums beat and trumpets blared and Pierre tootled his flute. Grapnels sailed across the short space between ships—gripped—held—and with a perfectly diabolic din, led by Anne, the pirates swarmed aboard. . . .

And Jade stayed where she was. Like the slap of a giant hand across her mind came revulsion. A young, scared, resolute French face vanished in the melée, to haunt Jade forever. A cry of pain cut her ears. This was what happened, then, when the victims had the courage to turn and fight!

Below, the battle surged across the quarterdeck and down to the waist. Anne, yelling and blazing like a fiend from hell was enough to scare anyone to death without a blow. Domino and Joshua, shoulder to shoulder, wreaked impartial havoc, as if avenging themselves on all white men in general. Tom was in the middle of it looking bewildered while Mark protected him with big-brotherly concern. Even Calico Jack fought with an aggressive skill that reminded Jade of the name and fame he still had. And all for what?

Those poor seamen weren't at all the ones Jade wanted to fight! This wasn't reform, or justice, or even vengeance. It was plain ordinary pillage and murder, quite as ugly and vicious as the other evils men committed against each other. Sickened, she clung to the shrouds in a fog of disillusion. She wanted no part of it!

And then, almost before battle had reached the waist, it was over. The French were throwing down their arms. There seemed, after all, only a few casualties. The pirates at once became a splendidly organized team, rounding up prisoners, disarming them, searching the ship for loot, even keeping discipline when gold was unearthed from the captain's cabin. When everything of value had been taken aboard the *Queen Royal*, the crew was good-naturedly invited to join the company of Free Brethren. There were, explained the pirates, no hard feelings.

Then the two who accepted were brought aboard, the grapnels were thrown off, and the hapless *Belle Marie* cut adrift. Rudder still locked, she heeled over slightly, main topsail flapping like thunder, to drift off in the sweep of trade winds until the remaining crew could get her under control again. And the *Queen Royal* jibbed and came about to a starboard tack, to sounds of rejoicing.

Jade came down from the shrouds at last, stiff and numb in body as well as mind, still trying to sort out her bewilderment.

Anne, passing, gave her a withering look. "Chicken-hearted?"

Having once proved her courage, Jade felt not the slightest need to defend it. She just turned her head to stare at Anne squarely and silently.

Anne laughed a little and conceded the point. "Oh, all right then: squeamish." But her voice still held a certain amount of scorn. Anne was anything but squeamish.

Jade considered the matter. It was true she had been

quite sickened by the bloodshed. But she didn't think that was the real point. She hadn't been squeamish on the *Pearl*, and she didn't think she'd have been squeamish if *Belle Marie* had been a slaver.

"I don't know," she said at last. "I have to think."

Anne, still wildly excited and inclined to be aggressive, lifted a condescending shoulder. "I was a good deal younger than you when I first killed," she bragged.

"Oh?" Jade looked at her without approval. Sometimes she didn't like Anne Bonney at all. "Who was it, your baby sister?" she asked, scathing.

Anne reddened. "A bond slave drew a knife on me!" she snapped.

Jade, wondering what Anne had done to goad the bond slave, merely curled her lip, deliberately infuriating. Anne looked ready to slap her. Very well, let her try! Jade was spoiling for a fight.

But Anne confined herself to words. "Very moral and virtuous, aren't you?"

"Well, if I were a plain robber and bully, I'd say so, and not call myself Robin Hood or St. Nicholas! You're as big a hypocrite as all the rest!"

"What an odious little jade you are, after all!" said Anne, angry and amused at once. "I begin to sympathize with the late captain of the *Pearl*. And you needn't expect a share of today's loot, you know, since you didn't help."

"Well, of course not!" said Jade blankly. It had been the last thought in her mind. They stared: a long, baffled, green-and-hazel stare. But Anne had got fighting out of her system for the time being. She shrugged and was about to move away when the grizzled head and scarred face of Barton loomed up, scowling.

"I told yer we shouldn't sign on little girls," he told Anne, aggrieved. "Scared, she were. I seen 'er. Scared ter fight!"

All Jade's frustration and bewilderment exploded into a fierce need for action. Action against this brute of a shipboard bully would do splendidly: she'd enjoy taking out her anger on him instead of the unoffending French crew. She smiled.

It was her straight, slit-of-bared-teeth smile, eager and menacing, and highly disconcerting to a man accustomed to intimidate.

"Am I?" she crooned softly. "Am I really scared to fight, Barton? Want to find out?"

Barton looked at her in sudden doubt. She wasn't reacting at all the way she should.

And Anne laughed. "Go on!" she urged him. "Challenge her to a duel, Barton! Enhance your reputation! And it will give her the choice of weapons, don't forget. Have you ever seen Jade with a rapier, Barton?"

Barton blinked, frowned, shook his head. He didn't like Anne's laughter any more than Jade's smile. It occurred to him that there was no use killing a green girl, not yet even blooded in battle. Besides, he didn't like the rapier. Fussy, twiddly things, not fit for men's fighting. He growled and turned to look for a better fight to pick.

"Say you're sorry!" Jade challenged him, and was rewarded by another grumble. She sighed, deprived of an outlet for her bad humor, and said a word that she had just recently learned. But there wasn't much satisfaction in it, because there was no one to be shocked.

Anne moved on, puzzled but tolerant, and Jade headed for her favorite spot on the fo'c'sle to brood. But it was already occupied by a glowering Rory, who would doubtless produce a few caustic remarks of his own about Jade's failure to join in the battle. Glaring at him, she took an unsociable position on the opposite side of the bow, back firmly turned, and stared down at the surging smoothness of the bow wave.

Unhappiness swelled over her. She thought she had found her place in the world—and she hadn't. There was no point to piracy—except loot, and that meant nothing whatever to Jade, so long as she had enough to eat. She had supposed, somehow, that it would be a kind of righteous revenge on the world, setting slaves free, and punishing horrid men like Chidley Bayard and Governor Lawes.

A black thatch and beaky nose loomed over her, and Rory glared down. "What's the matter?" he demanded.

Jade hunched her shoulders disagreeably, but he just turned her around to face him. It wasn't her nature to struggle uselessly; she met his angry eyes with her own.

"What's the matter?" he repeated. "Why didn't you fight?"

At least he knew without asking that she wasn't chickenhearted. Jade shrugged in a vast helplessness.

"Didn't feel like it," she muttered. "Wasn't angry at *them;* why should I try to kill them?" Then, as Rory still stared down at her, a sardonic look on his hawk's face, she gave a small, impatient, bare-footed stamp. "It's no *good* saying we're Robin Hood, because we aren't. Unless he was just an ordinary robber, too. And I don't see any use in it, just stealing things." She turned away from him again, blinking against the sun which was just exploding into sunset.

"What did you think piracy was, you daft little loon?"

Rory demanded harshly. Jade whirled back again to peer into his face with sudden suspicion. She searched it carefully.

"You feel the same way!" she discovered with a sense of profound relief. "What shall we do?"

But Rory's face was set tight. "Drink our own brew," he said tersely, and stalked away.

CHAPTER FOURTEEN

The Second Armada

"Oh, a pox on you!" cried Anne irritably. "Stop *nagging*, you young vixen! D'you think we're a flaming Crusade, or something? What do you want, anyway?" She threw herself across the width of her huge four-poster and glowered at Jade, while Jezebel squeaked and chattered from the top of the canopy and both parrots tried to out-shout her.

Half a dozen other pirates were lounging in the salon in the heat of the afternoon, and they looked up from various amusements, all interested in the running battle with this cheeky youngest member of the crew. Pierre lowered his flute and Mark a captured book and Toby paused in the act of dealing cards to Domino (who had grasped such games with astonishing brilliance and was becoming richer by the day) and Joshua. Only Sam went on stroking the purring Morgan. Rory, an unsociable soul, was doubtless aloft somewhere.

"What d'you want?" repeated Anne, sounding exasperated.

Jade frowned. "Well—*something* besides just robbery. We have a big strong ship; why can't we pick on people that deserve it instead of just ordinary harmless ones?"

Morgan, falling into the spirit of the thing, began sharpening his claws in the deep pile of the carpet. Mark tilted his fair head, quizzical.

"But my dear girl, according to you the entire world needs punishing, and that's just what we're doing."

Everyone laughed except the militant Domino, who nodded with vigor. Jade grinned sheepishly, scowled, scratched her nose (which still tended to sunburn a trifle), and sighed. She felt in danger of becoming greatly muddled. "Well, yes—but—but some are much worse than others." Morgan jumped on her lap and curled up, purring. "I mean, like that Mr. Bayard."

"And your uncle," suggested Domino, unforgiving. "Kill he."

Jade shifted uncomfortably on her stool, causing Morgan to dig in protesting claws. If it really came down to it, she wasn't at all sure she wanted Uncle Augustus to be actually *killed*, however arrogant and bullying he was, and however infuriatingly certain that he had some God-given right to order other people about, and however much he considered slaves and females and horses to be inferior creatures . . . But by now her blood was beginning to simmer again, and she was more inclined to agree with Domino after all. It was all extremely confusing. She sighed again.

"In any case," pursued Anne, sensing victory, "you don't really expect us to stop and cross-examine everyone on board the ship we're fighting before we cross swords with him, do you? Or even tell a Good Ship from a Bad Ship before you grapple and board?"

"You can tell a slaver." Jade hated giving in. "I know,

because Rory told me. They're low and fast, without much hold space. We could go for them."

Domino made a small fiery sound of agreement, and Joshua put a restraining hand on her arm, as she seemed ready to go search for one at once. Anne looked at her with understanding, and Toby entered the conversation. "We does when we sees 'em. Got yours, didn't we? Don't see 'em all the time."

"*Aussi*," added Pierre, coming out from behind his flute with a surprising flash of practicality, "we could not at all make a living at freeing slaves, *voyons*, unless we should then to turn around and sell them instead of setting them loose. And where would we to find a crew who will remain if there is no loot and no food? Hmm?"

Jade ground her teeth, infuriated. People were so—so *mercenary!* Being right was never enough reason for doing a thing; it had to be safe and practical and profitable as well!

"That's what's *wrong* with the world," she muttered, and dug her fingers into Morgan's side so hard that he fled, outraged, to Anne. Rory, entering at that moment with Tom and Mazer, slanted his eyebrows with cynical amusement that didn't reach his eyes. He had given up any real hope of changing human nature. Tom sat down beside Mark, who first smiled and then looked away with an expression of flinty aloofness that at once caused Jade to forget the world's iniquities.

It wasn't the first time she had noticed Mark behaving rather oddly toward Tom. Jade had thought at first they were rivals for the attentions of Anne, but that didn't make much sense. Nothing could have been less romantic than their behavior toward Anne—or Anne's toward them. Anne and Mark and Pierre in particular were like brothers and sisters, laughing and thinking up mischief, and protective of one another. But as for Mark and Tom, they behaved like two people who couldn't for the life of them decide whether to be friends or enemies.

Jade shrugged and began to coax the yellow-and-green parrot away from Joshua, who was stroking its head. People began to seem a great deal more complicated than they had. Hypocrite and victim, brave and weak, were inadequate categories after all.

The parrot pigeon-toed his way along the settee to Jade's black velvet knee and began to climb it. Anne's voice penetrated her consciousness. "—have to tell Vane next time we see him."

Jade looked up, startled. "Do you mean Charles Vane? But I'd have thought you'd be enemies."

Anne looked surprised. "Whatever gave you that idea?" In her rich ivory brocade gown, with a bit of dainty sewing on her lap, she looked so unlike a pirate queen that Jade was thrown doubly off her stride, and just sat blinking until Rory came to her rescue.

"Och, I can't think," he drawled, "unless it was the story about his being kicked out of his captaincy and set adrift in a smallboat."

"Oh, that!" Anne laughed. "You don't understand. There was nothing personal in it. We're all still good friends, those of us who are still alive."

Rory and Jade looked at each other, shrugging in astonishment. What extraordinary people pirates were! They, now, would take such a gesture very personally indeed.

"Anyway," added Mark, "we can't afford not to be friends, especially since Governor Rogers closed New

Providence to pirates the summer before last. There's few enough of us left."

"Where do you go now for provisions and water and turtles and to sell the loot?" asked Jade curiously. "Do we have another Pirate Republic somewhere?" The parrot was now sidling up her arm, digging in its claws to keep from falling off.

"No," said Anne. "But there are ports here and there who find pirates very profitable indeed, and open their doors to us. We're heading for Trinidado now, on the south coast of Cuba. But there's St. Catherine's Island, or Bermuda, or places in French Hispaniola–"

"But–" Jade sat up straight. The parrot, having reached her shoulder, was now chewing amiably on her short, sun-bleached hair with sharp grating noises right in her ear. "But–Cuba's Spanish, isn't it? And aren't they on bad terms with England? Unofficially, I mean?"

Mark chuckled. "So are we, my pet. And officially, too."

Jade giggled, and the parrot at once began nibbling her ear. "Yes, but I mean, we're English pirates, and we've got some Spanish loot from the ship you took before the *Pearl*. Well, aren't the Spanish at Trinidado going to notice that and resent it?"

"Poor child," said Anne kindly. "You still don't really accept human nature, do you? That's why you and Rory are such cynics, you know: you're frustrated idealists who go on letting yourselves be disillusioned. Why should the Cubans resent it when those nice Spanish doubloons are going straight into their pockets instead of back to Spain?"

"Oh," said Jade, and curled her lip.

Half a dozen pirate craft lay at anchor in the bay, and Trinidado prospered. The pirates were having a jolly reunion, overflowing the larger tavern, to the great wonder of Jade and Domino who sat curled up against each other in an alcove drinking lemonade and giggling at the idiocy of the male species.

"Like much little boys," commented Domino as several of them capered past singing a naughty song with sideways glances to see how the girls would take it.

"Much sillier," countered Jade, remembering Matthew with a pang. But she looked thoughtfully at the nearest table, where Anne and Jack and Vane and the other captains laughed and joked together. They had that other childish quality, it seemed, of forgetting grievances as if they had never been. It was a nice quality. Jade, watching them wistfully, wished she had it.

"More rum here, Juan," Vane shouted happily. "Rum for the girls there, too. This is a party, blister it!"

"Girls drink lemonade," Juan reminded him, disapproval for this shocking habit all over his long mustachioed face. "My lemons," he remembered, cheering up a bit. "I bring you good news to toast, *señor*. Soon now some day you visit New Providence again. But only to see," he pleaded. "You come back here to drink, *si?*"

Everyone seemed perfectly happy to toast anything at all. Only Anne turned an alert head. "Why?" she demanded.

"I have good tavern, good rum," Juan informed her with simple dignity.

Jade giggled and Domino snorted. Anne glanced at them with brief mirth. "I mean, what news?" she explained. "How can we go back? Governor Rogers forbids it."

"Pah! Cold-blooded English also very soon kicked out now," Juan beamed. "Our great Spanish Armada, she is sailing now presently, perhaps yesterday or *mañana*, from Havana, and New Providence will be Spanish as God wishes." Nodding happily, he waddled away, leaving a speculative silence behind him.

Jade broke it. "But the Spanish Armada was about a hundred and fifty years ago! And in the English Channel."

"A hundred and thirty," Anne corrected her absently. "This is another one. They've been building it in Havana for over a year. Rogers knows about it; Jack and I warned him, months ago when we were on good terms for a while. Even then, there were four or five warships and more than a dozen sloops and brigantines and some two thousand men."

"Everyone knows Rogers has been begging London for help," put in Vane, fingering his brown beard. "They haven't sent so much as a longboat. He hasn't got a chance."

"The Bahamas will soon be Spanish," Jack sighed, looking as if he regretted it but wasn't at all sure why.

Another silence. Then Rory's harsh young voice and Rory's hatchet-carved young face blazed between Tom and Mark. "Well? Are we going to let them get away with it?"

Jade lifted her head sharply, and their eyes met. This was the sort of thing they wanted to do!

Vane was on his feet, staring at Rory. "No, by heaven!

I'm blistered if I want to see that! I may be an outlaw, but blast it, I'm an English outlaw! And I hate Spain far worse than I do Rogers!"

"Hear hear!" shouted the pirates.

Anne tossed her red head, laughed recklessly. "Right! If we all feel the same way, let's go stop them!"

Jade could restrain herself no longer. "Right this minute!" she yelped, leaping to her feet excitedly. She waved her mug of lemonade as if it were a torch. "Hurry up!"

Then Domino was beside her, loosing an African variety of war whoop that would have scared any listening Indians into day before yesterday. It caused Juan to go diving under the nearest table, and brought the entire party of pirates to its feet, cheering. And within the hour, the pirate Counter-Armada had set sail for New Providence . . . one schooner, one ship, and four swift little sloops.

Both Spanish and British histories show great reticence in describing that battle for the Bahamas in February, 1720.

"Our watch prevented the invasion," say the New Providence Council minutes with true English understatement—or just possibly a touch of mendacious embarrassment.

"Not worth taking," says the report sent from Havana to Madrid laconically and with an almost visible shrug. "Changed our minds."

No official reports mention the swarm of pirate ships that descended upon New Providence Island after the invasion had actually started. Only a number of unofficial eyewitnesses tell of the four little sloops that appeared from nowhere to cut neatly between ships and the Spanish troops already on the beach, and catch them both at once in a deadly double broadside; and of the *Queen Royal* and Vane's schooner who swooped around the point while the Spanish were staggering from this most un-Christian behavior—and did the same thing between the huge ships of war, causing the Spanish flagship to explode and sink on the spot.

At this, the Spanish lost heart at once, and Governor Rogers launched his tiny fleet of gadflies to join the pirate hornets. Together, buzzing, they harassed the large clumsy Spanish ships until their commanders decided that this was a dreadful place, and they didn't want it anyhow.

Then Rogers' craft—rather battered—put back to shore, while the pirates gleefully harried the would-be invaders halfway back to Havana, chuckling with the fun of doing such a very mortifying favor for the man who had chucked them out of the very island they had just saved for him.

"Now this," said Jade with satisfaction, "is what I meant!"

It was, said Anne, a perfectly typical descent from high drama to farce, that their next action should be the capture of a cargo of horses. It ended, of course, with bareback races around the heaving waist of the *Queen Royal*, half a dozen riders fished out of the sea, and only Anne and Joshua mounted at the end of it.

CHAPTER FIFTEEN

Mark

This time there was only one other pirate ship anchored at Trinidado, which, in the oppressive heat of spring, looked like a parched rubbish heap on the edge of the jungle. The *Queen Royal* tugged gently at her anchor on the turning tide, the town had its afternoon *siesta,* and the crew dozed or talked, or worked on scrimshaw, or played panpipes or guitar or flute or fife, in the shadow of stripped masts or in the salon. No point going ashore until the heat of the day was over.

Jade, standing at the wide salon windows running across the stern of the ship, contemplated Trinidado with an expression that caused Mark to grin mischievously.

"You think this is bad, you should have seen New Providence when it was our stronghold! Harbor cluttered with all sorts of pirate craft and the hulks of prizes, shore covered with huts and tents, and the most brawling, bawdy, riotous swarm of people you ever saw. Vultures of all sorts, come to prey on the pirates."

"Weren't they all pirates there?" demanded Jade, not pleased with the picture.

Mark shook his fair head. "Harpies! Parasites! They outnumbered us about five to one, the sneak-thieves, hawkers, escaped convicts, smugglers, fishwives, harlots, drunks— Sat in their garbage pit of a town waiting for us to go out and get the loot and bring it back—and then they tricked and plucked it out of us. Like jackals around a pride of lions. It's a good thing the punishment for piracy is hanging!"

Jade contemplated this last remark in silence for a minute, trying to tie it in with the rest of the speech. Failing, she peered sideways at Mark's handsome face, doubtful and questioning. "What's that got to do with it?"

Mark twinkled at her. "Simple. If it were a lesser penalty, the whole swarm of jackals would come out, too. The seas would be as overcrowded with rogues as the land, and then what would an honest pirate do for a living?"

Anne raised her head from a book and laughed. "There's sense in that, Mark. If you don't mind hanging, that is."

Mark shrugged. "Everybody dies. And hanging's less unpleasant, I dare say, than most ways. Illness, for instance. . . ."

Several heads nodded casually. No one worried about such things. Time enough when the day came.

"Like Black Death," suggested little Sam meaningfully. "Who'd be an honest man in Marseilles these days?" For Juan had told them that this dread plague was raging there. Brought about, he had added firmly, by the long pointed shoes which had recently come into fashion, and which, said many of the bishops, had proved so offensive to God that He had instantly sent the plague to indicate His disapproval.

"Whatever caused it," said Dickson firmly, "I'm for hanging or drowning or getting skewered in a good fight."

It was at this philosophical moment that Rory stuck his black head inside the door. "Jade?"

Jade turned at once. She preferred Rory's company to anyone's, growls and all. Besides, he must have something interesting to say, or he wouldn't have come for her.

"Barton's finally picked his fight," Rory added grimly just as Jade reached the door. "With that rattlepate Tom."

"No!" Mark turned sharply. "Not Tom Deane! He can't fight a duel with Barton; he's no more experienced than—than Jezebel! And Barton's a killer!" His face looked sharply pale in the half-light of the big cabin, and Anne threw him a hard warning glance that caused him to bite his lip and turn back to the window abruptly. The door closed, with Jade and Rory on the outside exchanging a long and puzzled stare.

"I *don't* understand Mark," complained Jade. "Why does he either snub Tom, or act like—like his big brother or something!"

"Aye, and why did Anne stab him with that dour look?" wondered Rory.

They both stood for a moment in the Caribbean sun that beat down on deck like golden hammers. Jade's sun-bleached hair glowed, Rory's blue eyes slitted against it, and they both thought of Tom.

"Race you to the masthead," said Rory, and they shot in unison across the deck and up the shrouds. Rory won by a small margin, and they both heaved themselves to the small platform where mast and top-mast joined. There was just room for the two of them to sit in the skimpy shade of the bare mast and stare downward, through a network of ropes, across the whole length of the *Queen Royal.*

Just forward of the mainmast Barton stood amid a group of the rougher pirates, bragging about what he had done to victims of his previous duels, all in a voice clearly intended to be overheard by Tom on the fo'c'sle. Tom, calm but undeniably pale, was talking to Joshua and Dickson and Mazer, who looked both grave and grim despite their loud cheerful words. Nobody was fooling anybody.

"He'll kill him," said Rory, anger in his voice.

Jade glowered, jutting her chin out like the prow of a Spanish warship. "It's ridiculous! It shouldn't be allowed. We can't just sit here and let it happen!"

"What d'you think we could do about it?" he demanded harshly.

"Prevent it, of course!"

"How?" jeered Rory. "You can defy law, but not custom. The men wouldn't let anything stop a challenge accepted."

"Well, it's a vicious, stupid custom!" Jade snapped, knowing he was right, and all the angrier for it.

Rory turned on her, so that his ringed eyes were close to hers and his sharp chin nearly butted her tipped nose. "You think you're right and everyone else is wrong, hmm?"

"Yes," said Jade, unintimidated. "And so do you."

He laughed suddenly, a short mirthless bark. "Aye, I do. And so we set our judgment against the world—and—"

"And so the world will squash us for it," Jade finished, baring her teeth. "I know; Monsieur Maupin said the same thing. I don't care! We *are* right, and the world is wrong, and we've got to save Tom."

Rory laughed again, genuinely this time. "You're just like Gran! Water-witch! Kelpie! Don't you wish you could put the Evil Eye on Barton?"

Whatever the Evil Eye might be, it sounded satisfyingly dire.

Jade nodded with enthusiasm. "Or ju-ju."

Rory looked intrigued. "What's that?"

"African black magic. They call it voodoo here in the West Indies. Domino told me about it. You can use it to make people get sick and die, and I'd like to use one that would make Barton get killed instead of Tom." She stared with bitter hatred at the swaggering bulk of the bully below, and then poked Rory excitedly. "Look! I think Domino *is* putting it on him!" For the magnificent figure of the African girl suddenly swung into the mainsail shrouds almost above Barton, and stood easily poised with one foot and one hand on the ratlines, glaring down at him with concentrated venom and making strange movements with her free hand.

Barton seemed to find it unnerving. He glanced up, scowled bellicosely, strutted to the port rail with an indifference that was distinctly overdone. Domino, encouraged, drew even more menacing figures with her hand, and Rory—brought up with Highland belief in such charms—watched with deep interest.

But Jade had no such background, and she was a girl of action. With a sudden annoyed exclamation she swung herself off the platform and slid down the backstays. Mark, looking distraught, was just coming out of the big cabin, and Jade confronted him with fists planted on her sailcloth-clad hips. "Look here," she said directly. "Aren't we going to do something?"

"Yes—" said Mark, determined but baffled by the unwritten laws of the brotherhood of pirates. "We can't prevent the duel, though."

Jade snorted. "I'll bet I could! . . . Oh, all right, I know. But we could do something . . . like getting Barton to challenge me, and I could choose rapiers and fight him before Tom can."

Mark's face had lit with interest even while he shook his blond head decidedly. "Not you. For one thing, he'd never challenge you and give you choice of weapons now he's seen you with the rapier. And you haven't enough experience with cutlass or pistol."

"And he'd be making a fool of himself to challenge a chit of sixteen, anyway," said Rory's gravel voice from behind Jade.

"Nearly seventeen!" she said indignantly.

"Never mind." Mark's blue eyes were gleaming. "It's still an idea. *I* can challenge him, and take him on with the cutlass, too." He looked pleased.

Rory curled a lip disagreeably, determined to be obstructive. "And you think Tom will just sit back and let you?"

But Mark was sailing before the wind now. "We won't ask him, of course. You'll have to help. Get him to go ashore with you early, as soon as possible. Teach him a new stroke, practice with him, give him a bit of rum when the tavern opens. Not the big one where everyone goes; the little one over there on the bluff with the sign of the sick-looking cock over the door. In the meantime, I'll challenge Barton. I'll fight him right here on board if I can—

but I doubt he'll agree. He likes his duels on shore, with an admiring audience around, after plenty of rum. They'll all go to the big tavern, I dare say, so I'll meet you and Tom in the little one, and we'll contrive some way to keep Tom out of the way until I finish with Barton. All right?"

Jade and Rory looked at each other, at the confident and intrepid slight figure of Mark, and then at the hapless Tom on the fo'c'sle, still trying to appear calm and light-hearted, but making bad weather of it. "All right," growled Rory with a disgruntled air that didn't in the least hide his approval of Mark. And he and Jade made their way forward.

"Going to prick Barton's bubble, are you, Tom?" called Rory cheerfully, and Jade tried to look like someone who hadn't the least doubt of it.

But Tom's smile was distinctly wan. "He's more likely to prick mine, I'm afraid," he said in a voice that wobbled as if his bravado was growing very thin. It was rather a poor show, really. Jade, who had put on a better one, herself, felt a swift flash of scorn. Then, as swiftly, came a memory of choking black fear, and her heart lurched in sympathy for poor Tom.

"Let's go ashore now," she said briskly. "Come on, Tom. We can practice a bit out of sight of the others. Warm you up, you know. Besides, I know a nice cutlass stroke Mark was showing me the other day, and I'll teach you. Just in case you find it useful."

Tom agreed quickly, with visible relief.

"Well, go change your clothes, water-witch," Rory suggested. "You look like a bilge-rat in those baggy breeches, and rather a scruffy one, at that."

Jade glanced down with a surprised grin at the loose sailcloth trousers reaching halfway between knee and ankle, and the equally loose cotton shirt that Pierre deplored, and the broad canvas waistband. Not really town wear, perhaps. She chuckled and hurried aft.

In the small aftercabin which she shared with Domino, she took out her black velvet breeches and coral silk blouse with long full sleeves. Gradually, as she started to change, her brow corrugated. All very well to prevent Tom being slaughtered like an affable and helpless lamb —but what about Mark? With his shining audacity, it was easy to forget that he was, after all, a slight man, smaller even than Anne or Domino. Barton must have a full six-inch advantage of reach on him. It took—as Monsieur Maupin had been at great pains to impress on Jade—enormous speed and skill to overcome such a disadvantage. And it occurred to Jade that she liked Mark very much indeed: even better than Tom, and it seemed a little hard that Mark should risk his life for a young man whom he didn't even seem sure he liked. What an extraordinary thing, come to think of it! Surely that kind of reckless chivalry was unusual, to say the least, outside romantic tales, and Shakespeare, and ballads, and—

Jade's train of thought suddenly fell flat over on its nose, and she paused with one arm halfway into the coral sleeve to backtrack and see what had tripped it up. Some important and relevant word? Romance . . . ballads . . . Shakespeare . . . Shakespeare! *AS YOU LIKE IT!* Rosalind! Jade's eyes widened, narrowed, widened again. She took a deep breath, grinned crookedly, and finished putting on her blouse. Carefully she belted on her rapier, tucked a pistol into her belt as well (this being both high fashion and standard uniform in pirate circles), and went into Anne's big cabin.

Anne and Mark were alone, talking quietly together at the far end of the room. Jade closed her door quietly, leaned against it, and proceeded to study Mark with quite new eyes. It was a most enlightening study. It explained a great deal. It explained, for instance, why a man surely old enough to have a beard, didn't. It explained that odd warning look of Anne's today, and the easy friendship between them, and Mark's contradictory behavior toward the bewildered Tom. The only thing it didn't explain was everyone's incredible blindness, including her own. Jade drew a very slow, very deep breath, and smiled. Tight bandages around the chest, of course, to flatten any awkward curves. All the same, it was quite staggeringly improbable!

Her curious stillness caught Anne's attention, and she looked at Jade narrowly. "Anything wrong?" she asked, snappish. Had she been telling Mark that Tom wasn't worth it? Or was she annoyed (as Rory was) at not having thought of a counter-challenge first, herself? It was hard to tell.

They eyed each other, mutually inscrutable. Jade shook her tousled honey-colored head and smiled her small, slanted, secret smile. This wasn't the time for her questions and comments.

"See you ashore," was all she said.

CHAPTER SIXTEEN

The Duel

Mark found them sunk in the gloom of the tiny tavern trying to radiate cheerful confidence and not doing it at all well. Jade was in an anguish of apprehension for Mark, and Tom for himself, and the others were in varying degrees of dark brown depression. Mark brought a shimmer of light, and a friendly hand clapped on Tom's shoulder.

"Hello. They're all at the other place. Been limbering up, Tom? Did you show him that undercut, Jade? Let's make sure you've got it. Finish up, Tom, and we'll go down to the cellar here. There's enough room, and Diego won't mind. Will you, Diego?"

Diego, a brown slender man with black curls, didn't flick an eyelid, but his hand curved over the coin Mark sent sliding toward him. It was clear that he didn't mind. For two more like that, Mark could have owned the place.

The cellar stretched into barrel-piled dimness.

"Need a light," said Mark, picking up a barrel stave. "Should be flint and steel and a lamp just over there by you, Tom. See them?"

"No," said Tom, groping. "Uh!" he added, as Mark hit

him firmly over the head with the barrel stave. "Nnng," he finished, collapsing neatly into Rory's waiting arms.

"What you do?" demanded Domino, preparing to fight. Joshua restrained her, and Mark's wide firm mouth flickered briefly into a smile.

"Take care of him!" he urged them. "If he comes round too soon, don't let him out until you're sure Barton and I have finished."

Jade looked at Domino and Rory, bent over the sleeping figure, and decided that they could do very well without her.

"I'm going after Mark," she announced, and did so, Joshua behind her.

On a spot where the ground rose from the beach near the large tavern, they looked down at the lone figure of Mark standing outside the door while a boy ran in with a message. And then the doors opened again, opened wide, and a stream of pirates poured out with the fuddled but happy expectancy of boys coming to see a dog-fight. Barton, massively at their head, paused at the sight of Mark, planted his treetrunk legs apart, wiped the rum from his mouth with the back of a hairy hand, and let out a bellow.

"Ready, are you? Let's see if you are!" And with the simplicity of the natural killer, he drew his pistol and fired at Mark.

Jade gasped and clutched at Joshua—just as a second shot rang out, not two seconds after the first. Mark, it seemed, was not unprepared for Barton's peculiar notions of how to start a cutlass duel. Acrid smoke swirled and blew away. Both figures stood unharmed, energetically drawing cutlasses.

The pirates cheered on general principles and formed a solid circle around them, betting wildly. A few booed Barton, but with some caution, as the odds were running heavily in his favor. Anne appeared from somewhere, red hair blazing and face set and angry, forcing her way to the front of the ring. Jade and Joshua stayed where they were. Here they could see everything; down there little would be visible but the backs of dirty necks. And Jade found, at the cost of chewed knuckles, that the role of expert as audience is sheer torture. To be helpless to do anything—and yet to see everything: every feint, every opening, every hair-breath parry or missed riposte . . . She moaned.

The fight went on and on. Mark, defending, didn't try to close against that long arm, but contented himself with riposting against the arm itself, over and over. The sunset faded with the disconcerting swiftness of the tropics, and the sea became a burning shield of silver in the brief colorless twilight. Mark was bleeding from half a dozen cuts in his shoulders and one perilously near the artery of his throat, and the sky darkened further, and the sea faded from silver to pewter.

But Barton was losing control of his right arm at last. His cutlass slowed and drooped as the muscles weakened, and his face curled in anger that had not yet turned to fear. And at last Mark began to attack effectively with hoarded strength, forcing Barton to defend himself at last. The slight figure took new authority, using his sword as a skilled tool instead of a battle-axe, adapting it brilliantly to a style of speed and subtlety that had never been intended for it, and that completely bewildered the larger man.

And then, at last, just when Barton was beginning to adapt himself to this unfair style, Mark changed with shattering speed to something different still. A whistling downward sweep, a circle unpausing, a swift horizontal arc—and Barton fell where he stood, like a tree.

A moment's awed silence. "E's dead," announced Toby without regret, and Mark quietly crumpled upon the sand.

Anne reached him as he fell, and Jade was already halfway down the rise, crowding in as Anne tongue-lashed the clustering pirates back. "Give room!" she barked dangerously. "Stand back, you scurvy dogfish! Throw me your kerchiefs or anything else I can use for bandages, you calkheads, he's bleeding badly! Stand *back*, I said— Oh, it's you, Jade. All right, you can help."

And Jade—no nurse at all—became a veritable miracle of efficiency as Anne's aide, helping to staunch long gaping cuts. She didn't bother to look up when the fringe of her attention glimpsed Tom, staggering from the lump on his head, escorted by the impenitent Rory and Domino.

"Somebody hit me on the head!" he bleated. "They said— What's happening, anyway? They kept me in that accursed grog-cellar! What's going on, I said? Where'd Mark go? I want to talk to him!" And then as his muzzy vision began to focus on the scene before him, he stood quite still and stopped bleating. "What's happened?" he repeated sharply, this time directly at Anne.

And Anne looked up briefly, her expression just visible now in the dusk. Her eyes glittered almost cat-like. "Your duel's been fought for you," she told Tom, and the bright gaze swept the crew, mocking. "By *Mary* Read," she added softly.

And in the dead silence her eyes met Jade's unastonished ones, and the two girls bent once more over the third.

An air of stunned disbelief hung over the *Queen Royal* as she tugged quietly at her anchor. In the waist men shook their heads, blinking, and counted up again how long they'd known Mark—er—Mary. She'd been a pirate at least three or four years. . . . "Signed on wiv Sam Bellamy, 'er did, in '16 or '17". . . . Ridiculous for no one to have suspected!

"Well, I *thought* it was funny he didn't have no beard!"

This was greeted with hoots of derision and half a dozen more claims from men who had always thought there was something odd about Mark, and still more jeers.

In the salon, Anne's huge four-poster had been turned once more into a hospital bed. Mary, bandaged in her own blood ("Best way to prevent mortification," said Anne wisely, and Domino agreed), lay looking suddenly frail and white but a trifle smug for all that. Tom hovered beside the bed, shining with devotion and bewilderment.

"What a woman!" he kept murmuring. "I *knew* there was something wrong! . . . Well, I mean it stands to reason! I wouldn't have started feeling this way about a *man*. . . . Thought I was losing my mind!"

Mary gave him a feeble but decided smirk. And Tom, quite carried away, promptly announced their intention of being married the minute they could find—or capture—a minister to do it.

Out on the fo'c'sle, Jade and Rory stood watching the quarter moon over the horizon, sending a long glittering trail of silver toward the ship. They said nothing at all.

CHAPTER SEVENTEEN

Prison Ship

There was no church for pirates, nor any minister conveniently aboard any of the *Queen Royal*'s prizes. So Mary and Tom were married in a solemn shipboard wedding: an outlaw wedding: sacred and binding—and altogether illegal as far as church or state were concerned. This worried Tom, who was at heart a conventional young man. Jade blazed at him furiously.

"What are you fussing about, Tom? Do you think God only lives in churches? Or that He's too stupid to understand why you haven't got a vicar? Or that He cares more about parish records and things than He does for your heartfelt vows? Don't be such a dolt!"

Tom looked sheepish. "To tell the truth, I wasn't so worried about God as I was about—well—society. I'd hate people to call my Mary a wicked woman or anything."

Anne laughed. "They do and they will. Along with me, and Domino, and even our righteous-minded pacifist Jade."

Anne's eyes sparked mockery at Jade, who simply

shrugged, uncaring. She still sat and sulked aloft when they took a merchant ship, and she wasn't to be taunted out of her convictions.

"Pooh, who cares what anybody says?" She tossed her head, as she had done, months ago, at Monsieur Maupin. "The thing is, they just can't *stand* females who decline to be inferior, and they can't think of anything bad enough to call us. I've heard them."

"Aye," said Rory, her ally in this. "But just you wait! Some day they'll have to back down and change the laws to give equal rights and respect to women. You'll be able to own property, and go to court if need be, and be defended by women lawyers and judged by women judges—"

"And there'll be woman ship's captains," Jade burst in, carried away by the splendid vision, "and crew, too! And doctors and ambassadors and vicars and bishops and governors and generals and—"

"*Black* women generals and bishops and doctors," Domino put in truculently.

Tom and Pierre and even Anne looked slightly shocked, being unable to imagine any such drastic changes in the world of reality. Surely this was going a bit *too* far? But Rory was nodding matter-of-factly. Why not? Ability was ability, wasn't it?

"The hard thing is to get the education and training to prove your ability," he frowned, as if it were all to start tomorrow. "And to do that, we have to change the laws so you *can* get them . . . I tell you what, if women and Blacks and Indians had the sense they were born with, they'd all be working together to free each other." He glowered, incensed at the stupidity of people who let themselves be trampled.

Mary, radiant bride of two days, just laughed at them. "Why all this fuss? We're outside society, free of it. We have equality here on the *Queen Royal,* and Anne's captain, isn't she?"

"Except in name," Joshua pointed out unanswerably. "That's the whole point, isn't it?"

Anne shrugged. "What does that matter? So long as I have the power, who cares about labels?"

But the quartet of reformers stared at her unbending. It *did* matter, and they cared a great deal.

It was a leisurely occupation, piracy. Days and even weeks could drift by, smooth as the swells that slipped beneath the *Queen Royal*'s hull and out again in the perpetual summer of the Caribbean, without ever a sail breaking the circle of the horizon. Jade thought she had never been alive before. Within the loose fellowship of the pirates, she and Domino, Rory and Joshua became a foursome, caring about the same things, more and more in harmony, until a look exchanged could be a whole conversation.

They took to seamanship avidly, for even Domino had soon got the best of her seasickness. Together they went aloft, learned to reef a sail, began learning to handle the helm and to read the quadrant. Rory, who was now intensively studying navigation, proceeded to organize a class of three—which probably taught him more than it did them, observed Joshua tolerantly from his comfortable place as average pupil. Domino was the shining light, and Jade, embarrassingly, the dunce.

To make up for it, she wheedled Toby into teaching her how to cripple a rudder, and worked ferociously at the cutlass to make speed and skill more than make up for size and strength—as Mary had done.

Only sometimes the four of them acknowledged a slight uneasy sense of having cheated. That wall of injustice was still there, back in the world from which they had escaped—and what were they doing about it? What, for that matter, *could* they do about it? There being no apparent answer to this, they did nothing. But whenever they took a ship that fought back, Jade became as squally as July, and either sulked in the rigging or went and picked a fight with Rory.

"We signed on as crew, didn't we?" Rory pointed out implacably. "We knew what it involved. If we can't keep our bargain, we should sign off and leave."

"You hate it too," she retorted. "Fighting ordinary seamen, I mean."

Rory grinned at himself, sourly. "Aye. But not as much as I hated serving on a nice legal slaver. You can't have everything. When I find something better than this, I'll take it, and in the meantime I play fair with the pirates."

Jade, silenced but unconverted, stomped off, to find Domino and challenge her to a race to the topmast and back. It was an unfair challenge, because Jade was smaller and nimbler, and because Domino could not feel really comfortable with the distracting swooping of the masts. "Now we go shoot pistols," she suggested vengefully after Jade had won by a length. "After I beat you down," she added, launching herself into the topsail shrouds.

They landed on the deck in a laughing tie, and would

have followed this by a race to the fo'c'sle, but the way was blocked by one Joseph Rafferty, a short stocky fellow with a long Irish upper lip and the pugnacious eye of a born trouble-maker. He had half a dozen men behind him —the ones who were cronies of Calico Jack and *liked* trouble—and they all had belligerent gleams in their eyes.

"Look, you, Jade," said Rafferty. "We're needing no part-time pirates. You fight, or you get off."

Jade glared back at him, always delighted to pick up anyone's gauntlet. This was much more promising than letting Domino show her up in marksmanship yet again. "Who says so?" she challenged. "Who made you captain?"

"I say so! And crew can kick you off any time, or Anne Bonney, either."

This was true enough. But Jade didn't believe Rafferty could get even a quarter of the men to vote against her. She was well enough liked, she did her share of the work, and if she didn't fight on some occasions, neither did she take a share of the loot those times. A reasonable and conciliatory person would have pointed these facts out, coolly and logically. Jade, being neither, did not. Instead, she looked him levelly in the eye, reminding him of his own galling shortness.

"I fight when—and whom—I choose," she said, chin jutting and teeth bared and a positively hopeful look on her face.

The other men laughed approvingly. They liked spirit in a wench, so they did. And while Rafferty contemplated this sudden loss of support, Domino—magnificent in her deep violet breeches and fuchsia shirt—took the offensive right away from Jade. Towering above them both, she looked down, tapped Rafferty's collarbone lightly with a long black finger, and purred at him in English that by now was almost as fluent as she chose it to be.

"You saw me put ju-ju on Barton, yes? And what happen to Barton, hmm? Anyone who annoy my friends, I put ju-ju on him, too." And she smiled. It was a smile of great beauty: one that would have put any sculptor into ecstasies over line and plane and curve, but it entirely failed to enrapture Rafferty. He muttered himself away, and no more was heard about Jade not fighting.

But Jade turned a reproachful stare upon Domino, who *knew* she liked to fight her own battles . . .

Domino knew, all right. She transferred the smile to Jade. "Lock me in cubbyhole, hmm?" she remembered. "Leave me out of venture, like baby, hmm? Now I start to get even."

"Beast!" said Jade, and laughed helplessly.

And as it happened, the next ship they took was a Dutch slaver, and the ferocity of Jade's fighting this time was awesome. The Quartet—a fighting team—launched itself in a wedge across the deck, annihilating all opposition, driven by devils of scarlet rage. They could probably have taken the slaver alone. Even Anne almost forgot to fight, watching them.

When it was over, it was Domino who talked to the poor half-dead Africans emerging from 'tween-decks. Knowing half a dozen African languages, she found one that most of them spoke, and explained that they were to be set free, not back in Africa, but on the beautiful island of Hispaniola just visible on the starboard beam.

The other pirates stared, amiable but baffled, at the passionate gentleness of their foursome toward the slaves. Odd thing, to care like that about a bunch of Blacks who didn't even speak English. Still, they were a tolerant lot, and didn't begrudge a certain amount of eccentricity. The only one to jeer was the smarting Rafferty, and Dickson stuck a huge elbow in his stomach, which at once discouraged any more.

"Worthless haul, that," grumbled Jack when the slaves had been set ashore in a lovely cove, and the *Queen Royal* spread her wings again and sailed away. And he looked rather sourly at Jade, who laughed aloud. Worthless! It was worth her whole life! Nearly a hundred human beings who—God willing—would never be slaves now, after all!

"*Eh bien,*" Pierre shrugged philosophically. "Who knows, perhaps tomorrow we find for ourselves *un veritable* Spanish treasure galleon!" And everyone laughed. Such things were rare indeed. Even Jack and Anne had captured only two in their entire careers.

Nine days later they really did overtake a Spanish treasure ship. Pierre at once announced, awed, that he clearly had prophetic powers, in addition to his many other talents. After which he put his flute away and armed himself to the teeth, with no foolery, for the Spaniards were well armed and preparing to fight.

Jade, stubbornly refusing to bend her principles even for Spanish treasure, went aloft, where she watched with disapproval and wild excitement warring within her. One anxious eye on the other three-fourths of the Quartet (she hated letting them go into battle without her!), she also managed to see Calico Jack Rackam give an exhibition of sheer cowardice that she could hardly believe.

It was a corpse that unmanned him: a headless Spanish corpse, still running in reflex action, straight for Jack, before it fell to the deck. And a horrid enough sight it was, too—but hardly worth what Jack made of it. His mouth opened in a yell of sheer funk, he threw his pistol to the deck, turned, and began to stumble blindly back to the safety of the *Queen Royal.*

Anne caught up with him as he was climbing the bulwarks. Her own pistol was in her hand, her eyes afire, her face relentless.

"Take your choice, Jack!" she snarled, and with the pistol pressed firmly against his head, very little explanation was needed. "Fight—or not."

Jack, who had a well-developed sense of self-preservation, at once perceived that even being chased by headless Spaniards had something to be said for it. He chose, prudently and at once, and turned back into the battle that was by now all but over, anyway. After which, seeing the contempt on every face and the undoubted writing on the wall, he banished himself once more to his den in the hold, not even waiting to see the treasure.

It was finally all aboard, piled in Anne's salon in astonishing profusion. Bars of gold and silver were there, and bags of ducats and doubloons, sovereigns and pieces of eight, and jewels that caused even Jade a pang of covetousness. She sat on the narrow window ledge while it was shared out, watching with detached interest.

"Do you really not want any?" demanded Tom with astonishment, and she shrugged.

"What for? I don't need to buy anything."

Nothing at all was said—out loud—about Jack's cowardice until they put ashore on the lovely small island of St. Catherine for fresh supplies of water and live turtles and other supplies—and also to spend some of their loot. There, in front of the tavern, before anyone went in, the crew gathered and Rafferty spoke.

"I move we vote to depose Calico Jack. No coward ought to command a pirate ship, or any other."

No one was taken by surprise. It had been in the air. But Jade and Rory exchanged worried glances. All very well about Jack—but what of Anne? Rory stepped forward.

"He doesn't command it, in fact," he pointed out. "And we're getting along very well as we are."

"Well, if he don't command, he oughtn't to be captain."

"Well, 'tis Mistress Bonney who captains us, and what's wrong with that, then?"

A vivid argument burst out, and then Anne made a moving speech about the perils of rocking the boat. Rafferty scowled.

"Oh, and you would be saying that," he sneered. "You're wanting to go on running the ship yourself, and living in that fine cabin of yours, don't you? Well, I say down with cowards and females, and let's get rid of the lot, and here's my vote for it."

"And here's mine against it," said Anne briskly, and pulling a pistol from her waistband, she calmly shot him. "Any more votes?"

Jade gaped with the rest, stunned and sickened. Anne had violated written and unwritten law—had killed a man for expressing his opinion. There was an ominous muttering from the others. Where she stood, alone before them all, she could herself be shot down at any instant, easily, by any one of them. And the pirates were in the mood.

Anne knew it, flung their anger back at them with laughter, challenging them to do it. Her hair blazed and blew in the wind, and the fired pistol hung carelessly from her hand.

"I've used my vote," she taunted them, thrusting it back into her waistband and standing as defenseless as Rafferty had been a moment earlier. "Any more?"

There were no more. They were defeated by her defenselessness, outbluffed by her boldness; they loved and hated her for it. Moreover they were practical men, and there was no other among them with Anne's imagination and cleverness and audacity in battle. The subject was quietly dropped, and they all trooped into the tavern.

But Jade, deeply shocked, avoided Anne Bonney for days.

And Anne, nothing if not observant, finally taunted her with it.

"Did I offend your fastidious notions of fair play?" she jibed, and narrowed her light hazel eyes at Jade.

Jade narrowed her green ones back again. "Yes," she said, uncompromising.

"Sail off the starboard bow!"

The Quartet abandoned cutlass practice and raced for the shrouds along with a score of others. There it was, hull down on the horizon. "Some sort of British official flag," reported the far-sighted Rory, squinting.

"Take lookout," Anne told him. "We'll go have a closer look, but sing down if it begins to look like a man-of-war, and we'll just put about and fall over the lee horizon.

Especially," she added wryly, "if it should turn out to be the *Diamond*, *Winchelsea*, or *Ludlow Castle*."

Everyone grinned appreciatively. Last month they had captured a shipload of wretched lunatics on their way to slavery on plantations, and had considered it only right to set them ashore, kindly, on the Jamaican coast. Now the infuriated Governor Lawes had no less than three warships out hunting the *Queen Royal*.

"We fight him anyway," Domino urged, dissatisfied with the notion of running, but no one paid any attention. There was no profit at all in clashing with a warship, even if they should win; and only a fireater like Domino wanted battle for its own sake.

But this, it was presently clear, was not a warship. It was a puzzle. There was something wrong about that ship, and it grew more evident the closer they got. For one thing, it was neither running nor preparing to fight . . . and now it could be seen that the captain was rushing about the deck screeching at his crew—or was it marines?—who stood in a well-disciplined but stubbornly unmoving line, as far from the pirate ship as the bulwarks would permit. And in the middle of the waist was a sight that made a shudder run over Jade—and not Jade alone.

"Prison ship," muttered Dickson hoarsely, staring at the whipping post, the multiple rack, the chains and shackles—and the four limp bodies hanging there.

In deathly silence the ships closed. Waves slapped against the hulls, the wind hummed sorrowfully in the rigging, a sail flapped, and the captain of the prison ship—a ludicrous little bald man with a black eye and bruised face—indulged himself in a shrill tantrum.

Anne broke the silence at last. "We're pirates," she announced rather unnecessarily. "We're coming aboard." She stood on the bulwarks holding easily to the main shrouds, a vivid figure in her sapphire shirt, and with a grim eye fixed on that grim rack.

"You shan't!" yelped the captain, but he was altogether wrong. They did. Came aboard with no opposition more than the little man's petty fury; came aboard and found things that Jade could never bear to think of later. The ragged, filthy, beaten men who hobbled, cheering, from the deck house, chained painfully foot to neck, turned out to be the lucky ones—the trusted convicts, far better off than those in the writhing black hell below decks. . . .

Jade left the scene precipitately.

"Squeamish!" said Anne some time later as she opened the salon door and saw Jade's greenish face. "Said so all along. Mind the stool, Pierre. Put him on my bed. . . . Easily. . . . There! Never mind, young Jade, you aren't the only one this time: most of us lost our dinners. If you've got your stomach back, you can give me a hand with this fellow. He's far more damaged than you were when we found you."

Jade swallowed and crossed to the bed, to stare down, wincing, at the mangled flesh of the tall young man, unconscious there. "Who is he?" she asked, wondering at Anne's expression—as though this were someone who mattered terribly.

"Dr. Michael Radcliffe, they said. Ship's surgeon. He's the one who blacked the captain's eye, protesting the treatment of the prisoners. Just before they did this to him."

"Oh," said Jade comprehendingly, and her own eyes lighted up. She loved courage as Anne did; loved gallantry even more. This man was not going to die if they could help it!

Nor did he. Courageous still, he fought his way back from death, nursed by Jade and Domino, Pierre and Mary and Tom—but most devotedly of all by Anne.

CHAPTER EIGHTEEN

Hurricane

As summer moved along and the hurricane season drew near, when prudent ships lay to in some sheltered cove for careening and general repairs, as the *Queen Royal* sauntered over blue seas, as Dr. Radcliffe slowly fought his way back to vigor—Anne Bonney blossomed. Her hard beauty softened until she looked like what she was: a very young woman, just twenty, and really in love for the first time.

The crew (sentimentalists almost to a man) watched with benign interest. Anne's husband was dead, and mourned by no one, but what of other matters? Suppose Radcliffe ungratefully failed to return her love? Or suppose he was already married? For it was clear to everyone that this was no casual flirtation. And Jack, who had discarded many women only to have Anne turn the tables on him at last, growled and grumbled and glared.

"Watch out for that harpie," he told Dr. Radcliffe on the first day the invalid appeared on deck. "She eats men. For breakfast."

The doctor laughed, singularly unconcerned. And, as Jade had already noted with satisfaction, his eyes had a most satisfying tenderness when they rested on Anne.

It was a great shock to everyone when he refused to sign on.

"Me turn pirate?" He looked startled and amused. "But why on earth would I do that? Let me be quite honest with you, my friends." His intelligent brown eyes smiled around at them all, kindly and tolerant. "I'm a surgeon, and my business is saving life, not taking it. I'm sorry if I offend you, but your life seems so pointless to me."

There was an astonished silence, broken almost at once.

"That's exactly what I keep saying!" yelped Jade, leaping up.

Jack glowered, most of the pirates looked bored, and Michael Radcliffe eyed his unexpected supporter with mild surprise. "You agree? Then why on earth are you here at all, a nice young thing like you?"

"Because it's less intolerable than anywhere else," Rory growled, bristling at the slight air of condescension. "All very well if you're a doctor, but what's an ordinary person to do if he wants to make the world a little less foul? Here at least we can destroy a few things now and then that need destroying, like that prison ship of yours. And where would you be if it weren't for us?"

"Touché," he admitted good-naturedly. "But a young girl—"

"Isn't supposed to be a person at all," snapped Jade. "How would *you* like it, being marked down as a sort of second-rate human just because of the body you happened to get born into?"

"I see." He looked thoughtful. "Well, that bears thinking about, I confess. But as to piracy— I shall gladly stay with you for the time being, and be your temporary surgeon. But not permanently, I'm afraid. Only until I—er—

get my bearings and do a bit of planning and sorting."

And his eyes turned automatically to the silent Anne, who had confided to Jade only yesterday that she was sick to death of piracy and only wished there were somewhere in the world where she could wipe out her past and be a respectable, law-abiding wife—er—woman.

That was what being in love did to a once proud and independent pirate! Jade looked along her own slim shoulder at Rory, and thanked her stars that *they* were only good friends.

It surprised no one in the least when Anne and her Michael, shining, stood hand in hand and proclaimed to God and the pirates that they were man and wife. Nor did it surprise Jade in the least when Michael remarked later that he was determined to have it done again, legally, as soon as he could figure out a way to cope with Anne's outlawry. He was a law-abiding man, was Dr. Radcliffe, and it must have been very disturbing to fall in love with a notorious pirate.

"We might go into the backwoods wilderness of America," he mused. "Shenandoah Valley, or the Piedmont, or Blue Ridge. Law will come in with settlers, but they won't ask too much about the past."

"Whose law?" spat Rory. "White man's law, making it legal to cheat and rob and murder the Indians whose land it is?" And he stalked away in a fit of black humor that reminded Jade of the days on board the *Pearl*, leaving an astonished Michael staring after him with so bewildered a face that Jade—stalking loyally at Rory's heels—was torn between laughter and rage that the righteous-minded Dr. Michael didn't even know how he'd offended them.

"I used to think I could always go live with the Iroquois," gloomed Rory when they'd planted themselves at their favorite spot at the tip of the fo'c'sle. "But it would be worse than this. You'd have to watch it all happening, and not be able to do a thing. I won't go!"

"Of course not," agreed Jade, who couldn't imagine ever leaving the sea, in any case. "Why should you?"

But Rory just growled blackly and called her a hen-witted idiot, leaving Jade to figure out by herself that when Anne left, a number of things might be quite different.

And then, as if Mary and Tom had started a positive epidemic, Joshua and Domino married themselves, by the rituals of Domino's old home, now wiped from the earth. There was something strangely exalting about it. Jade couldn't imagine God taking offense because it was a pagan rite. But for herself, she wasn't at all sure she approved all this romance. It was uncomfortable. She found herself turning more and more to brusque, comfortable, unsentimental Rory, who saw no romance even in the lyrical beauty of St. Catherine's Island, but only a good place to wash clothes and get fresh water.

"And you can wash your hair first thing," he told her with unflattering candor, frowning at it. "It looks sticky with salt half the time."

Jade at once challenged him to a duel.

The sea was liquid light, patterned purple and green by shoals, with opal-tinted fish swimming among the coral. St. Catherine's was indeed a paradise, edged with crystal sand and palms, filled with shaded dells and mangrove clusters and scarlet flowers and an occasional flamingo to match. The *Queen Royal* floated at anchor on almost invisible water, in the shimmering morning light; and the pirates (except for half a dozen still ashore and sleeping it off) clutched aching heads and muttered that it had been a wonderful party, and looked enviously at the bright eyes of those who hadn't been to it. Even Joshua was looking unhappy, and Jade gave him no sympathy whatever.

"Well, you asked for it, didn't you?" she said tartly. "People *know* what's going to happen if they drink too much, don't they? So they've got no complaint when it does, do they?" And she hefted the armful of clothes that would be the better for a wash and airing at a nice pool they knew of, and smiled at him crookedly. "Come ashore and walk it off."

But Joshua shook his head cautiously, and Domino appeared beside him.

"Him work it off," she explained.

"While you lazy creatures idle among the flamingos," Rory grinned, joining them, "we will be hoisting sails and turtles. Here, how about washing a shirt for me, too?" And he calmly added it to the pile in Jade's arms.

Jade sizzled briefly, then decided that he wasn't really treating her as a mere female, but as a friend, and that he'd do the same for her. In fact, she'd see that he did. She hesitated just an instant, almost tempered to stay aboard for the run over to the Cuban coast. Then Anne called for the longboat. The lovely shore beckoned.

"Oh, all right," she grumbled without much conviction, and scrambled down the chains after Mary and Tom. They cast away from the ship, Anne throwing kisses at Michael as if he'd be gone for weeks instead of only a few hours. Jade shook a wondering and slightly scornful head. Really!

It was a lovely little spring, its water so soft and pure that things almost washed themselves. Out in the cove the *Queen Royal* raised sail and anchor, and soared majestically away over the translucent water. Jade bent again to her work, and presently looked up with a sense of astonished indignation. The sun was gone! The perpetual Caribbean sun; it was too annoying! How could anyone dry—

She squinted up at the sky and forgot the washing. The sun was gone indeed, and most alarmingly! The whole sky was scabbed with diseased-looking clouds, and growing blacker by the minute; and a malevolent stillness sat brooding over sea and island, pressing down like a baleful hand, silencing every bird and insect.

Jade glanced uneasily at Anne, whose red head had reared itself tautly erect, and at Mary and Tom. They all knew the thing that Jade was only guessing.

"Hurricane," whispered Mary, and the word was torn away by the howl of wind swooping across the island and on toward Cuba.

"Michael!" whimpered Anne, a frightened girl. "The *Queen Royal*! And a lee shore!"

The wind, incredibly, was still increasing, lashing and beating them so that Anne's hair was a bright horizontal banner, and Jade could feel her own standing straight out. Her loose cotton trousers and shirt stopped whipping and stood stiff as wood at the point where they could go no further without tearing. Palm trees fell all around without a struggle—one directly in front of them. Jade hardly noticed. She was fighting her way to the water's edge, Anne at her shoulder, to stare hopelessly out at the blind black maelstrom of the sea.

"Michael!" screamed Anne. "I've got to reach him!"

"Don't be crazy!" Mary yelled as a renewed frenzy of wind blew them all flat on their faces. Jade, nearly choked by the flying sand that cut wherever it hit, and hit everywhere, found herself being dragged crazily along the ground, kicked and buffeted by the gale. Something large and dark sailed over her head, and then she hit a not-yet-uprooted tree with such force as to knock her breath out. She hung there, caught like a weed on a snag in a swift river, until there was a slight easing of the wind. Then Tom's voice bawled in her ear.

"Tavern cellar! Take Anne. Help."

For Anne had quite lost her mind. She was, she said, going to swim out and get Michael. It took the three of them and a ferocious new violence of wind blowing in the right direction to get them at last, blinded and crawling, into the swaying tavern, which was announcing its intention of going to sea almost at once. They reached the hurricane cellar just before it did so, and joined the silent huddle of refugees.

Among them were Calico Jack, who was almost sobered by the shock of the storm, and his four drinking companions, who weren't. And there they all crouched while the storm tore the lovely island to shreds. Anne still had to be held while she shrieked defiance at the winds, but Jade hunched lonely in a corner, saying nothing and staring at nothing.

In all the months of fighting and laughter, of competition and companionship and study and jeering at romance, how was it she had never suspected until now, too late, that she loved Rory?

CHAPTER NINETEEN

No Quarter

The little sloop waved her single mast against a gentle sky, and the sea was pale satin. Jade, one hand on the tiller, stared with angry eyes and tight lips at the beauty about her.

There was nothing left of the *Queen Royal* but smashed and mangled wreckage scattered pathetically along the coast of Cuba. For days Jade and Anne and the other survivors had searched in a borrowed sloop, not daring to hope for survivors—and quite rightly. There was only death. Only a thousand bits of spar and timber and carved mahogany, only here and there a pirate who would never be hanged now. They found little Sam Clarke, and Pierre with the drenched fur of Jezebel's body clinging pitifully around his neck—but there was no life; no life at all. Even birds lay dead and battered amid the uprooted trees, and it was altogether mad to hope that anyone could have survived, and the sea was atrociously the richer.

Even Anne had to face it at last. The sloop's owner went back to St. Catherine's with it, and the stricken handful of surviving pirates were left to pick up the pieces of their lives. But Jade had no pieces. Joshua was gone, and Domino—and Rory! Mary still had her Tom, and was going to have his child as well. Even Anne had had a few weeks of happiness with Michael—and she was going to have a baby, too. Only Jade had nothing; nothing but a belated knowledge, a great emptiness, and a haunting question. Had Rory loved her, too? Had he, perhaps, discovered it in the same instant she had? She would never know. Oh, it wasn't fai—

She stopped herself roughly on the thought, jerking a defiant chin at the blind sky. She would *not* whine, or ask for quarter like a coward fencer who can't stomach defeat! . . . or break, like Anne . . . It was pride, more than courage, that kept Jade going.

Her stomach growled hungrily, and she tightened her lips again. There was no food. Fishing lines hung empty, and turtles had apparently ceased to exist. As for piracy, they might contrive to take a banana from a child, but not much more; not reduced as they were to a tiny stolen sloop manned by a crew of nine—five of whom were the most worthless scum of the *Queen Royal*—and armed with little more than cutlasses. Even then, Anne Bonney might have led them once more to brillant success, but the hurricane had blown out her spirit with Michael's life.

The jib flapped on the dying breeze. Jade ported the helm a little, and turned to scowl blackly at the tall figure who appeared to relieve her. Flame of the Caribbean, indeed! A gutted candle, a shell, a thing whose eyes had gone out and whose hair seemed less red. Jade surrendered the tiller and then stood for a moment glaring.

"Crybaby!" she blazed out of the savagery of her own grief. "Poor loser! Just because you don't like the way the game's going, you quit playing!"

Anne looked at her with dull surprise. "Why shouldn't I? It isn't my game, and I don't like it, so why should *I* be a good sport?"

It was a blow at the roots of Jade's code. She clutched. "But–you have to! It's what it's all about! I mean, the only way you *really* lose is if you snivel and quit." Anne just looked at her. "And–and it *has* to be fair play in the long run, or else God would be a devil."

"Yes," said Anne. "He is."

"Coward!" yelled Jade, appalled lest Anne be right. "You liked it well enough when you were winning! Cheat! Rotten sport! If I acted like that, Rory'd come back and haunt me as long as I lived, and–" her voice choked humiliatingly. "–and he'd be right, too."

Anne's hollow eyes produced a flicker of interest, and she studied Jade for a moment. "You and Rory too? I'm sorry, Jade; I should have guessed. But you couldn't possibly care the way I do."

Goaded, to fury, Jade slapped her. And then felt worse than ever when Anne–murderous, hot-tempered, imperious Anne Bonney–didn't even slap back. Jade gritted her teeth, stormed from the tiny quarter-deck, and ran into Jack coming up from below.

She looked ready to eat pirates for breakfast, and something behind the arrogance of his face winced. Annoyingly, Jade found she couldn't take out her rage on him, after all. She didn't even hate him anymore; felt only a tolerant contempt without rancor. How could you hate a great, cocky, not-very-bright dog who tried so pitifully hard to hide his weakness from himself that he all but wagged his tail at a kind word?

Not that he wasn't a great nuisance these days, lording it around the *Juanita*, acting the captain with great noise and swagger, now that Anne no longer bothered to sit on him. He never noticed that it was Mary who had quietly taken over the real command, with Tom as her loyal support. Ironically, there wasn't a strong-willed man aboard. Now, if Rory were here—Jade turned with a wrench, and made herself smile at Jack, lest he suspect she was almost in tears.

Jack all but wagged his tail. "There's Harbour Island up ahead," he told her, expanding his chest. "Mary says she remembers a fishing village on it, and we're heading there for food."

Jade nodded. Now they were reduced to raiding fishing villages, were they? Well, why not? They were hungry.

The villagers, it turned out, were very much annoyed about the whole thing. Not that any of them were hurt: they were merely herded into one of the huts and kept there while the raid was on. But such is the perversity of human nature that they resented it more bitterly than if some of them had been killed.

So, too, did the lone woman whom they met paddling back from a nearby plantation in a canoe filled with fresh provisions. She walloped Jade smartly on the side of the head with her paddle—the flat of it, fortunately—and poked it in Ned Bixby's stomach. Jade, her head ringing, hastily prevented his instant vengeance by giving him another blow in his stomach, this time with her elbow.

"Ooof!" said Bixby, doubly aggrieved.

"Leave her alone!" ordered Jade. "I don't blame her a

bit! In fact, I'd be hitting even harder." And she ducked another vigorous swing of the paddle, laughing . . . and surprised at her own laughter.

She laughed again, without much mirth, when they looked over the loot later on. The loot! There it lay—or squealed or clucked: four pigs, six chickens, a sack of rice and one of sugar, a basket of yams, a pot of potatoes snatched cooking from the fire, a quarter of beef, a side of salt pork, three loaves of bread, and a nice bag of crusts intended for chicken food.

Still, food was more welcome than gold. They ate that night. And they ate again in Hispaniola, by the straightforward process of going ashore and killing some wild cattle.

But luck was determinedly against them now. Every boat small enough for them to take turned out to be empty of cargo. A rich-looking French schooner—heroically taken against superior numbers—provided them with nothing but one meal, some rum, and two more hungry mouths named Besneck and Cornelian who insisted on joining them and who inevitably ate more than they contributed.

"Never mind," said Mary philosophically. "Once we've collected enough men, we'll be able to take a larger boat and work up the way we did before, until we have a big ship." And with this in mind, they headed back to Jamaica.

October proved to be a highly distressful month for the Jamaicans. A schooner, two fishing sloops, and a whole series of coastal villages sent indignant messages to Governor Lawes, demanding that he instantly capture the rampaging pirates. Anne Bonney again, *and* with two more female pirates, they informed him darkly, causing the governor to tear off his elaborate wig and stamp on it furiously.

"I'll see that woman hanged if it's the last thing I do!" he yelped for at least the hundred and fortieth time.

Nor was he the only one to express such an intention. Most of the pirate's victims did—and to their faces, too. And with impunity. The youngest of the female pirates saw to that, shouting that she loved courage, and anyone brave enough to defy pirates to their faces deserved to get away with it.

"*Fine* reputation you're giving us," grumbled Jack. "Next thing, *they*'ll be robbing *us*."

"Serve us right if they did," returned Jade coldly, and went up the rigging to work off the enormous anger that still possessed her. By now she had learned to swing by everything but her tail, exercising hour after hour until she was tired enough to fall asleep without any time to lie and think. She stayed aloft while the *Juanita* nosed along the northwest coast of Jamaica in the westerning sun, nosing into every cove and inlet. Twilight fell, and swift darkness, and Jade came down, but still they ghosted westward in the tropical night, to anchor at last safely off the shoals of Montego Bay.

The green mountains of the Cockpit country shone fiery in the dawn, and Jade remembered how she had once toyed with the idea of trying to find Domino a refuge there. Well, Domino had found her refuge . . . under the sea. Jade shook her head violently and ran up the rigging to take her station as lookout. The anchor was hoisted and they set off again toward Negril Point.

But it needed no lookout to spot the fat little turtling

boat wallowing just off shore. She was easy prey: shamefully easy—and she yielded all of four turtles and a barrel of rum which Jade felt they could easily have done without. It was a final ironic twist of fate, surely, that the five worst tipplers on the *Queen Royal* should have been saved by their own hangovers and thereby inflicted on the *Juanita.* Jade exchanged a glance of angry resignation with Mary as the rum barrel was discovered with yells of joy and transferred instantly to the sloop.

Mary shrugged and turned to the skipper of the plundered turtling boat. "As long as we've robbed you," she suggested politely, "won't you join us for the party?"

Jack scowled and Jade grinned knowingly. Three more to share the rum made that much less for each.

The skipper was clearly a philosopher. He shrugged wryly, nodded at his two assistants.

"Since we're furnishing the food and drink, why not?" And they all came aboard.

It was a long and noisy party—especially for the four who hadn't stayed more than twenty minutes after the food was gone. It went on, noisily, all night, penetrating easily to the cabin which Anne and Jade shared, and also, doubtless, to Tom and Mary's. It was still going on, though feebly, when morning came. Jade looked with disgust at the staggering or sprawled figures and wondered anew how people could so degrade themselves. Her new compassion didn't extend this far—not *nearly* this far; and she stood and watched with curling lip while the three fishermen tottered to the bulwarks, fell more or less by sheer good luck into their own boat, and set a wavering course around Negril Point. She would be surprised if they got very far.

She would also be surprised if the *Juanita* got anywhere at all that day. Jack and his cronies were now leaning against one another in the waist singing a bawdy song—or, more likely, two or three different ones. Driven by a need to put as much space as possible between herself and them, Jade started up the shrouds again, and then paused, her eye fixed speculatively on the triangular sails just coming around the point.

"Deck, there!" she called down. "Sail rounding Point Negril!"

Anne glanced up without much interest, Mary frowned, Tom picked up a spyglass and peered.

"Just a sloop," he pronounced. "Harmless enough."

But Jade dropped uneasily back to the deck, and Mary had already leaped down into the waist and was kicking the lolling Jack smartly in the ribs. "Get up, you bilge-rat! Sail ho!"

Jack mumbled. Jade, catching Mary's alarm, ran down and kicked Besneck, who looked the nearest awake. "Get up fool! Ship approaching!"

The men, awake now but exceedingly reluctantly, looked at their tormentors with hatred. "Leave's alone," they grumbled, and added a number of highly impolite remarks to put the point across.

And then Anne's voice. The old Anne—the Anne of battles!

"Stand by to repel boarders!" she yelled, and Jade, whirling, saw that the harmless sloop had become an extremely harmful one, bristling with soldiers. In an instant it had crowded on sail, caught the breeze, and was swooping down on them, virtually brandishing a pair of four-pounder guns.

The world became a kaleidoscope in which incredible things happened all around, as slowly as if it were under water. A roar and a crash, and the mast lazily toppled, missing Jade by a full four feet—and felling Anne with a mass of tangled rigging. The drunken crew instantly became cold sober, leaped to their feet, and dived without hesitation into the doubtful shelter of the hold. Mary was screaming at them to come out and fight like men, while Jade ran to the unconscious Anne.

But things were happening too fast. The enemy sloop was now only a few yards away, grapnels already swinging. No time to help Anne! No choice! Jade and Mary and Tom must fight alone. They raced for the rail, the three of them, pistols and cutlasses ready.

And then there were only two of them. A musket cracked and Tom fell—killed instantly—at Mary's feet.

Mary went berserk. She forgot the enemy, about to board; turned to the hold with a twisted face.

"Filthy cowards!" she shrieked, and fired into it. A howl rose. "Desert my Tom, will you—" She fired again, and was again rewarded by an anguished yell. Jade only half saw. Alone by the bulwarks, she was standing by to repel boarders.

It wasn't much of a fight, she was later annoyed to remember. She fired both pistols and then drew her cutlass. But they swarmed over her before she had time to do any serious damage with it. And Mary hardly had time to turn from the babbling and wailing hold before she, too, was seized.

The commander, one Captain Barnett of the English Navy, stared at the captured pirates with moderate satisfaction and considerable awe. The victory, somehow, lacked—er—something. Mary, entirely unsubdued, raged like several tigers in the hands that held her, while Jade—scorning useless struggle—simply stood still and looked at him as if he were something particularly slimy that had just crawled up from the bilge. Anne, pulled unconscious from under the tangle of rigging, still held a pistol in one hand and a cutlass in the other. And out of the hold, stumbling and mumbling and demanding protection from Mary, came five uninjured pirates carrying a dead one and Jack, limping from a bullet in his leg and claiming bitterly that she'd shot him—as she had. Mary at once announced that she was sorry she hadn't done a better job of it.

Jade contradicted her. "I'm glad you didn't kill him," she announced fiendishly. "Now he'll hang, and he'll hate that, the crybaby! I hope he hangs before we do, so we can laugh at him."

"So do I!" agreed Mary, who seemed to be in a state of crazy shock, unable to feel or care about anything. Jade, for her part, was in a spirit of wild exaltation. There was nothing to lose! It was all over now—and instead of feeling hopeless, she felt recklessly free to say and do anything she liked.

It went to her head. She grinned with unholy joy, laughed aloud at the expressions of her captors, and especially at Captain Barnett, who was regarding the three of them incredulously.

"Furies!" he said, fascinated. "Amazons! Right out of Greek drama! By gad, what couldn't Sophocles have done with these three!"

The soldiers and Mary, not in the least versed in the classics, merely looked blank. But Jade grinned again, her most irreverent lopsided smile, and announced pleasantly that she'd gladly play Medea. And then laughed again, with genuine delight, at his face.

It wasn't until the captives had been heavily shackled and transferred to the enemy sloop, and the order given to head at once for Port Royal that reality sobered Jade as if she'd been dumped into a cold ocean.

Port Royal!

It really wasn't fair, she decided, staring with mild astonishment at the chains on her wrists. It really wasn't. Why should her own personal consequences reach out to hurt other people? Why should her family have to drink her brew? Hadn't she given them enough heartache already?

CHAPTER TWENTY

The Prisoners

The sloop sped on its way, rejoicing and incredulous. They had actually got Anne Bonney at last! Right there, in that cabin, unconscious and shackled and triple-guarded. Nervous lest she somehow vanish after all, a guard opened the door for at least the tenth time in half an hour and poked a mistrustful head inside.

No one stirred. Anne Bonney lay with closed eyes on the only bunk, and Mary Read sat staring numbly at nothing, and the little one was curled up on the floor, her face invisible.

Crying, no doubt, said the guard loudly, and bent to look.

Jade instantly feigned sleep, stirring a little as she felt his peering stare, and snuggling into her own arm like a child disturbed.

"Zeuks!" said the guard unbelievingly. "She *can't* be asleep!"

"Mmm," Jade murmured, snuggling harder. "Was. G'way."

She listened to his baffled retreat with mild satisfaction, and returned to her problem: that of not being recognized in Port Royal, even by her aunt and uncle. And having finished a tentative plan or two—all she could really do now—she sat up and turned her contrite attention to her fellow prisoners.

They were both altogether dazed: Anne from the falling mast and Mary from the shock of Tom's death. And Jade, selfishly engrossed in her own problems, hadn't even noticed! Remorsefully she bent over the cut and bruised Anne, received a groggy flicker of smile, and turned to poor stricken Mary with almost motherly concern. She was the strong one now. Later she might be frightened or despairing—but right now hanging didn't appear nearly as terrible as being flogged or losing Rory had been, and she had survived both of these things with head held high.

It was almost a relief to have it all but over, and a well of gladness was in her that for Rory it had been the keen clean death of a storm at sea. . . .

The thought told her how to reach Mary.

"Listen!" she said, and kneeling, put an urgent hand on the limp manacled wrist. "Listen, Mary! What we told Jack is true! We can be glad for Tom; he's lucky; he never felt any fear or pain! And he'd have hated hanging worse than we will; you know he would."

Mary stirred, took a deep breath, raised her head. Slowly her face came to life.

"Yes, of course! How stupid of me!" She sobbed once, buried her face in her hands, and looked up with wet serene eyes. "I'm all right now," she said firmly. And from then on nothing moved her, nor could. Calm and gallant, she would play the farce to the end—but she wouldn't care how or when it ended.

Anne spoke from the bed, in the weak but rational voice of someone awake long enough to have sorted things out quite accurately.

"Is Tom dead, then? I'm glad, too, Mary. Lawes–" She didn't finish–nor need to, as far as Jade was concerned. She remembered far too well the malevolence when he spoke of Anne Bonney.

But they were too tired and too drained to worry. There was nothing they could do. They had always expected this to happen some day, had discussed it with cheerful fatalism. Now they settled down quite easily and comfortably with the hard reality. As Anne observed wisely, there was no hope to torment them with uncertainty, and one can always come to terms with the inevitable.

"Though easier fed than hungry," she added, wistful. It was a long time since they had eaten.

"I suppose this is the last time we'll feel a ship under us," said Jade regretfully as the sloop heeled over again, tacking against the wind. And for some irrational reason this was a more pangful thought than that of the gallows. They all fell into sad silence just as a new guard opened the door, stuck his bushy head in with the air of a cannibal making sure his dinner hasn't run away, and leered.

"No fight left in this lot, either," he announced, pleased.

Three heads turned to regard him coldly. Jade elected herself spokesman. "Where's our dinner?" she demanded, tart as lemons. "How can Lawes hang us if you starve us first? You go tell that captain of yours that the Furies are *hungry!*"

The head gawped and retreated, sped on its way by what sounded remarkably like a chuckle from the bed. "That'll show 'em," said Anne with great satisfaction.

The arrival of the sloop back in Port Royal caused a crowd to start gathering at once as rumors flew. Anchor dropped, and a small-boat went ashore. "To get Lawes, I dare say," said Anne philosophically. But it came back bearing instead the lean gray-wigged figure of Dr. Hughes. Jade drew a sharp breath, withdrew from the tiny window in haste, and fell into frantic thought.

"Our first public reception," murmured Anne, and looked with discontent at their worn and slept-in sailcloth trousers and jackets, and the rumpled cotton shirts. "Oh for velvet breeches and silk blouses and a hairdresser!" And she turned to the door as it opened to admit the doctor.

"I'm sorry to see you again in these circumstances, Mistress Bonney," he said with grave courtesy, and fixed a sharp professional eye on her battered face and shoulder.

"So am I," returned Anne drily as he bent over her, clearly here to make sure she didn't cheat the gallows by dying first. "But I rather think the rest of Jamaica will be in whoops of joy over it."

"Mostly," he agreed, not mincing matters. "Mmm—that hurt? No? Good. Just cuts and bruises here; no bones broken . . . There are a few people here who remember you kindly, though I don't suppose you'll find it noticeable. They—" He straightened and found himself confronted by a thin, deeply tanned figure with cropped honey-gold hair and a fined-down face all eyes and mouth and jutting cheekbones. It looked almost familiar.

"Good heavens!" he discovered faintly. "It's Mistress Melanie! What are you doing alive and in such company, poor child?"

"Being a pirate," said Jade, uncompromising.

Behind her, Anne and Mary exchanged glances and launched instantly into a conspiracy.

"We captured her," they said firmly. "Held her prisoner. Forced her to be a pirate. But," they added with slightly more truth, "she always sat in the rigging and refused to fight."

"Don't be silly," said Jade, struggling somewhere between annoyance and affection. "Anne never forced anyone to be a pirate," she told Dr. Hughes. "Besides, just you try to tell *that* lot—" She jerked her chin at the door. "—that I never fight! How many wounded have they got in the crew?"

"Four." Dr. Hughes still looked bemused. "Two with bullet wounds and two with cuts."

Jade smirked. "Me!" she bragged, and then came to her own urgent business. "Anyway—" She cocked a quizzical but worried head at him, wondering how best to present her case. "I'm not who you think," she tried. "I'm Jade—er —Green."

He stared down at the pointed brown face. "You're not," he said with conviction. "You're Melanie Lennox. You've changed almost out of recognition, I admit, but you can't fool a doctor. We notice things like bones and the shape of an ear. Besides, I remember when you cut off your hair. How did you come here, child? We all supposed you drowned at sea."

"Yes, I know, and it's better that way. To stay drowned, I mean." Jade felt that she was not explaining this as lucidly as she might. "Melanie, that is. And I'll be someone else, like Jade Green. Oh, please, *can't* you see?"

He narrowed gray eyes as if he might be starting to.

"What is it you want, exactly?" Dr. Hughes asked, direct.

"Bandage my face so no one can recognize me, and don't say anything," she replied, as direct. "And when they hang an ordinary pirate named Jade Green, my aunt and uncle—"

He shook his head, startled. "Your aunt and uncle? My poor child, of course you wouldn't know. Your aunt's dead. Of yellow fever. She never even knew the *Pearl* had gone down. And your uncle sold everything and went back to Prussia."

She stared, shocked. Poor Aunt Louisa! Or was she lucky? She had never seemed very happy to be alive. Muddled, Jade fixed her eyes on her chains, and then looked up again to find them all watching her. This was a time for practicality, not sentiment.

"There's still my name, and other people who might recognize me. My family in Virginia *mustn't* find out!"

"But my dear child, they think you drowned!" he protested. "Surely they'd be happy—"

But she leaned back against the bulkhead in a pose of unconscious grace and quite deliberate mockery, pulling her mouth into its one-sided smile.

"Oh, yes," she drawled, her voice harsh as Rory's. "Overjoyed to have their dear daughter raised from the sea to hang for piracy! Delighted! Oh, do please be sensible and help!"

Dr. Hughes stared at her for a moment, and then nodded, his gray eyes warm.

"If you really want it. But I don't think the bandage is needed. You've changed completely. I saw you more than anyone here I think, and I'm the only one to have seen you at all after you cut off your hair, am I not? And its been nearly a year since then." He stared at her with keen eyes, perhaps regretting the young softness gone from her face. "No one will recognize your face, my dear. If anything gives you away it will be your voice and personality."

"Behold how I am French," suggested Jade at once, in Monsieur Maupin's best accents. "And I name myself Jade –uh–Loupin." She grinned briefly to herself. Jade Wolf. Monsieur Maupin would have appreciated that. Had she chosen it partly because it was similar to his name, and she was suddenly longing unbearably to see him? The grin had died, and she set her chin strongly.

"Yes, yes; that might do." The doctor sighed, looked at the three of them sadly. Such a pity! "Be careful in front of Governor Lawes, child; you're liable to see a good deal of him, you know."

"Oh, he won't much notice anyone but me," predicted Anne wryly, and no one argued with that.

And so, in a strange mood of calm practicality quite unsuited to a funeral, one Melanie Lennox was buried forever; and Jade Loupin, pirate, was led with her fellow-prisoners to the dungeons below the fortress of St. Jago de la Vega.

There was no conversation between the half-dozen aggrieved men pirates and the unforgiving female ones as they clanked their way down the stone steps into darkness. A heavy iron-barred door opened, swallowed the men. And the next one down the corridor creaked open in turn . . .

The lantern in the corridor outside sent a dim flicker of

light through the bars and across solid stone walls of the cell. They needn't, as Anne observed at last, waste their time with any thoughts of digging out.

Mary shivered. The cell was no warmer than it was opulent, and it was as if the sun's warmth had never existed. A pile of straw and a thin blanket, a bucket in the far corner, two wooden benches . . .

Anne and Mary sat down on them wearily, and Jade—already chafing for air and exercise, herself—regarded them with worried eyes. Pity filled her, for them and for the unborn babies who must die with them.

And then footsteps clomped down the steps at the end of the corridor, and she set her mind against pity, which could only weaken them against their enemies.

The footsteps materialized, became the portly form of Governor Lawes, looking, in the murky yellow light, as expectant and happy as an enormous child on Christmas morning. He applied his nose to the bars, squinting into the gloom, clearly half fearful that St. Nicholas had deceived him after all. Anne's red hair gleamed dully back at him, convincing him that it was really true, and the governor whooped with glee. His rosy face turned rosier; he chortled, he capered, he crowed; his joy was unbounded.

Jade, one shoulder leaning against the cold stone of the wall, watched him with an oddly detached interest. Governor Lawes was no hypocrite, as she had noticed before. He was gloating unashamed, enjoying his revenge with simple wholeheartedness, glorying in it. Magnanimity in victory was not for him; he believed in rubbing it in.

"Ah, Mistress Bonney," he announced at last when he could stop bouncing long enough to bellow for more lanterns and peer through the bars again with a joyful blue eye. "You can't imagine how delighted I am to see you here!"

Anne, smouldering at him from hooded eyes, said she could easily imagine, at which Lawes beamed with the loving look of Morgan the cat with live rats to play with, and added that he had been waiting a long time for this.

"*Told* you I'd catch and hang you, didn't I?" he burbled, and waited hopefully for an explosion of the famous Bonney temper.

Except for clenched fists, Anne failed to oblige him. "You took long enough," she shrugged, disappointingly mild.

Lawes drooped, recovered, sniggered. "You're very meek all of a sudden," he jeered. "Such fierce bold pirates! Come, ladies, show me how fierce and bold you are!"

They declined. Mary yawned delicately, Anne turned an indifferent shoulder, and Jade contrived to look faintly amused. They were no fun at all.

Governor Lawes was beginning to look like Morgan disappointed because the nice rats wouldn't play anymore. "I thought you had more spirit," he mourned. "Who'd think you'd break so easily, the deadly Anne Bonney? Oh, do show a little fight!"

Jade couldn't possibly keep quiet an instant longer. Her eyes gleamed green. She carefully arranged her French accent. "Me, I think you are a very silly man," she drawled huskily.

Lawes turned startled and interested attention to her for the first time. "What's that?" he demanded, not missing the insolence of her pose. Good! He was going to get something besides this infuriating show of unconcern.

"A very silly man," she repeated with relish. "We, *voyons*, are not so silly. We do not fight when it is not now the time for fighting. You wish, *sans doute*, that we undignify ourselves by beating at the walls, or cry to be let out, or scream at you, *non?* That would amuse you very much, I think. But we do not wish to amuse you, silly fat man."

Lawes regarded her with appreciation. "You can't help amusing me," he retorted genially. "It amuses me to see you in there, and it amuses me to see the bold face you put on it, and it will amuse me even more to watch you hang, my dear. And how will you like that, hmm?"

Jade had a gift for the disconcerting.

"*Tiens*, it will not amuse me very much at all," she admitted with a cheerfulness that utterly discomposed him for the moment.

They eyed each other like swordsmen found worth each other's mettle. Jade, idiotically, felt better than she had since the hurricane. Life promised to be not without interest, after all—what was left of it.

Then Lawes turned back to his pet enemy Anne with brand new affability.

"I'm having a new scaffold built on Gallows Hill," he informed her with gleeful menace, watching for a sign of flinching and getting none. "Imagine yourselves standing there," he urged them, "with the noose just slipping over your necks!"

They did, of course. The invitation was compulsive. And although the idea had long ago lost the terror of novelty, yet here, in the dank cell and the cold reality of here and now, it bared its teeth again. Something clenched its fist briefly and unpleasantly in the pit of

Jade's stomach, so she slitted her eyes and contrived to look more amused than ever. Anne shrugged, and Mary appeared to be so bored by the whole subject that she could scarcely keep awake. It was a really splendid performance, and Jade was proud of them all.

Lawes concealed any disappointment very well indeed. One might almost have thought he was Morgan discovering that the nice rats had decided to play some more after all.

"I'll be back," he promised gaily. "I'm giving a party tonight to celebrate your capture. Sorry I can't invite you, but never mind; I promise we'll be thinking of you."

"We'll be asleep," said Mary firmly, and yawned again.

True to his word, Governor Lawes did return, every day of that long three weeks. Jade looked forward to his visits and the verbal duels with him as the one taste of seasoning in unsalted time. Malevolent though he was, he played the rules she knew, neither giving nor asking quarter, even seeming to enjoy the points she scored almost as much as the ones he did. And although they detested each other, it was with a measure of grudging esteem.

He stood peering at her speculatively one day when her accent had slipped, as it frequently did.

"I know you," he said, groping in his memory.

"You don't!" Jade contradicted at once.

"I do!" He remembered suddenly, and his protuberant eyes widened, disbelieving. For an instant they glared at each other like gladiators deciding whether and where to strike first. Then common sense asserted itself, and he shrugged his mustard taffeta shoulders. "Perhaps not," he decided, vaguely baffled.

"*Non,*" Jade agreed, relieved.

But Anne was a great disappointment to him. She refused to fly into helpless rages and declined the game of repartee, leaving it all to Jade.

"You're better at it," she said. "I'd just lose my temper. Besides, why give him the satisfaction of arguing?"

"For *my* satisfaction," snapped Jade, and girded her loins to do new battle with a newly-arrived flock of gaping and jeering public.

For the public came at all hours to see and taunt the wild pirates in their cages. They thrust malignant faces against the bars to peer, ogle, comment, and to hurl abuse like dung. Jade longed daily to jump into the clean salty sea to wash it off. It was far more loathsome than the running duel with Lawes—but it did keep her in battle spirits. Unthinkable ever to quail before those cruel and malicious eyes, avid for any hint of weakness! And Mary's bored silence, or even Anne's sinister air of a brooding volcano, weren't even very effective as defense, much less as attack.

"You can't be subtle with yapping dogs," Jade fumed. "They just think you're too despairing and broken-spirited even to answer back. I've heard them say so, and so have you!"

"Who cares what they think?" asked Mary from the depths of her own indifference.

But Jade cared. So did Anne, at last. Together they worked out half a dozen different kinds of verbal stop-thrust—a riposte without parry, said Jade contentedly, that even Monsieur Maupin would have approved. There was no need for defense now.

The most effective was to discuss gallows and hanging

even more cold-bloodedly than their would-be tormentors. This not only shocked and confused the enemy, but it also wore such callouses on their own nerves that they were almost immune to any attack on that subject.

"You ought to see the new scaffold we're building!"

"See it! We're going to try it out!"

"It's a huge one, especially for you cursed pirates."

"Well, I should hope so, it's the least you could do for anyone as important as Anne Bonney. We're expecting a brass band and fireworks, too, you know."

"Have you repented?" asked one long-faced man with lugubrious malice.

They looked at him, gleaming. "You'd be surprised at what we repent," they told him.

And when threatened with the torments of hell, the female pirates had the insensitivity to remark that it sounded terribly interesting, and they could hardly wait to see some of their old friends.

Next, Jade developed the distracting habit of keeping in trim by doing acrobatics at odd moments, whenever she felt the need to express her feelings or stretch her muscles or confuse the enemy. And visitors found it difficult to keep their minds entirely on the subject with someone persistently grinning at them upside down or bending into a wheel. It was, to say the least of it, a highly unsuitable attitude.

And if Jade had her hours of black depression, when the fear so well bottled up beneath the floor of her mind banged and shouted to get out and the long nights dragged without end, no one had any cause to suspect it. Especially not Mary and Anne, who doubtless had their own dark hours to cope with. For some reason Jade felt it her responsibility to keep up their spirits and lead the counter-attacks.

One day, newly inspired, she informed Governor Lawes with ghoulish glee that she had decided to become a ghost.

"Think how Jamaica will be famous," she pointed out zestfully. "To have the only haunted gallows in the world! I cannot think, me," she decided in surprised tones, "why it is that no one has ever done it before."

"Lovely idea!" approved Anne. "But I certainly shan't waste my time haunting the *gallows*." And she looked meaningfully at Lawes.

But this fell disappointingly flat, for the governor was too elated with news of his own even to notice what they said.

"Charles Vane has been caught, too!" he announced, pink with jubilance. "They're bringing him here, and you'll all be tried and hanged together."

The dismayed silence lasted only an instant. They rallied under his sharp eyes.

"Very sociable," they said brightly, not fooling him for a moment, but at least not giving him any more satisfaction than they could help.

When he had gone off jauntily to throw another party of celebration, and the door was temporarily empty of mockers, the cell sank into dismal silence. Mary leaned back against the damp wall with a sigh and a cough, Anne slumped into bleak dejection, and Jade hugged her knees and rested her forehead on them with a sigh. This dreary captivity was a part of the consequences she hadn't foreseen, and it was getting harder and harder to bear without self-pity.

"Poor Vane," said Anne.

Jade said nothing. She liked Vane well enough, but he was no worse off than the rest of them—especially Mary and Anne. Any pity she dared indulge in, went to them.

"At least he'll have that much less time to spend buried alive," she muttered sourly. "I'll be glad when it's the fifteenth."

Mary coughed and nodded fervent agreement, but Anne turned on Jade, tempestuous.

"Will you! Have you thought what the trial will be like?"

Jade had. All the venomous tongues and virulent faces and pitiless eyes, all at once. Hundreds of them—and in broad daylight, with no protective dimness. . . . Oh yes, she'd thought! She shivered.

"Yes," she said, defiant.

"Well?" blazed Anne, caustic with nervous strain. "Well?"

"Well what?"

"But I suppose you won't mind, will you?" Anne's sneer was withering. "The heroic Mistress Iceberg-without-nerves; you never mind anything, do you?"

Jade shoved her chin out. "I'll mind. I'll hate it!"

Anne stared. "Well, I'd have thought you'd be too proud to admit it," she said in tones of deep disillusion.

"Oh, would you!" snapped Jade, and scowling, paused to think about it. Denial was defense, and against her principles. "I'm too proud to deny it," she discovered, nose in the air.

"Stop it, both of you!" Mary pleaded. "Don't take it out on each other! It'll be all over soon now, you know; it's just the waiting."

Anne sputtered and glowered for a moment longer, then laughed and crossed the cell to put a pacifying arm around Jade's sullen shoulder.

"Sorry," she said. "I'm even sorry I encouraged you to sign on with us. You could have been back home in Virginia reading about our capture with faint regret."

It didn't sound as heavenly as it should have done: not even the thought of light and warmth and space.

"Virginia's only another kind of prison with a longer sentence," Jade sighed. "I'm glad I joined you. It was the only time in my life I was free and alive. And I never had a single beating!" she remembered, astonished.

"You might still plead compulsion, though," persisted Anne, eager to make amends. "After all, you were less a volunteer in coming aboard than Cornelian and Besneck, and they're doing it."

Jade wrenched away angrily. "Yes, I'd be likely to, wouldn't I?" To try to sneak out of consequences, and betray her friends as well; how dare Anne even suggest it? "Anyway," she added, dropping into prosaic realism, "what would I do if I *were* set free? Crawl back home to make my family wish I really had drowned? Sell myself as a bond slave?"

She stopped there, other possibilities being even less attractive. The subject was dropped. There was no place in society for a girl like Jade.

CHAPTER TWENTY-ONE

The Trial

The light was blinding, the heat was an astonishment after the cold dimness of the dungeon, and the noise was an assault. The courtroom was filled with a gallows mob, lusting for blood and scandal. Ribald and sadistic, they overflowed the building and swarmed in the street as at a devils' carnival, eating and drinking, laughing and staring, buying miniature gallows as souvenirs from prospering hawkers.

A roar arose at the sight of the prisoners, causing Jade to shrink inside her own skin like a panic-stricken snake trying to escape by shedding. This was far worse than she'd imagined; surely a bit of hell itself, fed with pure essence of hate. For a moment she thought she really couldn't face it. Then she pulled herself together with a small gasp and an even smaller smile of self-mockery. As if she had any choice! Or, rather, the only choice was whether to face it with dignity or without—and that was no choice at all.

Clanking, the prisoners were wedged through the bloodthirsty crowd. Jack shook as he walked, his face wiped blank by fear. His cronies shuffled sullenly. But

Charles Vane studied the crowd with a clinical interest that Jade found admirable, and Mary was wrapped in her cloak of indifference. As for Anne, the target of all the worst and loudest abuse, she was like a queen. The flaming hair was pulled severely back from her pure classical profile; she was tall, remote, altogether magnificent.

Jade, comparing Anne with the mob around them, was suddenly and fiercely glad to be where she was, against them all. She stared at them, tingling with loathing and battle-joy. No matter that she was a prisoner, that she was ragged and dirty in cotton trousers; no need to wish for velvet breeches and her flame blouse! She was better than any of them, could out-scorn them right to the gallows. Not with Mary's detachment or Anne's majesty, but with her own style of irreverent flippancy. Her head lifted proudly on its slim neck.

"Stretching it for the noose?" jeered a pimply youth as the file of prisoners jangled past.

"But of course," she flashed back, even remembering her accent. "It will be of a good fit, *non?*"

There was laughter, not sympathetic, but definitely appreciative. The mob was here to be entertained, and the better show put on, the better they liked it. And Jade promised to be the most entertaining of all the pirates.

"Ah, they like you," came Vane's dry voice from just behind.

She turned an inquiring look over her own shoulder, carefully calm, matching his dryness. "Dogs like bones, too," she retorted.

He chuckled, so naturally that Jade wondered whether he too had walled away his fear deeply, or whether he truly had none. "You'll do," he approved. "Actually, I was thinking of bull-fighting. They *do* like a spirited bull. . . ."

It was horribly apt—and just the thing Rory might have said. Jade grinned at the thought, and imagined she could feel him beside her, disrespectful and unyielding.

They were squeezed into the prisoners' dock now, the target for all the pitiless eyes. Jade, in the front row between Anne and Vane, was grateful for the sheltering height of one and bulk of the other. She no longer felt flippant, and it took a certain amount of effort to keep the insouciant smile fixed in its place.

Governor Lawes—now Judge Lawes—was in his place, no longer a clownishly vindictive little man, but a powerful and baleful magistrate in a huge gray judge's wig, pounding his gavel for quiet. The crowd buzzed itself into silence. A town crier settled himself on the broad windowsill where he could repeat all the proceedings to the avid hundreds outside. And the trial was on, as solemnly as if there were any doubt about the outcome.

In danger of becoming very much oppressed by the whole thing, Jade raised her impudent face to Judge Lawes, who was eyeing her with a kind of affable ferocity that was not in the least comforting. He reminded her strongly of Morgan when he had finished playing and was out to kill. Moreover, he was making no pretense at impartiality. His opening speech, addressed to Anne, was a small masterpiece of invective, and one which left very little for the Prosecutor to add. The kindest thing he called her was "a lusting, thieving, oathing female, best made use of on the gallows."

Jade stood still, trying not to be sickened. The town crier was repeating it all, zestfully, to the outside audience, and the crowd murmured approvingly, and Anne—Anne stood erect and unashamed, like Antigonë under the flaying tongue of Creon. Jade's heart lifted in admiration. She curled a derisory smile at the mob, who were clearly irritated at such unflinching stoicism, and she stood proudly closer to Anne.

Considering everything, it was a fairer trial than Jade had expected. To be sure they had no barrister to defend them, and this might have been a distinct handicap had they been innocent. As they were blatantly guilty, it didn't matter except in principle. And Judge Lawes, ignoring the shouts of "Get on with the hangings!" scrupulously called witness after witness to testify against them.

"As if we needed all this proof!" murmured Jade. "We've never denied any of it, not even Jack."

"Proper legal form," said Anne from the side of her mouth. "Besides–" She grinned shrewdly. "He does love to rub it in, you know."

Astonishing how many witnesses appeared! From all around the Jamaican coast they came: from the fishing boats and villagers and small trading ships that had been robbed. All were delighted to testify against the pirates; all were particularly eager to punish the females who had dared so affront masculine dominance.

Jade listened, cynical and embittered but not at all astonished, until the woman from the canoe–one Mistress Thompson–took the stand and behaved in exactly the same way. Why, demanded Jade in an aggrieved whisper, should she turn against her own sex that way?

Mistress Thompson turned at the sound, met her indignant stare, and returned it dourly. "You're the one I hit with my paddle," she remembered with satisfaction.

The judge's gavel beat through the noisy tittering and

bawling crier. "You hit her?" he echoed, incredulous. "That one? You're sure?"

Mistress Thompson asserted indignantly that of course she was sure, and Jade at once supported her.

"Of course she did, and poked Bixby in the stomach, too. You men think just because someone's a female she shouldn't have any spirit or courage, and if she does, you either won't believe it or punish her, and if you ask me—"

"Silence!" brayed Lawes as the crowd broke into booing, applause, and imprecations, and the town crier gabbled out the window. Mistress Thompson stared at Jade doubtfully, getting the point and bewildered by it.

"She didn't hit back, nor let the others," she conceded fairly, and was at once dismissed from the stand, to be replaced by the skipper of the turtling boat. After that Captain Barnett testified with damning admiration that the women and the late Tom Deane were the only pirates to show fight on the day they were captured.

Finally came Besneck and Cornelian, saving their own skins by swearing that they'd been forced into piracy. And if they were at all embarrassed or shamed by the eight pairs of contemptuous eyes boring at them from the prisoners' dock, they never showed it. Probably they didn't even notice, being single-mindedly devoted to the business of self-preservation.

"Slimy dogs," said Jade between her teeth, but Vane smiled down at her philosophically.

"What does it matter? They aren't hurting us any. And would you be in their shoes?"

"No!" Jade hissed, and meant it. For just one instant she had glimpsed their world: a place where the end always justified the means. It was a terrible world.

Besneck was being questioned now about life on the *Juanita*. "And what about the orgies?" demanded the judge with an air of expecting to be deeply shocked but not surprised.

"Orgies?" Besneck looked confused. Nobody had told him about any orgies, and although he was perfectly willing to invent anything that might please the court, he had no idea what to invent. Perplexed, he fell back on the prosaic truth.

"There wa'n't any, Y'r Honor."

Deep and audible disappointment filled the room. Governor Lawes beetled his skimpy brows skeptically. "None? Nonsense, man! Tell the truth, now: what was it like living with a band of evil, vicious pirates?"

Besneck looked apologetic. "Uh— Well, Y'r Honor, us men got drunk whenever we could find any rum," he offered hopefully.

Jade giggled. Sharp from the crowd came one curt bark of laughter that made her catch her breath and stare. There was a distraction rising from the far door, a narrow swathe cut through the unwilling pack, a rising murmur of protest. Judge Lawes banged for order, and in answer there came a new urgency to the ripple, a new volume in the murmur. A seedy little man popped into view, looking as if he wished he were somewhere else, but prodded unmercifully by the two figures behind him.

Then Anne gasped and clutched Jade's arm, but Jade stood engulfed in stillness, for she had known since that laugh whom she would see.

"Barrister for the pirates," said Michael Radcliffe, looking confident and professional. And behind him was a shock of black hair and two angry, slanted blue eyes.

The courtroom was a blurred roar in the background, and only one face was real and sharp; a fiercely inscrutable face, like a bad-tempered Indian tomahawk, or something carved with one. . . .

And all Jade's cherished fatalism melted away, and she wanted to live!

Faint hope crowded into the prisoners' dock, and died almost at once.

"Deuced decent of them to try it," muttered Vane appreciatively.

Jade hardly heard. She and Anne stared with joy and despair while the court still buzzed, and the judge still banged, and Michael explained with respectful dignity that he and his friend had felt a moral compulsion to provide for the prisoners some sort of barrister (and he looked regretfully at the nondescript and hangdog creature who went under that label) even as belatedly as this.

"Too late!" rumbled Lawes angrily. "Trial's all but over, damme! Out of the question to repeat it. Not worth it, anyway: cut and dried. The fellow can sit here for the rest of it if he likes, but the witnesses have been heard; I tell you, you're too late!"

And Rory's still face glared dauntingly at him, and Anne's was a pale mask, and Jade could feel her own turn to smooth wood, with a crooked little smile fixed where she had carefully set it. But her eyes glared green at Rory, almost hating him for having returned to life at this impossible moment. Rory blazed back, forbidding her to weaken, and Jade stiffened. As if she would! She'd show him!

Interminably the summary dragged on, saying nothing

that hadn't already been said. And at the end of it, Judge Lawes turned to the dock with terrible triumph.

"You've heard the evidence against you. Have you any defense to make?"

"No!" Four voices spoke in defiant unison, a great disappointment to those who had hoped to see them grovel abjectly. Michael looked quietly desperate, but Rory looked dourly at Jade, as unyielding as she. He'd have done the same.

"Hang 'em!" chanted the crowd. "Hang 'em!" bawled the mob outside.

"Have any of you any pleas to make!" Lawes asked them, almost hopefully. Jade and Anne, hands gripping in misery, regarded him with stony scorn. Mary looked bored and Vane amused.

But Jack, losing his nerve, mumbled hopelessly that he was sorry, and he'd never do it again; and Bixby indicated sheepishly that if anyone were to offer him mercy, he'd accept it. The others just stood sullenly, knowing it was no use.

And then Jade, to her own astonishment, heard herself speak.

"I want to plead for two people who—who can't plead for themselves."

There was instant silence, all eyes on her, breathing suspended. Judge Lawes leaned forward avidly, the seedy barrister tried to look alert, Rory's face was strained and challenging.

"It's—" Jade hesitated, felt herself blushing, was furious at herself for it. "It isn't for any of us—but—my Lord, if you hang Anne and Mary, you'll be murdering their—

their unborn babies. Surely they have a right to live, even if they can't speak yet."

Scarlet, she subsided in a stunned silence that turned at once to pandemonium. The town crier nearly fell out of the window. Lawes gobbled and goggled. Michael, mastering his emotion, spoke to the barrister with urgent intensity. Anne and Mary were whispering to Jade agitatedly, but she wasn't listening, for Rory smiled at her suddenly, and quite lit up the room. The Crown Prosecutors were in a huddle that reluctantly took in the seedy barrister. The crowd was nearly out of hand. The trial, in short, was in as remarkable a state of chaos as had ever been produced by one sentence from a seventeen-year-old girl.

Lawes, his face quite unutterably annoyed, finally emerged from conference with the chief prosecutor and slammed his gavel down as if he wished Jade were under it.

"Court adjourned!" he squawked. "This trial will be continued later. Return the prisoners to their cells!"

Then he put the gavel down, turned, and glared at Jade.

"You little devil!" he said, not without admiration.

CHAPTER TWENTY-TWO

"I Don't Envy You"

Anne paced the cell like a tigress, Mary chewed her knuckles, and Jade stood kicking the hapless wooden bench as if she could punish it for everything. For they had done a terrible thing between them, she and Rory and Michael. They had unleashed first the wish and then a tiny hope to go on living—with perfectly disastrous results. Calm acceptance had collapsed, and now the cell was filled with raging uncertainty, rampant longing, regret, fear, protest—all the emotions so long and carefully blocked out.

"I wish you hadn't!" said Mary wildly. "I don't want to live any longer; not without Tom!"

Jade looked at her bitterly. "Well, I do—and I can't!" she spat, and then her anger fell apart. "I'm sorry," she muttered, forlorn. "I was only trying to help."

"Shame, Mary!" snapped Anne, and Mary turned, remorseful.

"Forgive me, Jade! I didn't mean that; you know I didn't. You've given our babies a chance to live—and nothing for yourself. There aren't any words." She came over to Jade and gave her a quick affectionate hug, and said no more. There was no more to be said. It hung in the air.

"I wish it had been Tom who came back instead of Rory," said Jade desolately.

There was no answer to that, either—unless one counted the faint clang of the door above, and then familiar footsteps and two familiar faces at the bars.

"Michael!" Anne flew to him, laughing and sobbing and reaching her fingers through to meet his. Mary came smiling to greet them. But Jade stood still. She and Rory searched each other's faces with fierce wonder. No word of love had ever passed between them, nor had they ever intended such a thing.

They looked at Anne and Michael, still babbling endearments. They looked at each other again, consciously superior.

"Hullo," said Rory gruffly. Their fingers touched through the bars. They glowered.

"I must say," Jade observed waspily, "you've picked a fine time to rise from the dead! Now you've got me right back in the mood for living again."

"And you would have to try to defend that silly sloop single-handed!" he retorted with acrimony. "How can we convince anyone that you're a poor delicate little victim of circumstances who wouldn't hurt a fly?"

Jade managed a small chuckle. "What happened to you?" she demanded, moving over to make more room for Mary between herself and Anne. (Poor Mary, left out of the reunion, looked as if she more pitied than envied the rest of them—and perhaps she was right.) "We hunted and hunted, and there was nothing but bits of ship and a few bodies! Are Joshua and Domino—"

"Safe, too," he growled, and Jade found herself smiling

happily. "They're here in Port Royal, too, posing as our slaves and staying right in our rooms in case anyone should recognize them."

Jade frowned. "Are you sure it's safe?"

"Safer than you are," he retorted curtly.

This was unanswerable. "Well, what did happen to you?" she asked again, and Mary, coughing, nodded.

"When *Queen Royal* broke up, about a dozen of us managed to get in one of the longboats and more or less stay afloat," he said simply. "The hurricane tossed us ashore in the wildest bit of jungle I've ever seen, and it's taken ever since to patch ourselves up and get back to St. Catherine's and then here. No trouble finding out where you were, anyway." He regarded her sourly. "Everyone's talking about the female pirates. Especially about Anne, of course."

Anne had stopped babbling and was looking scared. "Michael! What if they should suspect you?"

"Now calm down," he said gently. "No one will. And if they did, there's no evidence."

"And pirates don't inform on each other," Mary reminded her. Anne relaxed. This was perhaps the first rule of the Brotherhood of Pirates; not even Jack and his cronies would break it . . . particularly when it could gain them nothing.

"We only arrived last night," said Michael. "Had a terrible time getting even that wretched cur of a barrister, Thrumpton; the others won't touch your case. But we'll turn Jamaica upside down to get you three reprieved."

There was a moment's silence. They all looked at Jade. She shook her head. "Not me," and she managed to sound unconcerned, through the lump in her chest, and even to shrug and smile. "It's all right; I—"

"Shut up," said Rory crossly, and he and Michael began to explain their plans for arousing public sympathy (Jade snorted at that), get up petitions, and generally bring pressure on the governor.

It was a feeble enough hope, and they all knew it, but nobody said so. Easier not to—although Rory's eyes were hagged with the knowledge and raging at the prudent part he must play. Better even her shoes than his, Jade realized with a stab of compassion.

"We've talked to a Doctor Hughes," said Michael, filling the pause. "He's sympathetic to you, and very much annoyed about this dungeon you're in. I see his point." His face was taut. "It's a foul place—and in your condition, too! A terrible health hazard! I'll go tell the governor at once."

"Dr. Hughes already did," Jade broke in irrepressibly. "Only Governor Lawes said it wasn't for long, and the noose would be an even worse health hazard."

Michael looked outraged, but Rory chuckled reluctantly, and Jade twinkled back. A good quip was a good quip, even when it was on them. She wished she'd thought of it first, herself.

For a few days there was intolerable suspense. The doctors consulted the Chief Prosecutor, who sighed and advised the governor to reprieve Anne and Mary until after their babies were born.

Lawes, agreeing with great reluctance, saw no reason at all to include Jade in this—which didn't surprise Jade in the least. Their encounters of late had been spiced with rather more malice than usual.

"They're re-trying you and the men tomorrow," Rory told her that evening, his voice expressionless.

Jade nodded, impassive. It was what she'd expected, wasn't it? And if the sour taste of fear was suddenly in her mouth, making it hard to speak or swallow, the more reason not to show a trace of it. Not just for the sake of her pride and her code—but also for her friends, who felt bad enough as it was, and above all for Rory.

"Well, it's one way of getting out of this cell." Amazing that her voice could come out so nonchalant. Michael swore softly, and Rory's fingers hurt her cold ones. "You'll be there?" she went on deliberately casual. "I'm twice me when you're around."

His eyes burned; his voice was as matter-of-fact as hers. "Oh, aye; I'll be there. If they sentence you, they'll just have to hang me, too," he added almost apologetically, as if the thing were far too obvious to need saying.

"Yes," said Jade, and found she'd known it all along.

But Anne turned sharply. Anne was in love with life again, for everyone else as well as herself, and she'd have died ten times to keep her Michael alive once.

"What d'you mean to do?" she demanded of Rory.

He laughed. "Och, just stand up and demand my rights as a pirate."

Anne raged at him. Rory showed her his most inscrutable face, and looked at Jade quizzically. Anne turned on Jade.

"Are you going to let him throw his life away?"

"Yes," said Jade placidly. "And he'd let me. And neither of us could stop the other, anyhow."

Michael—being a doctor—looked pained, but Mary smiled, understanding perfectly that neither Jade nor Rory feared to die, but only for either to leave the other alone in an alien and infuriating world.

"Well, we're going to try to get you off," said Michael. "Tell her our plan of argument, Rory; I'm going along to talk to Vane and Jack, and then see if I can batter some sort of intelligence into Thrumpton. He's got to word things exactly right."

"What things?" demanded Jade, beginning to bristle. "I won't beg, you know. And I won't lie the way Besneck and—"

"Of course not, daft loon," said Rory tolerantly. "Now hold your tongue and listen."

Again the courtroom was packed, but with a crowd of a slightly different mood, for the intensive propaganda of the past few days had not been altogether without effect. Besides, their pet hate Anne Bonney wasn't here on trial today.

Heads craned as the file of shackled prisoners came in, and attention centered this time on the only female—the little French she-wolf who'd broken up the last trial so neatly and dramatically . . . and not even to her own benefit, either, as that hawk-faced young fellow had been pointing out.

There she was—looking very small and forlorn and valiant amid all those burly unshaved pirates. A few of the women began to develop distinct symptoms of maternal sympathy. Some of the eyes once so avid to see her broken and hanged now held traces of favor—even of pity (which would have wounded Jade's pride severely had she known). They nudged each other, noting that she seemed even skinnier than before, and had a new shadow on her pointy face, but she could still trade quips with the hecklers and laugh about her own execution! A game 'un she was and all, keeping her head up that way. And so young: no older'n our Sukey.

Only sixteen or seventeen, 'twas said. Came from a fine aristocratic family, 'twas said. Kidnapped by the pirates, 'twas said.

Proud little vixen! Never pleaded for herself, did she? No, nor wouldn't neither. Bets were laid at once, and then more bets on whether she'd cry. Looking pretty worn, wa'n't she? Pity, 'twas. Some folks were saying around town that 'twere only fair to reprieve her at least as long as them other females. . . .

Jade wasn't aware of all this; only of the usual hecklers, which her tongue could handle almost without thought while her eyes searched for Rory. This second trial failed to arouse her love of battle; it was too much of an anti-climax. Instead she felt rather as Mary did these days: remote and detached and unreal. It was a state of mind that lacked zest.

There was Rory, carefully apart from Michael lest he incriminate him, as near as he could get to the dock, and smouldering at her in a manner altogether heartening—although some people might fail to find much comfort in thick scowling black brows and a ferocious mouth. Jade thought him beautiful.

She took her place in the dock again, this time between Vane and poor shaking Jack, who stared around with hunted eyes. Judge Lawes peered down at her with his old genial malignance. Triumph rode his smile. Jade returned it with a high chin and even a touch of mischief. For, one way or another, Lawes still had a surprise or two coming to him.

The resumé of the first trial was short and decisive. There seemed nothing left but to declare them guilty and pass sentence. And then the seedy barrister who rejoiced in the name of Thrumpton rose sheepishly to his feet.

"May it please Y'r Honor, before testimony is finished I'd—er—like to question the girl—er—Jade Loupin."

He was certainly not much of a barrister, said Rory's expression dourly. The crowd leaned forward expectantly, hoping for a new sensation. Lawes raised a thin eyebrow and nodded with an air of martyred patience. A waste of time, it was clear.

Thrumpton shuffled his feet nervously, and turned to Jade.

"Is it true, Mistress Loupin, that when you were—uh—aboard the pirate ship you—uh—refused to take part in piracy?" he asked with the air of someone grasping at straws.

Jade felt rather the same way herself. She regarded him with antagonism.

"Sometimes," she admitted as grudgingly as if it were a crime to refuse to take part in piracy. "If they were just helpless merchant ships. Except, *voyons*, after the storm, when we were very much hungry," she added, remembering her accent.

Vane gleamed down at her, amused, and Lawes looked unimpressed.

"But before the storm—" Thrumpton managed to produce a note of dramatic passion that set Jade's teeth on edge. "Before that, you refused! You were too noble, too honest, too gentle and ladylike to have anything to do with piracy!"

He had gone much too far, made it ludicrous! Jade hesitated—met Rory's helpless eyes—was lost.

"Actually," she said deflatingly, "it was merely that those were not the people whom I *wished* to kill."

The crowd guffawed and the crier shouted. Michael—just visible behind the lawyer—looked furious, and Rory inscrutable, and Lawes spiderishly amused. Thrumpton lost his head and dropped his sheaf of notes in the same instant.

"But isn't it true you were taken aboard against your will? No, I mean—" He'd worded it the wrong way. He pawed his notes, stammering. "I mean taken aboard without your consent?"

Judge Lawes looked deeply suspicious. "What *do* you mean?" He looked questioningly at Jade, who lapsed suddenly into mulish silence. It was Michael's idea, this tack, and a blatant attempt to stir up maudlin sentiment for her. She couldn't go through with it. Besides being shockingly undignified, she saw more clearly than ever that it was useless and irrelevant.

"Well, Mistress Loupin?"

She shook her head mutely, let her eyes pass over the despairing Michael, apologetically seeking Rory and his wry but unastonished grin.

The crowd buzzed, scenting mystery. Lawes rapped, scowled. "The prisoner is directed to answer."

Jade grinned at him defiantly, having nothing to lose. The crowd booed her, but with a faint note of approval. And then Charles Vane cleared his throat.

"Mistress Loupin doubtless prefers not to speak of that day," he said, so accurately that Jade tilted an indignant cropped head to stare at him reproachfully. "I understand that she was indeed taken aboard without her consent."

Jade found his toe and stamped on it vengefully but not very effectively. He smiled down at her. The judge demanded to know what he was talking about.

Then Bixby roused himself. "She were unconscious," he announced. "Been flogged, she 'ad."

Speechless silence for an instant, even from the town crier gaping from the window sill.

"In the name of heaven, why?" demanded the astonished governor, staring at Jade's sullen face.

"I loosed some slaves," she informed him aggressively, hating this. "And I'm not sorry, either." She felt pierced by eyes. Better their hate than their pity!

"Hmm!" The judge's blue button eyes regarded her with uncomfortable shrewdness, turned to Thrumpton. "What's all this got to do with the charge?"

"Uh—" The barrister shuffled his notes, flustered. "If she—er—If it was without her consent—"

Lawes silenced him with a contemptuous glance, turned to Jade. "Did you consent willingly to become a pirate?" he asked, coming to the heart of the matter. And Jade rose almost gratefully to the challenge.

"Yes, I did!"

In the heavy silence Thrumpton sat down, a broken reed. One could almost hear the clash of figurative rapiers between Jade and the judge, almost see his point at her throat.

"Have you any more pleas to make, Mistress Loupin?"

The crowd held its breath. Bets were hanging on this

moment. For an instant Jade was back in Williamsburg, with Father inviting her to back down rather than take another beating. She jutted her chin, stared back at him in unyielding silence and with the small lopsided smile by habit on her still face. A sigh swept the court.

"Then I sentence all of you to hang by your necks until you are dead," said Lawes with infinite satisfaction.

Rory, poised, at once shoved forward purposefully, demanding equal treatment. But his voice was drowned by the sudden growl of a mob discovering that they had after all, a soft spot for the French wench. "Reprieve!" shouted someone, and the word was picked up. "Reprieve for the girl! Treat her like the other females!"

For an appointed governor, Lawes had an extraordinarily strong sense of political expediency. One might almost have thought he'd been prepared for this, for he instantly banged his gavel with an air of a man interrupted in mid-sentence.

"Silence!" he bawled. "Or I'll clear the court!" And when order once more prevailed, he resumed as if he had never paused at all. "I further declare that the hanging of the male pirates shall take place three days from now, on November 28, and that the girl Loupin shall remain imprisoned with the other female pirates to be hanged at the court's pleasure."

Jade stood still, dazed and vaguely depressed. Rory, halted in his tracks, turned baffled eyes to hers. And Vane smiled down at her wryly.

"Well, I don't envy you, girl. It's having your tail cut off an inch at a time. Better to have it over."

And Jade was strongly inclined to agree.

CHAPTER TWENTY-THREE

Mary's Escape

The sound of feet and the clash of fetters in the corridor brought three somber faces to their cell door on the morning of November 28. Heavily guarded and chained, the little procession would have clanked on past but that Vane brought it firmly to a halt, wearing a look of exasperation that fitted ill with a man about to be hanged.

"For heaven's sake, Anne, see if you can talk some courage into Jack!" he said curtly and fixed a commanding eye on the about-to-protest jailors. "You're not going to deny the poor man a last word with Mistress Bonney, are you?" he asserted, so reasonably that the protest died unspoken. In any case, it was quite clear that without something potent Calico Jack would probably have to be carried to Gallows Hill. He was ashen and shaking, and he looked at the three faces in the cell as if he didn't recognize them.

Pity and contempt fought in Anne's voice. "Lud's blood, man, pull yourself together!" she said impatiently. "The least you can do is go out there and die with your head up!"

He shivered, in the grip of sheer panic. "You can talk big now, but when it's your turn—"

"When it's our turn we'll laugh in their faces," retorted Anne, "and you know it. Where's your pride, Jack?"

But that, Jade suddenly realized, was precisely his trouble. He'd never had any pride; only conceit, which never yet produced courage. He looked at Anne blindly.

"But I'm going to die *now*," he bleated in piteous terror.

"And serve you right!" Mary broke in, still unforgiving. "If you'd fought like a man six weeks ago, you wouldn't be about to die like a dog now." And she turned a pitiless back on him—the more pitiless, perhaps, because it was really just as well Tom had been killed that day, and saved from this.

Jack looked like a kicked puppy. Anne shrugged helplessly. But Jade suddenly felt herself in Jack's skin, reliving that dreadful night on the *Pearl*. By the narrowest of margins she had kept from breaking; who was she to judge Jack? Moreover, she had discovered something in those hours of fear. . . .

"Jack!" she said quickly. "I'll tell you the secret! It's all a big act! Courage is nothing but pretending you aren't scared when you really are."

He was looking at her doubtfully, but at least with focussed eyes. She pressed her point.

"You can act it as well as anyone. You're Calico Jack Rackam, remember? Be a bold pirate and a dashing hero; die proudly and bravely; think of a joke to make at the very last." Jack flinched at this, but he had an air of dawning discovery. Jade put a thrill into her voice. "Play to the audience, Jack! Make them admire and envy your courage! Give them something to remember!"

He gripped the bars, stuck his haggard face close to

hers, staring with a kind of hungry hope. "Is that what you do? You've been pretending all along? Have you?"

"Of course! Everybody does!" But he was only half persuaded. Jade set her teeth and pretended she didn't loathe confessing her own weakness. "D'you think I don't *know?* You can be so scared you're choking to death from it, and still fool them! When I was waiting to be flogged—" Her voice quavered slightly, and she broke off, deeply mortified.

But it was the most convincing thing she could have done. Jack knew all about that episode; the recruits from the *Pearl* had told the story often enough, and with graphic detail. Jack had enviously supposed Jade to be a creature unfairly born without nerves. But if it was all an act, after all. . . .

He took a deep breath and straightened his shoulders. "Yes," he said. "All right." And he took his place quite steadily at Vane's side. The guards stopped leaning against the walls and looked alert.

Vane smiled. "Au revoir—and good luck."

The file clanked up the stairs and was gone, leaving a long long silence behind.

Jade stood still for many minutes, forehead pressed against the bars, feeling drained of everything. Vane had been right: better to have it over. Better to be free from this terrible damp dungeon and out under the hot sun, wits and pride and courage all rising to meet the last danger of all. She visualized it, and felt nothing except that it would be a splendid dramatic scene to be played to the hilt, like a Greek tragedy, but soon and finally over. Looked at like that, it wasn't at all a bad death; not at all.

She turned slowly to face the bleak dimness of the cell

and the painful wheeze of Mary's breathing, and Anne's ferociously bad temper. Six months more of it to be endured—and with a noose at the end, after all.

"I wish I were with them!" she said violently.

"Hold your tongue, crybaby!" snarled Anne.

They were ready to kill themselves or each other when Michael and Rory finally came. Rory was looking savage, himself, and Michael's forced manner didn't fool anyone.

"They were all magnificent," he reported, holding Anne's hands through the bars. "Even Jack. Do you know what he did? He not only got hold of himself and faced it like a man—"

"Or woman," growled Rory, insisting on fair play for the sexes.

Michael ignored the interruption. "He actually stood up there and pleaded for *your* lives to be spared! Said you suffered enough. Brave and dignified as a lion, he was, Anne; you'd have been proud of him."

"I'm glad," said Anne softly into the stretching silence.

And nothing more was said, and the men went off to protest once more about the cell and Mary's worsening health, and pass petitions among the possibly-softened Jamaicans.

The days dragged now. Few people even came to taunt them any more, for the novelty had worn off. Jade would have welcomed any number of malevolent faces against those blank bars, or almost anything at all to vary the monotony. And the only outlet for her driving energy was her self-taught acrobatics, which she practiced by the hour, even though it made her cellmates snappish and irritable.

Then even that had to stop, for Mary was really ill. Michael argued and shouted at the governor in vain; Lawes said callously that it was just a trick to get luxuries, and they *deserved* to be uncomfortable, and he'd have Michael and Rory jailed too if they didn't stop pestering him. Even Dr. Hughes failed to be convinced that there was anything very wrong. A bit of an ague, he said, and a wonder they weren't all three in a much worse state—especially Anne and Mary—considering everything.

But less than a week after the execution, Jade and Anne awoke one morning to find Mary talking to Tom, in high delirium.

The jailor, summoned, went reluctantly up to report it. In a short time Dr. Hughes arrived, and Mary was borne off to the infirmary, still babbling endearments. But as they picked her up, she stopped prattling, opened eyes that looked remarkably rational, and fixed them on Anne.

"I'm going to escape," she remarked conversationally but with determination.

And she did. A few hours later Dr. Hughes came down to tell them that Mary was dead. Anne buried wet cheeks in her hands, but Jade stared straight ahead, seeing nothing.

"I'm glad," she said stonily.

Governor Lawes visited them early the next morning, furious with Mary for having slipped through his fingers, and apparently harboring a dark suspicion that she'd done it on purpose and for spite . . . Perhaps in a way, she had.

Jade and Anne, grateful for the dimness that hid their reddened eyes, at once began coughing pointedly, and announced their firm intention of following suit.

And Lawes, suspecting that he was being manipulated but not daring to call the bluff, angrily had them transferred to an upstairs barracks room, barred—but with a window!

Light and air and warmth! Impossible not to bask in it! Impossible to grieve very long or deeply for Mary, who had never since Tom's death wanted to live, anyway—and whom they were to follow. Impossible to dwell on their own postponed executions, far off and insignificant. Their spirits soared; they nearly fought over occupation of the window with its view of the sea and the shaft of yellow sunlight that flowed in daily. How could they ever have taken for granted the heavenly blessing of sunshine?

But within a few days Jade plunged into deep and utter gloom. As always, her valor forsook her when she no longer faced a crisis. She couldn't bear being caged! She wanted wildly to be at sea again, a cobalt sea misted with frost-white spray of sundrift, and the wind humming in the rigging and masts swooping with the dance of the ship. Six months more of this would kill her! . . . Literally, she remembered with bitter humor.

Like a ferocious young leopard she paced and snarled, snapped Anne's head off, swore at the jailors, refused her food, sulked at Lawes (who, deprived of his verbal duels, went off in the sullens, himself), smouldered at Rory and even at Joshua and Domino when he brought them to cheer her up, and finally lapsed into brooding silence.

She was not whining. But she couldn't help her thoughts. And it seemed to her that it had all been useless. The world was ugly and unjust, and would never be any better, and it was a waste of effort to fight for anything—or even against anything. Her own life had served only to make her family unhappy, and it would be better if she had never lived at all.

Rory hadn't discovered this yet, was not yet tired of fighting man, God, and the devil. He and Michael were engaged in a passionate and tireless campaign for her life and Anne's. None of them believed it could succeed, but as Anne remarked wisely to Jade, "It makes them feel better to think they're keeping our hopes up. Besides, they have to do something, poor dears."

The something bore some fruit, at least, in the form of a petition signed by all the important planters and doctors in the area that Anne be allowed to take daily walks for the sake of her health.

And so the notorious pirate queen appeared again to the fascinated citizens of Port Royal, no longer shackled, but escorted by two guards, Michael, and an assortment of journalists and pamphleteers hardly able to believe their eyes and ears. This was Anne Bonney? This gentle and sedate young lady dressed so demurely in a new contouche of puritan brown which had been given her (and which made a magnificent setting for that bright hair, now in a smooth knot in back)? Mistress Bonney walked with a subdued meekness that was altogether disarming. Mistress Bonney did most heartily repent of all her evil ways. Mistress Bonney, said the pamphlets (which sounded suspiciously like Michael's style) had put down the demon within her, and would die before committing again any offense against the laws of God or man.

Which, as Jade observed sardonically, was *perfectly* true.

Anne Bonney, whispered Jamaica, was clearly a reformed character. But what of the little French vixen, they asked each other? Whispers swept the town—mostly started by Rory (who was developing a great talent for dramatic and tear-jerking propaganda) and helped on by Michael and even Joshua. She was ill, 'twas said. Dying, like Mary Read, poor soul. Broken at last by imprisonment and humiliation. Pity, 'twas. Spunky little thing she'd been. . . .

Jade wouldn't have cared terribly had she known. She forced herself to get up and dress and go through the empty routine of eating and listening to progress reports and pretending a kind of cheerful cynicism. After all, she owed that much to her self-respect; and anyway, it was surely part of the bargain to pay the piper with a smile. Even a pinched, crooked little smile that didn't fool anybody. . . .

And all the time, under the smile, she was drowning in bleak despair that was really almost worse than the black fear of the *Pearl*, or the weeks when she thought Rory was dead, and far worse than the pain of the flogging. Pain and fear and grief could be absorbed, or buried, or conquered. But endless dreary hopelessness. . . .

And then at last Rory's voice broke through it. "It isn't enough."

She focused her mind again, saw the hot sunlight edging the window, and Anne across the room talking with Michael and the ineffectual Thrumpton, and Rory standing looking down at her. He was gray and grim from the strain of trying to save her life in all directions at once, and the anger was almost drained out of him.

"What?" she asked huskily.

"I said, it isn't enough, is it? Courage, I mean. By itself it's just useless heroics."

Jade looked at him for a long time. It was true. And it didn't make her feel any better. "What, then?"

"I don't know." His face was more than ever like something carved with a dull knife—but under the weariness there was still purpose and intelligence and determination. He'd never be defeated! Jade sat a little straighter while he groped after an idea. "Something—that gives reason and purpose to courage?"

"Like reforming the world?" Her voice was bitter and low.

Rory's eyes had begun to gleam with that sardonic amusement of his. "Perhaps the world's just a wee bit big to take on," he suggested blandly.

"Then there's no use in anything! Are we supposed just to close our eyes and let things like cruelty and injustice go on happening, and not even try to *do* anything? Well, I won't play those rules, and if that's what God wants, I won't—mfffgh!"

Rory had placed his horny palm firmly over her mouth. "Shut up and stop fighting God," he ordered her kindly. "In the first place it's no use, and in the second place I don't think He's fighting back, and in the third place I think it's really yourself you're fighting in the first place. Whose good opinion really matters most to you, anyway?"

he challenged her, as she jerked her head away, glaring.

"Mine!" she sputtered.

"Aye. And quite right," he agreed surprisingly. "And your own good opinion says you have to try to do something about the awful way humans treat humans. But—" His eyebrows slanted, self-mocking. "Could it be you and I have taken ourselves a bit too seriously? Could it be we've even been a wee bit conceited, going out to reform the world and not stopping to think that we might need to reform ourselves first?"

Jade blazed. "Well, I like that! If we—" She stopped. She frowned. She thought about it. "Oh," she said doubtfully, and looked several questions at Rory. "Do you suppose we're being punished for that Greek thing in their plays? The one that meant arrogant pride, and always came to a fall?" It was a shattering thought.

"I don't know anything about Greek, but I don't think God punishes us. I think He just lets His Law take its course. I think He has just one Law, that sooner or later, in this world or another, everybody reaps just exactly what he's sowed. And I think the whole purpose of life is to learn some wisdom and courage from it."

He looked slightly astonished at himself, as if he hadn't really known he believed all that until he heard himself saying it. Jade, deeply impressed, digested it for a while.

"What good will it do us to learn wisdom if we both hang?" she asked, more as a point of argument than anything.

Rory grinned. "You've got it backwards. What does it matter whether we hang, if we've learned a little wisdom?"

Jade took a deep breath. Nothing had really changed—and yet everything was different. She was somehow coming through the gray fog and finding that there was light on the other side, and a new kind of serenity. She felt much better—well enough to launch into a spirited argument.

"Well, but what about the slaves? I don't believe they did sow slavery, especially the babies. And even if they did, God just *couldn't* want people to turn their backs and not care. You can't just sit there and not even try to do something—and I'm glad we let those slaves loose, and I'd do it again tomorrow, and I do wish we could have been pirates who only pirated slavers."

Something sparked between them. "Aye," said Rory, grinning briefly. "But not taking ourselves too seriously, mind."

Jade nodded. She smiled at him.

"I'm hungry," she decided.

CHAPTER TWENTY-FOUR

The Decision

Jade was herself again. She ate enormously, squabbled with Anne for the patch of sunshine, argued with Rory, teased Joshua and Domino when they visited, did acrobatics, and renewed the duel with Governor Lawes. She was also allowed to join Anne in her daily walks, and was anything but demure and subdued—to the delight of at least some of the townspeople.

"For heaven's sake!" Michael expostulated. "I'm trying to convince Jamaica that you're both reformed characters!"

"I'm not," said the unrepentant Jade, and added a couple of French swear words to prove it.

"I know you're not," retorted the harassed Michael. "But at least try to pretend you are—for Anne's sake if not your own. Rory, can't you do anything with that atrocious little wildcat?"

Rory just grinned and produced a pair of cerise breeches and a white silk shirt, made for a boy, but quite passable for the slim-hipped Jade.

"By the way," he reported with enjoyment. "Some of the other pirate captains have sent threatening letters to

Governor Lawes. Especially Bartholomew Roberts. He says that he'll attack every port in Jamaica if Anne isn't set free."

"Good heavens," said Anne feebly. "We've never even *met!*"

"Loyalty of the Brotherhood," observed Rory with wry amusement. "I must say he's got more guns than tact. Lawes is furious."

"We know," Jade chuckled. "He was in an awful temper this morning when he visited."

She was thinking about Lawes on the morning of Christmas Eve as she practiced handstands in her lovely cerise breeches. The governor seemed to be bewildered as well as furious of late, staring at Anne with an expression of aggrieved frustration while she sat quietly across the room and let Jade do all the fighting.

Jade glanced over, from her heels-over-head position, at the window where her cell-mate sewed tiny garments, wearing the gentlest of dreamy smiles. And Jade's memory produced with startling vividness a series of pictures. . . . Anne in a violent temper, her face murderous. Anne armed to the teeth and splashed with blood, leading a yelling horde of bare-chested pirates to board a hapless merchant ship. Anne boldly putting the ship between the guns of two Spanish warships. Anne shooting Rafferty down in cold blood, and then laughing in the face of imminent retribution . . .

The handstand sagged. Jade righted herself and stared again at this new Anne. No wonder Lawes was so upset! The pirate queen he hated didn't exist any more! Instead, this—this—

"I never *heard* of anyone changing as much as you have!" she announced with profound disapproval.

"Nor have I," agreed Anne, clearly pleased with herself. "It was loving Michael that did it. Now I'd want nothing more than to be a good wife and mother, and the whole idea of piracy revolts me."

She looked unbelievably virtuous, utterly smug. Jade peered at her with suspicion, and then shook her head.

"They might just as well let you go free," she said, disgusted. "Even Williamsburg would approve of you now. You've got no spunk left."

Anne laughed, then winked shamelessly. The jailor had just sauntered down to the far end of the corridor. "Don't be too sure of that, young Jade." The jailor was turning, coming back. "And you've changed, too, you know."

"I haven't!" Jade stared, indignant. "*I* haven't repented everything, and turned into a sweet proper young lady, and all that. Anyway, Rory wouldn't like it if I did."

"No. But you're twice the person you were, all the same. I can't explain how, but there's more to you. You aren't quite as cock-sure and intolerant, and you've even got a tiny bit of humility. Not much, mind, but some. And would you want to go back to piracy?"

For an instant Jade was aboard a ship, with wind driving across sapphire seas to belly the sails, and flying fish skimming off in a panic before them. . . . She caught her breath in an anguish of longing; then thrust the picture deep down in the well where fear lay buried. She daren't even think about it. Instead, she closed her face and launched herself so ferociously into another handstand that it went on over into a backbend.

A guard's voice interrupted her inverted reverie. "Governor Lawes wants you both brought to see him in half an hour."

This unusual command caused Jade to remain perversely upside down for a moment, to think about it and to annoy the guard. But he went on talking, more puzzled than irritated.

"And there's a man here says he's Mistress Loupin's grandfather."

Jade, just about to start the difficult business of turning the backbend into a handstand, paused to consider this remarkable statement. Both of her grandfathers had been dead for years, and of course neither had ever been related to anyone named Loupin.

"Couldn't be," she decided with finality.

"But of course I should have known very well that I should find you *sens dessus dessous*, with down side up," said a familiar voice. "How else? And how else should I have recognized you, *ma petite-fille*, my so-wicked Jade?"

Jade instantly collapsed to the floor, righted herself, scrambled to her feet, and hurled herself at the barred door.

"Monsieur Mau– Mon Grandpère!" she yelped, correcting herself just in time and staring with incredulous eyes at the self-possessed and exquisitely dressed figure of Monsieur Maupin, actually standing there smiling at her.

"*Ma foi!*" he said, astonished. "How you are different!" He walked through the door that the guard obligingly opened for him, and bowed to Anne with delight and reverence. "And this is the so-great Lady Pirate whom I very much admire! Do not hang your mouth open in that way, *petite* Jade; it makes you to look amusing but very much stupid."

Jade pulled herself together. "How— How did you know?" she demanded. "Does Father—" She could not go on, just stared pleadingly, as if he could choose whether or not her family knew.

"*Non, non,*" he assured her instantly, and she let out an enormous gust of breath. "No one questions at all that you are, *hélas*, drowned at sea."

"But then how did you guess? How did you get here? What—"

He laughed at her, his old faded eyes twinkling. "*Ma chère petite fille*, how could I not to know? I am not your father, me; I understand you very well; moreover I could not make myself feel you dead of a mere storm. And when I heard of a very young audacious female pirate, who has the name, *enfin*, of Jade Loupin, I asked of myself who else could it possibly be? But I did not say this to your family, who have long ago forgotten the old nickname." He cocked his bald head. "I thought you would not like it that they know, or you would have given your real name and sent them a message. Moreover, I think that it would not be a kindness to them if you were to resurrect yourself, *non?*"

"Yes, that's what I thought, too," said Jade wistfully. His presence caused her to be smitten with the most dreadful wave of longing for them all—for the porcelain primness of Lavinia, and the ebullience of Matthew, and Mother's plaintive sweet voice, and even Father's exasperated frown. She set her lips and stared for a moment at the blurred floor, before the painful memories could be pushed back down the well. Then she stiffened her shoulders.

"Did they– Were they very sad about me drowning?" And she didn't really know whether to hope that they were or weren't.

"But of course," he said gently. "How not? Moreover, being human, they at once discovered virtues in you that no one ever suspected before. Now Melanie begins to be a legend–which is, *voyons*, much more easy to live with than Jade in the flesh. Matthew, I think, will step a little into your shoes, and begins more and more to challenge convention, a thing which your sister disapproves."

He waited tactfully, smiling at Anne, while Jade once again got her homesickness in hand.

"And you came all this way?" asked Anne, staring.

"*Mais oui;* what else?" He shrugged, nodded. "But I was very much afraid that I would be too late–" The remark hung on the air awkwardly, a reminder of that death sentence. But the awkwardness died because none of them would give it tongue or recognition. Monsieur Maupin went on.

"I took passage to Charleston, and there I waited, cursing all ship's captains because none of them would to bring me to Jamaica, however much I demanded it. *Enfin* one of them said rudely that I had better buy a ship of my own–so I did." He beamed. "And, also, *mes petites*, while I was cursing and arguing and purchasing ships in Charleston, I was also doing another thing."

He paused dramatically, looking like a wicked elderly elf, so filled with glee that even Anne put down her sewing and leaned forward.

"What?" demanded Jade, a trifle breathless.

"I met a man who knows well the famous Anne Bonney,

and who said to me with much regret that he once treated her unjustly, and that she twice rendered him great service which he now wishes much to repay."

He had his audience. The honey head and the red one were frozen in attention. He beamed at them.

"He gave to me a letter, this man, and desired that I should deliver it to this Governor Lawes who so much likes to hang pirates. It is a plea that he should set free this valiant young woman who saved New Providence first from a plot by one Chidley Bayard—*mon dieu* what a name!—and then from a Spanish invasion."

"Governor Rogers!" yelped Anne, her eyes shining.

"*Mais oui*, that one. He has a fine regard for you. And this pouter pigeon Governor Lawes was in solitude with that so-splendid letter for two hours, after which he sent for me again and also for some other people whose names I did not recognize, and for you. I think he is very much annoyed, that one. We will see what he will do, *non?* It is very difficult for him, *voyons*, because he is a man wishing to run in two directions at once; and also because I have remarked, oh very casually, you understand, that if he should hang my granddaughter, I shall take my fast little sloop which I have named *Sea Wolf* in honor of my new name, and harry the coast of Jamaica with it. I think he did not *quite* believe me, but he is worried, which is most wise of him, for I mean it."

And his affable smile took in both girls and the bemused guard as well.

Anne began to laugh helplessly.

Governor Lawes awaited them in his small reception room.

"Sit down," he said curtly, and let them wait in brooding silence until a servant announced that Dr. Radcliffe and Mr. MacDonald and the barrister Mr. Thrumpton had arrived. Then he kept them in more silence until Jade could hardly bear the suspense, and remained silent only because Rory on one side and Monsieur Maupin on the other both jabbed her with their elbows.

Governor Lawes was scowling at Anne alone now, with the disgruntled wrath of one whose heart is, unaccountably, no longer in it. He felt bereft.

"If I let you go," he said at last, ponderously, "would you solemnly swear to leave your evil ways and become a decent, law-abiding woman for as long as you live?"

Anne gaped, speechless. She had never seriously imagined—hadn't dared to hope—that this might happen. She nodded, dazed.

There was another long silence. The governor clearly was trying to recover his satisfying sense of vindictive hatred, but was unable to work up anything stronger than mild irritation combined with a most annoying tendency to like the woman! He looked challengingly at Michael, who at once put his arm around Anne.

"I can promise you that, sir," he said tensely. "I'll take any oath you like!"

He was so eminently a sober, respectable professional man, and Anne turned on him such a loving and submissive look that Lawes was visibly shaken. He cleared his throat, very judicial.

"And you'll take her right away from the West Indies and never let her near me again?" he persisted with the fretful air of a Jonah addressing a whale-keeper.

"We'll vanish in oblivion!" swore Michael, holding up a

dramatic hand. "We'll disappear into the wilds of Virginia or somewhere and never be heard of again. If Anne gets the urge to do any more fighting, I'll turn her loose on the Indians."

Rory grunted angrily. His eyes met Jade's. If they went west, they knew which side they'd be on! Lawes looked at him doubtfully. He found Mr. MacDonald daunting. Always had. He turned his attention pointedly to the fictitious Monsieur Loupin.

"As for this deplorable young descendent of yours, will you keep her out of my wig?" he demanded.

"*Mais oui!*" Monsieur Maupin spread his hands eloquently. "Have I not said so? Is it not that I have come just to take her from your wig? I shall at once remove her to my ship." He looked every inch a fine gentleman, from the gleaming silver buckles on his shoes to the delicate lace jabot and ruffles at neck and wrists. "Imagine to yourself how she will become a sweet and gentle young lady, well trained by her family or perhaps a convent."

Governor Lawes looked pitying. He strongly doubted this.

"Just don't bring her to Jamaica again," he grumbled, carefully avoiding Jade's impudent green eyes. Confound if he wouldn't miss the little vixen! Galled at this whole process of giving up the vengeance he no longer wanted, he made a long and baleful speech at them, reducing the unfortunate Thrumpton to timorous nods, and not affecting the others at all.

And at the end of it, bewilderingly, they were free.

The *Sea Wolf* moved gently at anchor, restless to be flying over the sea again, and Jade's heart leaped with it.

The small salon was crowded with the rejoicing company. Joshua hovered near Jade with tears in his eyes, and even Domino, smiling widely, refused to be pried from her side.

Jade, giddy with disbelief, leaned affectionately against the shapely black arm, and then twisted her head to glance up at Monsieur Maupin reproachfully.

"You don't really mean to try to make a sweet gentle lady of me?" she challenged him, outraged.

"*Mais non;* I said that because it was the thing he very much wished to hear, so that he should have a good excuse to release you. What wicked thing is it you want to do instead, my Jade?"

Anne raised an alert head from Michael's shoulder. "Now stop encouraging her, you incorrigible old man!" she scolded. "We're reformed characters now, Jade and I; we promised."

"Speak for yourself," said Rory, grinning like a wolf.

Michael sat straight up in alarm. "She did! She promised—" He stopped, remembering.

"*I* didn't promise anything," said Jade, demure.

"A technicality," Michael argued, but doubtfully. "If someone promises for you—"

"Me, I promised only to keep her out of his wig," said Monsieur Maupin happily. "And also to take her away on my ship. These things I will do. Now it is only to decide where we shall go, *non?*"

"Back to the mainland of America," said Michael firmly. "I've got it all decided. We'll have a church wedding here before we sail, and then go settle in the backwoods. And I think Jade and Rory should do the same. We'd get along well together. . . ." But here he sounded more doubtful than ever, shooting a wary glance at the objects of his plans. They didn't look as if they were going to be either docile or sensible.

The quartet were looking at one another with sudden secret amusement. Some decisions didn't have to be spoken at all—one of them being that they wouldn't be going anywhere that Joshua and Domino couldn't be free. They glanced speculatively at Monsieur Maupin, who twinkled back as irresponsibly as a boy. He didn't much care what they decided, so long as it was adventurous; and he could trust his wicked Jade for that.

"Where is it that we take ourselves, then?" he asked contentedly.

"Och," said Rory. "I like the one bit of Michael's idea well enough. We'll have that wedding a double one. Triple, if Joshua and Domino want a church one, too. After that—" He looked like an Indian delightedly off on the warpath again.

Anne jerked herself bolt upright. "You wouldn't!" she cried.

"Yes, we would," said Jade with her bared-teeth smile. "We're going to Africa and harry the slave-raiders. It's what we've wanted all along, to be a kind of pirate that just attacks slavers. We can get some crew in Trinidado, even if we have to pay some of them. They can have all the incidental loot."

"You're mad!" Michael was aghast. "You'll be killed or caught again and hanged sooner or later. Probably sooner!"

"We know," said Rory.

"You won't let them, sir!" Michael appealed to the old

man. "It's your ship; you won't lend it to them for such a purpose!"

Monsieur Maupin was fixing an extremely long and penetrating look upon Jade, who returned it unflinching. He looked at Rory. Then at Domino and Josh. He nodded.

"I am a crazy and wicked old man," he confessed impenitently. "I should take the *petite* Jade back to her family, *sans doute*. But I think, me, that this would be even more wicked and crazy. Besides, I also would very much like to be a pirate against slave traders, who steal human freedom. And I am a master swordsman. Behold, then, how we go to Africa."

Anne looked almost envious. "It was you taught Jade to fence, wasn't it?" She sighed. She remembered her reformed state and leaned contentedly against Michael. "Good luck," she said.

Jade chuckled. "We'll need it. So," she added ominously, "will they."

ACKNOWLEDGMENTS AND HISTORICAL NOTE

I am indebted to the British Museum Reading Room, the files of the London Times, the British Admiralty Court Records, and to John Carlova's very helpful biography (and bibliography) of Anne Bonney: *Mistress of the Seas.*

Readers may think that from the entry of the pirates, this story sounds highly unlikely even for fiction. I agree. The fact is, I should never have dared invent any fiction so improbable—and I didn't. I got it from records of the time—directly or indirectly. One of the best sources, for instance, is in a book called *The History of the Pyrates* published in 1724 and written by a man who calls himself Captain Charles Johnson. For a long time his vivid and detailed description of Anne Bonney's adventures was taken with quite a few grains of salt. But now even Encyclopedia Britannica says "recent research has proved again and again that . . . he had first-hand knowledge of his subject and is to be relied on in almost every detail."

And so all of the pirates are real people culled from Captain Johnson and a number of other books that I found in the British Museum and Mr. Carlova's biography. So are Governor Lawes, Chidley Bayard, Governor Rogers, Tom Deane, Michael Radcliffe, and even the pets. Only Jade and Rory, Domino and Joshua are fictional, and I've inserted them as accurately as possible into the real incidents. The trial is on record, too, and although I've changed it slightly, both to allow for Jade's part and for the purpose of the novel, it's still generally accurate.

As for Anne Bonney and Mary Read, I've hardly touched on their lives and adventures. Mary was brought up as a boy, joined the British Navy at fourteen, later served with the army in one of the Duke of Marlborough's regiments, and still later signed on a Dutch ship as a seaman. When the ship was captured by the pirate Sam Bellamy, she had no choice but to carry on as a pirate. She was by no means the first or last woman to get away with this sort of masquerade; there are well documented records of at least fifteen others, and heaven knows how many that were never documented at all. In any event, Mary was an outstanding fighter, courageous, and skilled with cutlass, pistols, and the tiller. Her duel with Barton really happened—and so did the whole romance with Tom Deane.

Anne's story is just as incredible, and I have only touched on her wild career—which ended in fact as it has here. She and Michael disappeared into the wilds of Virginia, and presumably she really did become a demure (well, more or less), law-abiding wife and mother.

But not my Jade!

About the Author

Sally Watson: Born January 1924 in Seattle, Washington. Picked up phonics from Mother's kindergarten before I was two; the next thing anyone knew I was reading independently–which I went on doing for 12 years of public school–under my desk instead of arithmetic or geography. Rotten grades, didn't know how to study–I just read and wrote. Mum said I wrote my first book when I was four. Four pages, lavishly illustrated, begun with total phonic accuracy: "The sun roze up." From that, she decided that I should grow up to write books for children. Well, it was true I loved words and had a collection–just for fun–of synonyms for "said" and adverbs to accompany it. But when Mum suggested that I might write books for children, I sneered. For one thing, I'd read a book that convinced me one had to be a total genius and collect rejections for ten years. For another, I was going to travel all over Europe and study Highland Dancing and Judo and be a Prima Ballerina, I was.

At 16 or so, I discovered that I wasn't. Not a Prima Ballerina anyhow, and darned if I was going to settle for the corps de ballet. Disgruntled, I further realized that alone among my peers I hadn't the least interest in marriage and families. Nor in office work–the only thing going for women in the '30's.

Joined the Navy in 1944 and after *that* mess was over, I decided to go to college–and applied to Reed without knowing enough not to. They took me, it turned out, on "possible potential," and I waltzed innocently in...and by the time I realized that I would have to commit several *major* and sustained miracles to stay there, it was too late to do anything else. I was hooked by the intellectual excitement. (An astrologer once told me I had "a jack-ass determination that never knew when it was beaten–and consequently seldom was." True, I guess. A useful–albeit sometimes uncomfortable–quality.) At any rate, it was there I learned the discipline to write–but still had no idea of *doing* it. That childhood conviction was still with me.

But what to do? I still wanted neither marriage nor the office work I was temporarily stuck with. Moved to San Francisco, and then L.A., where (on Hollywood and Vine, true to cliché) I ran into an old high school friend who had *just had a children's story published in a real magazine!* Mental barriers collapsed all around me with almost audible crashes. I rushed home and started *Highland Rebel* that night.

I must have had a lot of writing dammed up in me. The first draft wrote itself in three weeks, the final in another three. It was accepted by the first place I submitted it–Henry Holt–*without revision!* And I was such a novice I didn't even know this was remarkable luck. (Needless to say, it never happened again.)

After three books, I had enough money to go to Europe for five months. Three more books, and I went back to England for a year and studied Highland dancing and wrote some more books. Passport and money ran out, so back to California for five years, helping Mother put out the first-ever audio-visual phonics course (which I now see duplicated virtually everywhere I turn. Never mind, Mother had good material, and the more who use it, the better.) Once it was accepted for publication, I realized I could now *live* in England on royalties, whereas I couldn't begin to in the U.S. So I went there and did that, and joined in Mensa, and went on writing books, and took up Judo at age 45, and I reckon I'm the only woman ever to do that and make Black Belt. Third Dan, at that.

Then, in a bout 1972, the bottom fell out. Up until then, my books were selling slowly but steadily, mostly to schools and libraries; and every time stocks got low, they just printed up a new edition. Now tax laws, it seems, were changed so that it was now uneconomical for publishers to keep books in stock over the turn of the year. So all twelve of my books went out of print almost simultaneously. And I was engrossed in Judo and also in copper enameling, and gardening my English country garden, and raising cats. So I stopped writing. And old fans kept writing and asking for copies of my books–and there weren't any.

After 24 years in England, I came back to America–the Sonoma County (*not* Napa) wine country, and joined a cat-rescue-and-adoption group and helped form another; and old fans kept on pleading for copies, and I discovered that feisty heroines are more needed now than in the '50s and '60s...so...

Printed in the United States
By Bookmasters